Jackson

woman's
Howard

ain . . . a
haracters
plot, the
rst page.
sion ex-
into the
ard it [a]
ense, and
nner."
vs Today

writing
an emo-
Romance

nued . . .

"*Midnight Rain* is dynamic romantic suspense."
—*Midwest Book Review*

"This thriller has just about everything you could ask for . . . suspense, intrigue, a broad brushstroke of the paranormal, and topped off with a great romance that makes it sizzle. To put it bluntly, this was one heck of an absolutely riveting suspense/paranormal romance—totally awesome! Such an adrenaline rush, I could have jumped out of my skin. Bottom line—this is a superb, fascinating ride of a suspense-filled romantic thriller. Do yourselves a big favor and find this book for a great read by an author who I predict has a fabulous future in front of her."
—Suspense Romance Writers

"Lisle explodes onto the suspense scene with a book so chilling and a voice so original that she's sure to become a major player. Creepy and thrilling, this book is truly unforgettable."
—*Romantic Times*

"Though this is her first foray into romantic suspense, Lisle proves herself a master. . . . Her story does everything right. Lisle has also created one of the creepiest bad guys to come along in a good while—Michael could give Hannibal Lecter lessons. *Midnight Rain* is the first in what I hope will be many more thrillers from this very talented author."
—BookLoons

I SEE YOU

Holly Lisle

AN ONYX BOOK

ONYX

Published by New American Library, a division of
Penguin Group (USA) Inc., 375 Hudson Street,
New York, New York 10014, USA
Penguin Group (Canada), 90 Eglinton Avenue East, Suite 700, Toronto,
Ontario M4P 2Y3, Canada (a division of Pearson Penguin Canada Inc.)
Penguin Books Ltd., 80 Strand, London WC2R 0RL, England
Penguin Ireland, 25 St. Stephen's Green, Dublin 2,
Ireland (a division of Penguin Books Ltd.)
Penguin Group (Australia), 250 Camberwell Road, Camberwell, Victoria 3124,
Australia (a division of Pearson Australia Group Pty. Ltd.)
Penguin Books India Pvt. Ltd., 11 Community Centre, Panchsheel Park,
New Delhi - 110 017, India
Penguin Group (NZ), cnr Airborne and Rosedale Roads, Albany,
Auckland 1310, New Zealand (a division of Pearson New Zealand Ltd.)
Penguin Books (South Africa) (Pty.) Ltd., 24 Sturdee Avenue,
Rosebank, Johannesburg 2196, South Africa

Penguin Books Ltd., Registered Offices:
80 Strand, London WC2R 0RL, England

First published by Onyx, an imprint of New American Library,
a division of Penguin Group (USA) Inc.

First Printing, July 2006
10 9 8 7 6 5 4 3 2 1

To Matthew

ACKNOWLEDGMENTS

With thanks to the EMTs throughout the years who fought beside me in the ER and hung out with me after things slowed down to tell war stories; with whom I ran some hairy, scary transports; and with whom I have shared more than a few ten-second meals and missed bathroom breaks.

And to the volunteers and pros in the trenches now who remember, in spite of massive pressure from the real enemies of quality health care—corporate-owned hospitals and monstrous insurance companies—that the mission is saving lives, not saving the bottom line.

Chapter 1

". . . so then the guy sits up on the stretcher, says, 'I don't feel so good,' and turns this incredible shade of blue. And falls . . . *out.*"

Ryan, the shaggy-haired blond driving the ambulance, hit the air horn—as if the driver ahead of them might have missed the lights and siren—and skidded the ambulance around the man who refused to give them clearance. Dia Courvant's hand slid to the seat belt that held her to the shotgun seat as the wheels of the ambulance rode up over the median, then thudded back to the tarmac again.

Ahh, the joy of driving in Coral Springs, Florida. Dia tightened her grip on the sissy strap as Ryan careened around a couple of cars hurriedly moving into the right lane.

Ryan didn't miss a breath. "Dude's got no pulse, no respirations, no *nothing.*" He sped up for the yellow light and started hitting the horn to get the people packed into the three lanes ahead of him to start pulling to the right. He kept talking while he drove.

With a laugh in his voice, Ryan said, "And the Hounddog *leaps* into action. Beautiful, beautiful, beautiful. Tubes the guy with blinding speed, drops an eighteen into the jugular; we're bagging and compressing, the Dog shocks, shocks, epi, and shocks, and he gets us back a faint rhythm." Ryan took the ambulance around the obstacles, driving far faster than traffic warranted.

But they were running code three, which meant "lights, sirens, and wings if you have 'em," and with Ryan driving, they damn near did. Dia Courvant braced against the g-forces and shouted, "So then what?"

"Miracle stuff—the magic of the game. Pure Hound-dog. Dude's heart rhythm gets better, his color improves, his pupils react. All golden, you know? And the wife is standing there watching us work, and while the husband was going down the tubes, she had this weird little smile on her face and she wasn't saying a word." Ryan shook his head and laughed. "Soon as she sees the rhythm, soon as we send up a little cheer, the smile goes away, and in a voice that would have frozen Ted Bundy, she turns to Hounddog and she says, 'You miserable son of a bitch—I ought to kill you.' And the Dog goes pale as the would-have-been corpse."

Dia laughed. "Waiting to send her inconvenient hubby off, was she?"

"Indeed."

Dia shook her head. "Lot of love in that blushing bride."

"I'm guessing there might have been a lot of insurance policy. I mean, we're talking Westgate, right? She had that tight, tanned, resurfaced look of a woman just waiting to inherit a nice stack of bling and—"

Dia interrupted him. "Driver at one o'clock doesn't see us." And Ryan jammed on the brakes and swore as one of Coral Springs's many geriatric drivers pulled out in front of the ambulance, oblivious to the lights, the siren, and even the air horn that Ryan hit.

Both of them swore.

It had already been that kind of day.

It was eight A.M. Friday morning, not the thirteenth, not the first of the month. Dia, the paramedic, Ryan Williams, the talkative EMT-Intermediate, and Tyler Frakes, the EMT-CC, who was back in the jump seat with his iPod plugged into his brain and a blissed-out expression on his face, had started their shift at six A.M. with a big, messy shooting. Philandering husband came home late—very late. Psychotic pit-bull wife met him just inside the door with a shotgun aimed at the family jewels, informed him that he smelled like a five-dollar whore, and made sure the issue wouldn't come up again. So to speak.

Just after seven, they'd been dispatched on what turned out to be a milk run—elderly woman calling in heart attack symptoms so that she could have someone to talk to. At seven ten A.M., she had her suitcases already packed and was sitting prim and proper on the front step, waiting for them when they arrived, having already notified her next-door neighbor to keep her cat for her for a few days.

The lady had what Dia and Ryan called "positive suitcase sign" or occasionally "premature packing syndrome"—it was common in South Florida, which had the highest concentration of the elderly per capita in the country. Aside from her PSS, the woman had been, Dia figured, about as healthy as Dia herself. But she was alone, and lonely, and she was willing to go sit in the waiting room of the ER, where she would get to talk to the admitting clerk, the nice triage nurse, and finally to a nice doctor, who would listen to her talk about her health for a bit before sending her home or admitting her if he could find anything that might qualify.

Nuisance calls were, and always had been, part of the gig. Dia did them, she tried to maintain her sense of humor about them—but the reason she became a paramedic was to deal with situations like the one she, Ryan, and Tyler back in the jump seat were heading into.

This was their third call in three hours. They were running hot to a car accident on I-95 that, according to an eyewitness call-in, started when an eighteen-wheeler jackknifed across the road, then expanded to the immediate vehicles following too closely, and finally radiated out to involve drivers going too fast to avoid the expanding wreck.

On that stretch of I-95, seventy mph was legal, and ninety mph was common. A lot of drivers had been going too fast. It was, by first reports, a big, bloody hell of an accident.

All available units were being dispatched—light rescue, heavy rescue, fire, and police. Odds were that rescue crews would be calling in helicopters once they stabilized the most critical patients.

These were the moments that Dia lived for. This was where she knew she mattered—on the pavement or the thin median strip or in the home of a stranger, where the only thing that separated life from death was her immediate intervention, her ability to assess the situation and the condition of her patient and her skill in making critical, correct decisions.

Ryan reached the interstate on-ramp. "You still on for diving next Sunday?"

She glanced over at him. "Weekend after this one, right? I'm on duty this weekend."

"Yeah."

"I'm in. I need to get my underwater hours logged. We're still doing the old shipwreck, right?" She yelled to the back, "You change your mind, Ty?"

He didn't answer. She reached around and punched his shoulder, and he pulled the earbuds out. "Huh?"

"Earth to Tyler. Diving Sunday after this one. You in or out?"

"I have a date, dammit, and she hates the ocean. So I have been forced to provide other ideas on how we can get wet."

"Naturally." Ryan laughed as he pulled them onto the median again to get past the backed-up traffic, turned off sirens, and left lights on. Dia could see smoke, but nothing of the actual accident yet. It lay around a bend and behind three lanes of nose-to-tail SUVs, pickup trucks, and tractor-trailers. He returned his attention to Dia. "Howie and Kelly are going, but Kelly says she wants to bring Sam with her."

"The elusive Sam, who always cancels out because he has an emergency?"

"So she says. We could use one more person, if you know someone who'd like to come along. Boyfriend, maybe?"

"I'm not seeing anyone, and everyone I know, you know, too, so I'm sure you've already asked them."

"Nah. Didn't know Kelly was going to screw up the teams." He hit the air horn as one Lexus SUV tried to push into the median in front of the ambulance to get a little farther ahead in line. The blast scared the jerk into pulling his nose back in line quick enough. "But I'm sure one of the Beta guys will want to come. They're always bitching about missing out on our off-duty stuff."

"They don't bitch about missing this stuff, though, do they?"

"Evenings and nights get their own messes." Dia studied the scene before them and said, "You ought to be the one to bitch, Ryan—I swear, you've caught twice as many disasters lately as the rest of us combined."

His grin was wry. "Surprised you noticed. I'm

planning on having a serious talk with Saint Luke tonight about that very thing."

"You should." She laughed. "He clearly has it in for you."

They reached the outer periphery of the wreck. Other rescue teams that had been closer in were already working the scene.

Dia had her paramedic pack already strapped onto the gurney. She and Ryan ran to the back to grab it, while Tyler found the disaster-scene coordinator and snagged them an assignment.

The scene was chaos. The air was black with greasy smoke and the stink of gasoline and diesel fuels, burning rubber, and other scents darker and worse—smells that were better off not identified. Fire trucks were working the main fire from the rig, and putting down retardant to keep vehicles not already involved from catching fire. Men and a few women moved in and out of the clouds, rescuers and mobile victims seeming to float surreally through the shifting haze. Jaws of Life trucks cut cars apart to reach victims. Overhead a transport chopper made ready to put down on the clean side of the accident; the chopper would airlift critical victims to the closest trauma center. Looking at the wreck, she was sure rescuers would need more helicopters. Between the flames, the smoke, the blood, and the wreckage, it looked like hell had opened up and spit out a parking lot.

Dia tried to guess the number of vehicles crushed, overturned, and on their sides. Her best estimate was close to twenty, with considerably more run off the roads, or with bent fenders, or crumpled hoods or trunks.

This thing had happened at the worst possible spot, where the dip on the far side of an overpass and a curve created a rare blind spot on the interstate. And it had happened at the worst possible time—during rush hour.

A firefighter waved them over. "They've about got this car cut open. We have three victims inside; we're pretty sure one is DOA. The second is hurt pretty bad. Third is a kid in a car seat, looks okay."

Dia nodded. She crouched down and peered through the right side of the windshield, where she could see the unmoving passenger, the unmoving driver, and a little girl still strapped into her car seat, hanging upside down, sobbing. Dia's gut knotted. It didn't look like either mom or dad had come out too well in this one.

Ryan leaned over her shoulder. "What do we have?"

"Possible DOA on the driver's side. Air bags deployed; it's hard to see. On the passenger side I'm seeing probable crushing injuries, lot of blood. Neither front-seat victim is conscious. Could be two alive, two dead. No telling. Little girl in the backseat looks okay."

"Some good news, then," he said. His face was grim.

"Some. Not much." She looked over the wreck scene, where victims who could move on their own were calling for help for themselves, or for those who couldn't. EMTs were wrapping shocky family members in blankets, giving them water, loading them into the backs of ambulances.

The fireman yelled, "Clear," and Ryan said, "Let's be heroes," and Dia, kit in hand, ran forward. She got to the mother first, and quickly checked pulse and respirations; she got a weak, thready pulse and counted fast, shallow respirations, but something was a hell of a lot better than nothing. Blood bubbled from the corners of the woman's mouth, from lacerations on her face and scalp, and from her nose.

"Cervical collar," Dia said, "split board, then backboard. Fieldstrip her, and let's see what injuries we're working with, and what we need to stabilize."

"Don't want to scoop and run?" Ryan asked.

"With a possible pneumothorax or hemothorax? No. I want some idea of what is wrong."

Dia couldn't let the possibility of spinal injuries leave her mind for a second. If the woman had a fracture somewhere along her spine, one wrong move could grind the bones against each other, destroying the delicate spinal cord and paralyzing her or even killing her. Dia put on a hard cervical collar, and she and Ryan worked a half board behind the woman's back, then strapped her to it. They slid in head blocks to prevent her head from moving from side to side.

In the backseat, the little girl sobbed, "Mommy! Mommy. I want Mommy!"

Doing what I can to make sure you still have one, Dia thought. "We'll get you out of there as soon as we get Mommy," she yelled. "And you can ride to the hospital with her."

When the woman was immobilized, Dia, Ryan, and a cop got her turned right side up and moved her out. A fireman climbed in and brought the child out, and stood holding her while Dia and Ryan put her mother on a long board and did their assessment.

The woman had broken ribs, a broken leg, an open fracture of the right collarbone, numerous lacerations, and was unresponsive. But her pupils were reactive. She was still breathing on her own, and when they got pressure dressings on the worst of the wounds, got her on mask oxygen, and opened up the IVs to replace her fluid, her heart and her breathing both slowed down a bit.

"She going to make it?" a man asked her.

"She's going to be fine," Ryan said. "*We're* working on her."

Dia didn't look up—she was busy. She hated correcting Ryan, but he occasionally let enthusiasm and confidence run away with him, and she didn't want to give someone a guarantee; this woman wasn't stable enough for that. "She looks worse than she is," Dia amended. "I'm concerned that she's not conscious. But her pupils are good; deep reflexes are good. I think she'll come out of it okay."

"Good," he said.

She turned her head just enough to get a glimpse of the guy who'd asked. Badge on his hip, and shoulder holster over a white long-sleeved shirt, sleeves rolled up—so he wasn't a friend or family member who'd already been rescued. Detective, then. Not someone who'd been looking for a guarantee. Dia caught an impression of height and lean muscularity, of short, wind-tousled hair.

Detective. She was already back at work, but that pinged a little in the back of her mind.

Detective. Funny. They weren't regulars at traffic accidents.

And then the woman was ready to travel; she wasn't critical enough to require a helicopter evac, so Dia and Ryan and Tyler would drive her. She told Tyler, "Make sure we have her ID with her. And we'll take the kid in with us. We want to keep the family together. Black indelible marker on the mother and the kid, pull the last name off the driver's license, and add an identifying number so that everyone can keep them matched up. No telling how many other parents and kids are banged up in this—let's not give anyone an Amber Alert opportunity."

They rolled the woman to the ambulance, strapped the kid and her car seat into the front, and Ryan called in while they were en route.

"Early thirties white female, unresponsive, vitals BP ninety over forty, heart rate one-twenty, cardiac rhythm sinus tachycardia. Open fractures to the left clavicle, right femur, suspected closed fracture to the left femur . . ."

Tyler was in the jump seat. Dia monitored the IVs, breathing, and bleeding from the bench seat in the back, drug kit in hand but so far unused. She could do considerably more for a heart attack victim than she could for trauma.

The woman in front of her wasn't much older than Dia was. She had a husband—firemen were still cutting him out of the vehicle, and he might or might not still be alive. Dia hadn't checked. She got the woman and the child. Someone else would pick up the man when he was reachable, and haul him off to whichever hospital would take him.

Dia would drop off her two, and never know what happened to them.

She'd wonder, though. Wonder if this woman's story would have a happy ending, if the little girl would get her mommy and daddy back, if the woman would ever wake up, if she'd find out that her husband had lived, or discover that he'd died. Rescue was only the first piece of a long story—first chapter, and the people who lived and breathed rescue never got to finish a whole book.

Sometimes, she thought, you just wanted to know it all came out all right. But there were too many patients, too many emergencies, too many hospitals, and always too little time.

She took another set of vital signs, and the tall, lean detective wandered through her mind again. Why had he been there? Highway Patrol fit at an accident scene. Fire Rescue fit. Fire trucks and firefighters and ambulances and paramedics and EMTs fit.

How did detectives fit?

* * *

Detective Brig Hafferty walked away from the EMTs who were working on the unconscious woman, aware as he did of the little girl in the arms of the firefighter. Brig didn't want to feel that family's tragedy, but he did. The EMTs were fairly confident of the woman; the little girl was okay, but consensus was that the man, whom they were still trying to cut out of the vehicle, was already dead. And that if he wasn't, he didn't have much of a chance of surviving.

The death toll on this wreck was rising, and the accident had the feel of one of his. The wreck had occurred during peak traffic flow, it had happened in the Coral Springs area, and it involved more than one fatality in more than one vehicle.

That described a lot of accidents in South Florida, which had some of the deadliest highways in the country. But a six-mile circle with Coral Springs as the center had recently gotten a lot deadlier.

Brig was backtracking from the eighteen-wheeler that was the first wrecked vehicle, working his way down the middle of the highway where he could, looking left and right. Simple humanity made him want to get into the middle of the carnage and start pulling victims out with the rest of the people working there, but he couldn't afford to give in to that impulse. He tried to stay out of the way of the rescue workers, but he was on an unforgiving clock. He was looking for something that would be swept away by the equipment that would erase all signs of this mess from the roads. The pressure to clear I-95, one of South Florida's main arteries, was intense.

If Brig hoped to find evidence of the crime he suspected, he was going to have to find it in the middle of chaos. There would never be a better time.

He sought a few small shards of debris. It was worse

than looking for a needle in a haystack. In the middle of a massive traffic pileup, it was like looking for hay in a haystack—two or three pieces of hay of a slightly different color than all the rest of the hay. He had to look at every flash of metal, at every broken, twisted scrap, to see if it was *his* debris. If he found anything he'd call in a forensics team. Until he found something, this was just another wreck, and South Florida had enough regular crime to keep a small army of forensics teams busy all day, every day, without sending them on fishing expeditions.

This, though, felt right. His gut had that tightness it got when he was looking at murder, not stupid human error.

He worked his way through crushed cars, avoiding for the moment the images of bodies being pulled from wreckage, the screams of the wounded, the sobs of the grieving, the blood. He kept a silent space around himself, in which he and the road and a few faint charred marks would find one another. In which he and a handful of twisted copper shards would connect. He was going to have to go back a ways—eighteen-wheelers, like trains, had a lot of forward momentum to shed when outside forces stopped them. He could see gouges this one had left in the tarmac in its slide toward its final stopping point. Long arcing streaks of rubber marked the road, and in places peels of turf dug up along the berm lay inverted, dirt and pale white roots exposed, like lacerations in the earth.

The violence of physics collided with the violence of a man.

He walked in his artificial silence, careful of every step he took, letting gut and nerves and instinct pull him back. Back.

Back.

In the middle of blocked traffic, between rows of stuck onlookers parked in the middle of the road, he found the explosion point. One asshole was pulled out of line—the guy had been thinking about trying to pull onto the berm and then . . . well, the morons who did that never had much of a plan after they got themselves into the grass. The jerk had probably figured he could run up the road a ways along the side and magically by-pass whatever it was that had all these other people stuck.

Brig, though, saw a curl of copper where the jackass would have been had he not been a jackass.

Crouching down, Brig shined a flashlight under some of the cars that were where they were supposed to be. More bits of copper gleamed back at him. Under his foot, he discovered a shard of some electronic component.

And back another few feet, the scorch marks on the highway where the bomb had gone off.

Yeah. This was one of his, all right.

He pulled out his radio. "This is Kilo-twenty-two, on site on I-ninety-five at the Coral Springs exit."

"Yeah, Brig, I gotcha." The dispatcher was Mary Finkle, who had been dispatching since God created radio, and who was utterly unflappable. "Whatcha need?"

"Forensics team, and airlift them if you have to," he drawled. Got a code fifty-five here, and I need some folks to come take pictures of the pieces and sweep them all up before they get gone."

"Ten-four, Kilo-twenty-two. I'll send them right out."

He studied the fragments.

This was number five in a series for him. The fifth explosive device somehow set off in the middle of traffic that had caused a wreck with fatalities. He'd fallen into the first one when a sharp-eyed fireman had spotted something suspicious well back of the collision point, and had called for a detective.

Brig and his partner, Stan Chang, had been following up on accidents with fatalities ever since. So that they didn't miss anything, they had a notice in auto-body repair shops to call if cars with explosives damage to the undercarriage showed up.

This was one of about thirty active homicide cases on his desk at the moment. This one, however, had moved itself to the top of the pile.

Crouching near the debris, he thought about the EMTs who'd been working on the unconscious woman. They'd been focused, tunneled way down into what they were doing. Sort of like him while he was trying to find his bomb shards.

He wondered if any of the three of them had been seeing wrecks like this. If they might have some useful information for him that they didn't even know they had. They were, often enough, first responders to accidents.

In his experience, EMTs were useful only where information about victims was required. They were wound a bit too tight—in general—to see much more than the tiny circle that lay within their work. Still, he and Stan could canvass the local stations, talk to the rescuers, ask around.

Perhaps he could accidentally-on-purpose bump into her.

He wondered if he was being disingenuous by considering talking to the woman. Granted, she might have seen something. But she was pretty, too. Striking. A tall, leggy woman, but not thin. She'd been well muscled, sleek, built like someone who worked out to stay in shape for a demanding, physical job. She'd looked strong. And calm. Self-assured. Alert.

Well, he told himself, even if he was considering seeking her out more because she was hot than because of any other reason, she did look like the sort of woman who might pay attention to details.

He allowed himself a cautious smile.

It never hurt to ask.

Chapter 2

Dia and her crew were doing their second run to the same wreck. Most of the living had already been cleared away, taken to local hospitals or regional trauma centers. The ugliest part of the job remained—clearing the dead. The closer in to the truck they worked, the more dead they were getting. Heavy Rescue trucks pulled vehicles apart that looked like they'd been through a scrap-metal compressor. The Jaws of Life cut those vehicles open, and Rescue retrieved and carried off the bodies.

The detective was still there, watching. Silent, grim, shaken.

Dia actually took the time to notice him because, for a few moments, anyway, until Heavy Rescue extricated the car she and Ryan were waiting to work, all she could really do was stand around with her thumbs in her pockets.

He wore neatly pressed blue jeans, that white shirt, rumpled and open at the collar and sticking to his skin in the oppressive heat, his tie loose around his neck. He was tanned, windburned, lean and tall. His brown eyes, light and warm, focused on the same wreck Dia and her partner were waiting on. He wore his brown hair long on top, tapered to short—it looked good on him that way, she thought. It emphasized his jaw.

She found herself liking the way he looked, the way

he moved, the way he just stood there. It was kind of nice, noticing a man again.

And because she was watching his face, she caught the slight shift in his expression that told her something was wrong. She looked where he was looking, saw a dead child being pulled out of the wreckage, and her gut knotted. She walked over to him and rested a hand on his arm. "Accidents happen. We can't hold on to the ones we lose. We have to keep thinking about the ones we can still save."

He looked from the kid to her. Back to the kid. He licked his lips, and she saw brightness in his eyes. Watching. "It's worse when it isn't an accident," he said, so softly she almost didn't hear him.

Cold washed over her. She looked from the truck to the twisted, ruined metal scattered across the pavement as if an angry god had given himself over to an epic tantrum. She thought of the dead, of the dying, of those so badly injured their lives would never be the same again, of those who had survived only to have people they loved ripped away from them.

Not an accident? she thought, and her heart thudded hard against her ribs.

Someone shouted, "Hey, we have a live one in here," and there was the hope again. The adrenaline rush. She had her chance to matter. She raced over to the car, to Ryan and Tyler and her kit.

Tyler and Ryan got backboards and collars and padding ready, made sure all their straps were untangled.

Dia got down on hands and knees to see the man, to get a feel for her priorities; he looked at her out of a bloody, burned face, his eyes round and scared. "Am I going to die?" he asked her.

"Not right now," she told him. "We're going to get you stabilized and to a hospital."

"How's my little girl?" His voice was hoarse. Smoke inhalation, she thought, evaluating him for deviations in the trachea that might be caused by a punctured lung open to the outside air. Deviating the trachea could alter speech, too. So could screaming. He said, "She's all I have in the world."

Dia had seen the little girl. She had no doubt the child had died instantly. At some point, knowing that truth might be a comfort to the man—knowing that his little girl hadn't suffered. But right then it wouldn't be a comfort. Right then it might kill him. So Dia lied. "I'm not sure how she is," she said. "Another rescue squad took her. We'll be taking you."

He managed a faint nod. "That's good. I'm glad they got her first. If she's all right . . ." He closed his eyes.

Dia said, "Sir?" He didn't respond. "Sir?"

She checked breathing. Nothing. Pulse—nothing. He'd done a lot of bleeding—her first order of business was to make sure his body could use what little blood remained as effectively as possible. That meant getting it to his heart and his brain. "Ryan, Tyler," she yelled, "we're losing him! Get the MAST pants on him, fast."

He was on the board.

In the first seconds, the ABCs meant the difference between life and death. *Airway* first—that was oxygen to the brain, because if you didn't save the brain, everything else was for nothing, and without a clear airway, you'd lost the war before you started. *Breathing* second, moving the air in and out of the patient's body for him, if he wasn't doing it.

Circulation came third. That meant controlling any bleeding, because you could be putting all the oxygen in the world into the lungs, and if there weren't enough red blood cells left in his body to get the oxygen to the brain, you were done. It also meant keeping the heart

beating one way or another: pushing on it from the outside, hitting it with drugs that would kick-start it, jolting
it with electric shocks.

So airway first. While the guys put the MAST
trousers on the man's legs, Dia grabbed a laryngoscope
and a big endotracheal tube from her kit. She would use
these to establish a clear, usable airway. She got a good
look at the vocal cords with the laryngoscope, slid the
tube in with a practiced movement, and inflated the bulb
to hold it in place.

The guys had the MAST trousers on him. Ryan
started them cycling, inflating in a regular pattern that
would keep minimal circulation going in his legs.
"Tyler, get me an eighteen jugular stick," Dia said. She
was hooking the ET tube up to a device that would push
high-percentage oxygen from an O_2 tank into the man's
lungs. "Ryan, breathe him," she said, and Ryan moved
to the man's head and started squeezing the bag in a regular, slightly fast rhythm.

Dia, meanwhile, put electrode pads on the man's
chest. It was mostly hairless and wasn't burned—two
small blessings for which she silently thanked whoever
might be listening. She hooked electrodes onto the pads,
and watched as the thin green line on the LIFEPAK
started jiggling in an ugly scribble. No pattern. Could be
atrial fibrillation, which was what it looked like. Could
also be a bad connection between the electrodes and the
heart monitor, or the pads and the man's chest. She felt
for a pulse, stuck her stethoscope in her ears, and listened for a heartbeat—because the first rule a paramedic remembered about machines was that they lied.
She didn't want to hit with electric shock a man who
had a heartbeat.

But he was silent as death.

The shock paddles were already warmed up. She

covered them with gel—he already had enough burns.
Put them on his chest, high on the right, low on the left.
And yelled, "Clear."

Tyler had gotten his IV line in place and running. He
backed away. Ryan let go of the airway and bag. Dia hit
the thumb trigger on the paddle, and the man's chest
bucked beneath her hands. "Two hundred joules," she
said, telling them the amount of electricity she'd used
for the first shock.

Ryan squeezed more air into the man's lungs while
Dia watched the monitor and felt with her gloved fin-
gertips for a carotid pulse—checking at the juncture of
the neck allowed the EMT to feel even a weak pulse that
might not be palpable all the way down in a wrist.

Nothing.

She increased the amount of electricity that would
run through the paddles to three hundred joules, and
shouted, "Clear!"

Ryan backed off; Dia shocked the man again.

They checked. Nothing.

"Begin CPR," she told Tyler, who carefully checked
for his placement on the man's sternum and began
counting.

"One-one-thousand, two-one-thousand, three-one-
thousand, four . . ." he said, and as his hands came up on
four, Ryan squeezed air into the man's lungs. "One-one-
thousand, two-one-thousand, three-one-thousand . . ."

They had done this so many times, the three of them.
It was a clockwork thing, a precise dance. She grabbed
a premeasured amp of adrenaline from her kit and in-
jected it into one port of the IV line Tyler had estab-
lished. Tyler made the man's heart beat. Ryan kept him
breathing.

Dia, the paramedic, ran the code, read the monitor,
pushed the drugs. The responsibility for how the whole

thing went, whether the man had a chance of surviving or not, fell on her.

She shocked again, at the highest possible power setting, and still got nothing from his heart.

"We're going to get him into the ambulance and get him to the hospital," she said. "This is not a stay-and-play situation."

They started pushing the stretcher through narrow winding lanes between cars, Tyler running alongside doing compressions, Ryan pulling and bagging, Dia pushing and digging through her box for the next meds she could give.

They were doing everything they could to save the man's life. But she wondered if it would matter. If he would want them to save him if he knew his daughter was already dead.

Another story the ending of which she would never know.

Dia dragged herself home after seven that evening, having worked twelve straight hours without a single meal, and having managed to grab only a pack of crackers, a Pepsi, and a bathroom break during one ER stop. And having spent a long three-quarters of an hour after her crew went home doing paperwork.

She reeked of smoke and gasoline. Her entire body ached. She looked at the weight machine in the sunroom and just laughed—usually she'd find time for a workout during the day, but she'd already had her workout and then some.

All she wanted was a shower, a nice hot bowl of soup, and bed.

And the shower was wonderful. She stood there until she ran out of hot water. Until she ran out of lukewarm water. When it started coming out of the tap actually cool, she climbed out into the steam cloud and toweled off.

On the mirror was the note from Mac: *I'm with you, sweetheart.*

It didn't sting so much anymore. She still missed him. He'd been her best friend as well as her husband, and that was a lot of loss to take from one death. He'd been the other half of their team, the Mac and Dia show.

He never got to see her make paramedic. He never even knew that she'd passed the test on the first try. That she'd aced it. She wished she was the sort of woman who could believe that he'd known anyway—because God knew he'd wanted it for her as much as she'd wanted it. He'd cheered her on every step of the way, studied with her, tested her constantly when they were running calls.

It had been four years, and she probably needed to wash the mirror off. She needed to let go of that last tangible thread that connected her to him.

It wasn't that she was clinging to his memory. She'd gotten on with her life. After his death, she'd done her preceptorship and made EMT-P, and gone back to the station where they both had worked. She knew the guys there; they knew her. It had been a good deal. She had friends who went diving with her, who worked out together, who hung out after hours at the station and told war stories, who had cookouts at one another's houses. There was no romance in the station; no one hit on her, and she wasn't looking for any action either. It was like having a lot of brothers, a couple of sisters.

And Howie, of course. Howie totally failed to be brotherly—but she got along with him all the same. She shot him down, he laughed and got up, and she shot him down again.

The doorbell rang.

Rang.

Rang.

Wasn't that always the way?

Some damned vacuum cleaner salesman, magazine pusher, or kid hustling school fund-raiser chocolate would break up even the most wonderful silence. But this sounded urgent, so Dia yanked her terry-cloth robe off the hook on the bathroom door, ran down the hall, and checked the peephole before opening the front door. No one was there.

She frowned, walked over to the front window, and checked to make sure someone wasn't crouching off to the side—she didn't live in a great neighborhood, and she didn't want to take chances.

No one was hiding in the shrubs, either. But now she could see there were flowers on the front porch.

She opened the door, carried them inside, and closed the door. Locked it, dead-bolted it, and put the chain on, because intelligent young widows in questionable neighborhoods were responsible for their own safety.

Once she was inside she looked for a note. There was one, but it wasn't in a little florist's envelope, or held up by a florist's pick. It was on a lined piece of paper from one of those tiny spiral-bound notepads that left little danglies all over the place when you ripped them out. The note was written in nice, neat, careful handwriting, in blue pen, by someone with a heavy hand. All it said was:

Thank you for saving my life.

No signature, no identifying marks.

Dia frowned.

The flowers were lovely, and though she was no expert, they looked expensive to her. The arrangement had a lot of ordinary flowers, but also orange roses and

some of those exotic-looking lilies that, to Dia, looked
too pretty and perfect to be real.

It seemed like a nice enough gesture; she'd saved a
lot of people's lives. But generally she never saw them
again; hers wasn't the sort of job someone did for the
recognition. On the surface, this would seem to be
someone who had taken the time to say thanks.

Except the flowers hadn't been delivered to the station.
They had come directly to her home. They hadn't been delivered by a florist, either. Had they been, there would
have been some sort of identifying mark—a little card-
holder, a tag, *something* that would have let Dia know
where she could call. A florist would have been a good
thing; the employee who took the order would have been
able to give a good description of the person who had pur-
chased them, if he was a walk-in. If he'd been a call-in, the
florist would have had a credit card number and a name.
Either way, Dia would have had something tangible to let
her know where the flowers came from.

The lack of a signature bothered her most of all. What
sort of person thanked you for saving his or her life—
probably his—but didn't let you know whose life it was
you were being thanked for saving?

Dia breathed out. Should she keep the flowers? The
note? She put the note back in the basket. She'd touched
only the top right corner of it. She wouldn't pick it up
again. It might be that this was a shy person who didn't
want to be any bother, who just wanted to say thanks
and be done with it, letting Dia know that she was appreciated before vanishing again.

But Dia's skin prickled just a little as she looked at those
flowers. They were the wrong kind of flowers for a simple
thank-you-and-gone. It was the wrong kind of note.

It was just . . . wrong.

*   *   *

"So we've got number five for sure." Stan Chang kicked back and put his feet up on his desk. It was after hours, but about half of the detectives were still hanging around, working on cases, filing paperwork, checking leads. It had been a big day for Brig and Stan, and they were still trying to catch up.

"Twenty-three dead so far," Brig said. "About fifteen more critical—we could lose all of them, or just some. None, if we're lucky, but I'm thinking we won't be lucky."

"Doesn't sound like."

They looked at the pins in their map. "Bastard really likes Coral Springs," Brig said.

"I wonder how many of these there were before we caught on?"

"I don't know. I wonder if there were any more big ones. This guy just tripled his kills in one shot."

There was a long silence.

"My thing went well," Stan said. "And thanks for asking."

"The witness actually had something we could use?"

Stan grinned. "Better. I think the witness may be our asshole, trying to get in close to admire his ability to fool us. I have him coming in tomorrow to look at photos. I'll give him a cup of coffee while he's here, he'll dump it, and we'll get DNA and fingerprints, and then we can check them against what we have on file."

One of their other open, active cases was a multiple homicide—eleven people murdered in a bad crack house in what had been, not too long before, a pretty decent neighborhood. The victims had been shot by an unmodified AK-47, by someone with a lot of ammo.

Initially it had looked to Brig and Stan like a drug deal gone bad. But the spent cartridges all had fingerprints on them, and testing had shown that they'd been hand-loaded.

To Stan, hand-loading AK ammo spoke of a hobbyist, maybe a gun collector. And that pointed away from the dealer/supplier or enraged-customer theories. So Stan and Brig had gone back over their postshooting canvassing of the neighborhood, looking for interesting possibles. They'd come up with several, and set up appointments to talk to them under the guise of wanting to go back over witness statements. They'd been planning on going together, but then the auto accident had come up, and the guy who had been most difficult to get hold of had been scheduled for the same time. They'd flipped a coin, and Stan had won the interview.

Brig had drawn the wreck.

"If we get a fingerprint match on this, we can have a warrant inside of ten minutes," Stan said. "I already talked to the judge, and she's excited. Everybody would like to get this wrapped up."

"Mmm," Brig said. Stan was watching him, he realized after a moment. "What?"

"Where the hell is your head? We're going to look beautiful for solving this one. Neighbor gets pissed off that they can't get the crack house out of the neighborhood, goes over, and solves the problem himself in the middle of the night, vanishes back home to be Mr. Upstanding Citizen. Your idea, our bag, and you're like . . . meh?"

"Jesus, Stan—who are you today? Valley Girl Detective?"

"Like . . . what-*ever.*" Stan's voice went high, but behind the jokiness, Brig realized he'd managed to annoy his partner. Stan had his arms crossed over his chest, and had put his feet back on the floor. "Stop changing the subject. Where are you? This is big."

"Today was . . . rough," Brig said. "Up-close rough. And there was this . . ."—he knew he was going to regret saying anything to Stan, but he said it anyway—"this woman there. Paramedic. Tall, solid, nice curves. Very together. And I keep thinking about her."

Stan grinned. "A girl? Dude."

"And now he's Surfer Ken."

"I am all things to all people," Stan said, waving his fingers in front of his face in eccentric loops and curves. "I have ancient Chinese magic."

"Your ass."

Stan laughed. "Also has ancient Chinese magic. And how is that alimony, by the way?"

"She remarried, dumb ass. There is no alimony once they remarry. I must admit I'm amazed—I figured she'd just live with the bastard, and milk me while he was sugar-daddying her. I figure her current victim must have married her without a prenup, and I know the poor stupid sonuvabitch makes a shitload more money than I do."

"You really don't have to pay them alimony anymore once they remarry?"

"You really don't. Thank God."

"Then you're a free man."

"And I intend to stay that way."

"Pretty blonde at the wreck scene included?"

"She wasn't a blonde."

Stan said, "Wow. I'm stunned. Going to try something different this time?"

"Once was enough for me. For the first time in three years, my bank account is all my own. Why would I want to ruin that?"

"Keep reminding yourself of that fact when your flights of fancy take you to the pretty girl at the ugly wreck. It's a good thing to be free."

Brig remembered her standing beside him, watching him.

She'd put her hand on his arm. Had offered him comfort, not knowing that the dead at that wreck had all been murdered. She'd been kind and caring, not just to the people she was there to help, but to a man who had seen as much hell as she had.

He wished he'd noticed her name tag. It wasn't like him to miss a detail like that. She'd been so kind. And real. Women who became paramedics were interesting. They clearly weren't the makeup-and-nails-done sort. They had their priorities right.

Maybe, he thought, he'd run into her again somewhere. No guarantees that he would, but . . . he did need to see about getting witness statements from the EMTs who had worked that wreck.

"Yeah," Stan said. "I see your newfound freedom lasting a long, long time. Dumb ass."

"What?" Brig said.

The man pulled a windbreaker over his sweatshirt, and studied his reflection in the mirror. He wore sweatpants, running shoes, sagging socks. Simple clothing, but he'd had to have each item specially made—not even the largest off-the-rack sizes would fit his vast bulk. He smiled a little, brushed dark brown hair back from his forehead with one hand, experimented for a moment with a middle part—but that looked ridiculous.

He reveled in the power of his fatness. King Henry VIII had understood. He had been one of the greatest kings the English had ever had. It had been because he was massive. The fat man commanded space. He claimed more real estate simply because of his size. He was impossible to ignore.

And yet, at the same time, with the average American's aversion to fatness, he was also impossible to view clearly.

People glanced, and then averted their eyes lest they be caught staring. They caught glimpses and impressions, but rarely ever a clear, detailed view. They underestimated fat men. They attributed stupidity to them, gluttony, weakness, slowness. They were blinded by their prejudices, and the man delighted in that fact.

He walked to the front door and opened it, and called in his cats. He had three of them. He enjoyed them; he found their manners delightful and their weightless, effortless grace enchanting. And they came when he called, which was something most people didn't seem to get from their cats.

With them trailing him, he closed and locked the doors, bent down with difficulty and petted each of them, and then headed toward the back of the house. He much preferred custom-fitted suits, preferably pin-striped, with double-breasted jackets, white shirts, and silk ties. But *she,* the innocent and vulnerable she, had said something wrong, terribly wrong. She told him in one simple sentence that she had begun to notice his art, even though she had not begun to see him.

He wasn't yet sure what price she would pay for having done so. He didn't imagine things would end well for his lovely vixen, the object of his fantasies, a creature as graceful as any of his cats. She had the failing of being too curious. Curiosity . . . well.

And when he'd visited her, she might have seen him, and he hadn't wanted to stand out in her mind as a wealthy fat man, stylishly dressed, powerful, memorable. If she saw him at all, he wanted her to see him only as a fat man.

He smiled and pulled on latex gloves and, with his cats trailing him, went into his workroom.

His next bomb was coming along quite nicely. He was having good luck with pressure-sensitive triggers— he'd managed to have the latest one detonate itself under the wheels of an eighteen-wheeler hauling gasoline. That had been perfection.

Life and death. The powerful man, the king, held life and death in a single hand.

Chapter 3

Red and white lights strobed through the darkness, but from the wrong place, from the wrong angle.

No, *Dia thought.* Not here. Not again.

But her feet were on the ground . . . almost on the ground, and they were taking her down the embankment, down toward the lights that spun crazily.

No.

She had nothing with her. No kit, no drugs, no tools. All she had were her car keys, jangling in her left hand, and a radio at her hip.

She couldn't hear anything. She couldn't see anything but the lights, spinning, bouncing off of a concrete wall.

And then her hand dragged across the crushed, jagged ruins of the ambulance, and her heart started pounding crazily again.

It would end differently this time. They would be hurt but alive, and she would save them; they would be strangers and she wouldn't care; they would be figments of her imagination and she would wake to find the world had turned out the way it was supposed to.

But no.

There was Ricky Hammonds, tangled in his seat belt, impaled in his seat, transfixed by a spear-straight broken sapling run through the windshield, and crushed by buckled concrete.

There, beside him, was Lan Cordillo, crushed by the same buckled concrete.

And in the grass twenty feet away lay Mac, thrown through the windshield, not thrown clear. She knew without looking that what was left of Mac would not be enough to try to save. She looked anyway, and he was dead, gone.

He was watching her, whispering something that she couldn't hear. Dead, looking at her, reaching for her, trying to tell her something.

Everything was still silence, and she couldn't hear him. She didn't know what he was saying, she couldn't make the sound come back, and she couldn't save him—again.

Dia turned, as she had turned once in real life and a hundred times in this nightmare, and saw the car crumpled against a tree. In it, a pale figure strobing in and out of view in the horrible darkness.

She ran, trapped in the slowness of dreams, caught in the impotence of nightmare, and somehow, through the molasses air, reached him. Found a faint pulse, though he had stopped breathing.

She dragged him out, mindful of his spine, of the danger to his life, and began rescue breathing. In between breaths, she once again called in the wreck, this time her own voice silent, the responses she was getting from the dispatcher silent.

Doing something was better than doing nothing. Her husband lay broken on the mowed berm, beyond her reach, beyond hope. This one she might save. She did what she had to do, operating not out of compassion or even duty, but simply so she wouldn't have to sit down on the bank next to what was left of her best friend in the world and two of her colleagues. Doing something was better than doing nothing. When the man's heart stopped, she began compressing him.

She did CPR until someone tapped her on the shoulder, and she looked up to see a familiar face, tear-streaked. Kelly Beam, who'd responded to Dia's call. Kelly's old partner, Perry Hall. They took over CPR, and other squad guys had wrapped Dia in a blanket, led her away from the scene, bundled her up, took her to the station.

Behind her, Mac was pleading for her to listen to him. She didn't know how she knew this, because she couldn't hear him. But in the dream she knew. She turned to him, and saw him trying to drag himself after her, trying to reach her.

Dia woke up drenched in sweat, her throat raw from trying to scream.

Three A.M. She shuddered, got up, padded barefoot into the kitchen, and took an aspirin and a couple of Tylenol for the headache that came out of nowhere.

She hadn't had that dream in nearly three years, after having it most nights for the year after Mac's death.

The dream had changed, though. It had added new, darker twists. That first year Mac hadn't been trying to reach her. She'd been reliving the accident scene—finding the bodies, working on the nameless, faceless victim—almost exactly as it had happened.

The silence was new. Mac's watching her was new. Mac's crawling after her, trying to tell her something was new. And horrible.

Hell.

Dia paced the kitchen. It was three A.M. and she'd have to get up at five thirty to get to work on time. Did she want to go back to sleep? The nightmare lingered—she could feel it back there, suddenly fresh and new and painful.

Why?

She'd been better. She'd found her way through that year of pain and gotten back on the horse, gotten back into the ambulance, and become the paramedic she'd planned all along to be. She hadn't dated anyone, but it wasn't because she wasn't interested in dating. It wasn't because she was in mourning. It was because the only men she knew were the men she worked with, and she wasn't dating another adrenaline junkie. She had a hard enough time keeping herself off the ceiling—when it had been her and Mac, they'd positively ricocheted through their lives, spurring each other on to more and riskier adventures in private, being keenly competitive at work.

She didn't know any calm, settled men, and the few she met through work she ended up treating for trauma, or heart attacks, or any of the other events that marked her daily life.

But she'd been okay. She'd been good, even, and she knew she'd meet the right man sooner or later—an accountant, maybe, or a librarian—someone who had a desk in an air-conditioned office and whose idea of adventure was watching the news.

She was going to meet someone perfect for her.

Except there was Mac all of a sudden, staring at her from out of her nightmare. She could almost feel him watching her, even though she was awake. What the hell had he wanted to tell her?

"Nothing," she growled, and stomped into the bathroom. "He wasn't trying to tell me anything, because it was a goddamned dream." She turned on the shower and stripped out of her pajamas. Let the hot water pour over her and pound into her muscles, washing away the residue of nightmare. Breathed the steam deep into her lungs, pulling it in until her sinuses ached.

When she exhaled, the headache behind her eyes receded. She felt clean again. She shook it off.

She stepped out of the shower and toweled off—and there in the steam was the last thing he'd written on the mirror to her. *I'm with you, sweetheart.*

She stared at the mirror and at those blocky letters, and took a deep breath. She missed him. Every day, that last little bit of encouragement—written for her to see before she went to take the test that would clear her to work in a preceptorship to become a paramedic—had given her a little boost. Sometimes she resented the hell out of the fact that he hadn't kept his promise—that he'd died on her. But mostly she read it and smiled.

Maybe, though . . . maybe it was time to wash that off the mirror. Maybe it was time to let go of that last little reminder. She had no intention of spending another year in the hell of that nightmare.

She picked up bathroom cleaner and a rag, and looked at the note.

It would be her last time to see it. She was ready to let go of that final connection between them.

She wiped, and the glass squeaked, and she shed a few tears.

When she was finished, she trudged naked through the house into the bedroom and got dressed early. For once in her life, she'd have a full breakfast before she went to work. Something healthy and delicious.

Brig woke just after three A.M., rolled over, and stared at the alarm clock. Something was wrong. He sat up and listened, but aside from the low drone of the air conditioner, his condo was silent.

He got out of bed and walked through the place. Bedroom, bedroom, narrow hall, bathroom, great room, kitchen, laundry, bathroom, exercise room.

All the windows were locked, the door was locked, the place was exactly as it should have been.

Something was wrong, though, and his mind returned to the wreck on I-95. This was related to that, this sense of displacement, of things off-kilter, of personal and immediate danger.

He'd missed something, a little voice in the back of his mind suggested. There'd been something there he'd needed to see, or had seen but hadn't interpreted correctly. And now the scene of the crime was gone, swept away, and covered with traffic that would preclude any second look.

He stood in the great room with its ridiculously angled ceilings, and paced between the front door and the kitchen at the back. Straight line, fairly long, and while he walked it, back and forth, he half closed his eyes and looked again at what he had seen. The cars, the glints of metal that had been his proof this thing had been set, not a simple accident at all. Blood, bodies, living victims, rescue personnel, cops, the long, long line of cars held up by the tremendous wreck.

Something in that tangle had clicked in his subconscious mind and snapped him to wakefulness, but refused to reveal itself to his conscious mind.

Somewhere inside, he knew what he'd seen, but he couldn't get it to shake loose.

The EMT—the tall brunette who'd put her hand on his arm—his thoughts kept cycling around to her, and his gut tightened every time they did. But that was hormones talking; he'd liked the look of her, liked the way she moved, liked her calm confidence, the way she radiated a sort of peace in the midst of the chaos.

She hadn't woken him up.

Maybe she, personally, had seen something, though. He decided that he'd make a special point of tracking her down the next day, just to ask her.

Chapter 4

Saturday morning, way too early to be back again, Dia sat in the break room, eating a doughnut from the box one of the guys had brought with him from the local Dunkin' Donuts. So much for the healthy breakfast. She was going to have to buy stuff to make in the mornings if she was going to start cooking herself breakfast. Prepackaged microwave meals and popcorn weren't going to cut it.

Howie said, "So the death toll as of this morning was thirty-one. We did good though; it could have been a lot worse."

Howie "Hounddog" Nash was, like Dia, a paramedic. His crew had been working the same wreck, though they hadn't even crossed paths with each other the whole time.

"We got eight in six hours," one of his team members, petite, redheaded EMT-CC Kelly Beam, said. "How did you guys do?"

Ryan said, "Ten in six. We did a little creative stacking."

Howie told Ryan, "Fucking show-off," and turned to Dia. "And when are you going to do a little creative stacking with me, gorgeous?"

Dia laughed.

Howie laughed too.

Ryan, Howie's best friend but Dia's frequent defender, took offense that time. "Lay off, man. She's one of us. You don't get to hit on her."

Dia really didn't mind, because, well . . . it was Howie. He was called the Hounddog for a reason. Any woman of legal age was fair game. He'd hit on anorexics and fat girls, on bikini models and homely wallflowers, on eighty-year-olds and college coeds, and on women like Dia, who stood a good head taller than him in their bare feet. He was race-blind, equal-opportunity, perpetually on the lookout for the next woman who would say yes. And he was harmless. He dated prolifically, and the women who dated him adored him, even if he never went out with anyone more than a couple of times.

He took "no" with amused grace and usually moved on right away. South Florida, as he put it, was a veritable candy factory churning out eligible women—no matter where he went, there they were. He never seemed to get his feelings hurt by rejection, because—at least in his case—turndowns and acceptances ran pretty much neck and neck. He seemed to regard Dia as a hopeful challenge, though—he told her once that he had mountain-climbing fantasies, and she was in them.

If it were handled differently, she supposed she could have considered his behavior sexual harassment. But he was warm and friendly and easygoing. And not fixated on her. He had a life, he lived it with joy and broad enthusiasm, and he never crossed the line between funny-endearing and uncomfortable.

So Dia didn't choose to be a hard-ass about him. He wasn't hurting anyone.

Dia finished the doughnut and started into the breakfast crapwich she'd picked up on the way in. She had a little more time before the night-shift guys finished up with the trucks. No way to go to work until she had a truck to work in, so she enjoyed her food and listened to the guys one-upping one another about their big saves the day before. With the other ear, she listened to the radio traffic. It was still dark, but then, at five thirty A.M., the morning was still young.

Someone knocked on the break room door. Nobody who belonged there ever knocked, so this meant someone who'd made it past the captain, but who wasn't one of them. The guys cut the horseplay, and Dia swallowed a bite she'd taken that was a bit too large for prime-time viewing, and washed it down with Howie's execrable coffee.

Kelly yelled, "Come in."

The cop who'd been at the accident scene the day before came through the door. This time, in what passed for the cool part of the day in South Florida, and on what probably should have been his day off, he was still wearing a dark-colored, lightweight jacket. His white shirt was still buttoned, his tie still tied. His jeans were razor-creased, his shoes spit-polished. With him was a second detective, a bodybuilder with Asian features and a classy silk suit.

The detectives nodded to all of them. The cop Dia had talked to the day before said, "I'm Detective Hafferty. Some of you worked the big wreck on Ninety-five yesterday," he said.

Everyone in the room nodded. A few of them raised hands.

"All of you?" Hafferty asked.

Everyone nodded again. "Our station caught a lot of it," Dia said. "We were close; Dispatch could divert us easily to cover that and let stations farther away pick up the slack for smaller things."

Hafferty nodded. "I need to know if any of you had

patients who talked about what happened yesterday, or
who said or might have even just suggested that something seemed odd or out of place in the accident. Any
help you can give us on this could be critical to us; anything they said to you could provide us with information
we desperately need to reconstruct what happened."

Howie said, "You're detectives, right?"

Dia stared at Howie. They'd introduced themselves
as detectives. It was a stupid question from a man she
knew was far too intelligent to have asked it.

The detectives both nodded, but didn't say anything.

Howie said, "I thought reconstructing accidents was
the job of the Highway Patrol."

"Reconstructing accidents is," Detective Chang said.
"Crime scenes are our job."

A little ripple passed through the table of EMTs.

"Crime scene?" Kelly asked. She was Dia's friend, a
year older than Dia, tough, sharp—she had intended to become an ER RN, and had gone into emergency rescue as
a way of learning the terrain, but discovered that dealing
with emergencies where they happened was addictive in
its own right. She was an EMT–critical care, and considering testing for paramedic again. She'd panicked on the
practical twice, and swore that if she didn't make it the
third time, she'd give up and stay where she was.

Dia was watching Hafferty, remembering his reaction
to the little girl being pulled out of the car, his hint that
the wreck hadn't been an accident. She couldn't remember exactly what he'd said, but the implication had
stuck with her.

"So what happened?" Dia asked.

"We're not at liberty to give out details," Hafferty
said, "other than to say that we have reason to suspect
that the accident was caused by intent."

"Our patients weren't talking much," Tyler said. "We

had unconscious or pediatric patients. One talker, but she was hurt pretty bad and screaming about pain."

"It was a mess," Howie agreed. "If anyone saw anything they thought was out of place in a wreck, they didn't mention it to me."

Ryan agreed. "Anyone who could talk was horrified by what a nightmare it was. They were glad to see us, and that was about it." He shrugged.

Detective Chang said, "In any vehicular accidents you respond to in the next few weeks, would you mind keeping your ears open for people talking about anything out of place? This would be witnesses at the scene, victims, and of course anything that you folks might see or hear yourselves." He and Hafferty started passing out business cards.

"Call either one of us," Detective Hafferty said. "Anytime, day or night. Our access numbers are on the cards."

Dia took the card Hafferty handed to her. It had a handwritten arrow on the front. She flipped it over. On the back it said, *Thanks for yesterday.* And a scrawled home phone number, with the word "home" written underneath it.

"Anytime," he repeated, looking at her.

She studied the card, then looked at him with renewed interest.

He was exactly the sort of man she would pick. And for that reason, exactly the sort of man she would never pick again. It was important to her to think that she could learn from experience, and the experience of being married to Mac had been educational. Mostly it had been wonderful, but she had to remember the downside, too. She didn't need someone she could bounce off the walls with. She didn't need someone who would be competing with her all the time, pushing her to do more, to risk more, to get right out there on the edge of life every single second. She didn't need a man whose job it was to put himself in danger; that life was one of constant excitement, but one of constant worry, too.

When she came home at night, or in the morning, depending on her shift, she needed the equivalent of soothing classical music and walls painted in muted shades of green.

She could look at Hafferty and see that he was pure red and orange—a long, lean, out-of-place cowboy who rode those broncos and those bucking bulls and wrestled them to the ground, and once in a while got trampled or gored.

So she put the card into her wallet, and smiled politely to Detective Hafferty, first name unknown, and wrote him off.

Accountant, she reminded herself. Classical musician. Professional chess player.

Not an Eagle Scout ex-para-jumper from the air force who went on to become an EMT-paramedic legend. And not a police detective.

The night-shift guys who ran Dia's truck ambled in. Her night-shift counterpart, Vega DeGracias, said, "You ready to do the counts?"

She nodded and rose, and followed him out to the big box-model ambulance. They climbed in and started counting off controlled narcotics and signing for them—something that had to be done every shift.

Meanwhile, Ryan and Tyler restocked the rest of the truck. Dia was a fanatic about making sure everything was there before they rolled—sometimes they got a call as soon as they hit the doors and they had to bend rules to answer the call, but if they had even five minutes, they could restock everything the night crew had used up.

In theory, of course, each crew restocked before they left. Fact, however, lived more than a few doors down from theory.

"Longboards, five," Tyler said.

Ryan said, "Check."

"O-two canisters, five—levels full."

"Check."

Dia listened to the drone of them going through the back of the truck.

Once she and Vega finished the count and signed the narcotics accountability sheet, he took off for home, and Dia did the rest of the paramedic gear check on her own. Airways, syringes, EKG pads and gel, IV bags and tubing, essentials like tape and emergency meds.

When they were finished checking, they took quick bathroom breaks—one of the realities of EMT life was that meals and opportunities to go to the bathroom could be eight or more hours apart, depending on the day. Another reality was that if a code-three call was coming, it would invariably come in the second before the EMT's plate hit the table or her butt hit the seat.

This time, though, no call came. They hung around the ambulance doors for a while, listening to the scanner, talking about the day before and their upcoming scuba trip.

"I wonder what they found," Tyler said suddenly.

Dia had just finished an animated monologue about the new diving watch she'd bought. "Found? Who?"

"The detectives."

"I think they found Dia," Ryan said, and laughed. "Did you see Howie's face when he saw how the tall one was looking at her?"

Dia hadn't. "Howie?"

"I missed it," Tyler said. "The whole idea of that accident yesterday not being an accident—"

"You have your priorities in line," Ryan said, and grinned. "But Howie was just about growling."

"Why? The detectives wanted information, and they were talking to all of us. They didn't single me out."

"You didn't take an elbow in the ribs when Howie saw that Detective Whatever-his-name-was wrote some sort of note on your card. *I* did. Howie was not happy."

Dia's jaw dropped. "Howie noticed that?"

"Far as I can tell," Ryan said, "Howie notices everything you do. You're apparently a regular topic of conversation on their runs. It drives Kelly nuts."

"Howie notices women," Dia said. "But he's okay. He wouldn't be bothered by my getting a note from a detective. Not *really* bothered." She shrugged. "It wasn't much of a note, anyway. He just thanked me for what I said to him yesterday."

Ryan said, "Yesterday?"

"At the wreck. He saw a couple of firefighters pulling a dead kid out of a car. Right before the burned guy who coded on us."

Ryan and Tyler both nodded.

"I said something to him about focusing on the people we could save, not on the ones we hadn't. I guess he appreciated it, because he gave me a 'thank you for yesterday' note scrawled on the back." She shrugged again. "Not exactly a proposition, you know?"

"If it had a phone number," Tyler said, "it was a proposition."

"Just the one on the front of the card," she said. "Does that mean he propositioned everyone in the room?"

She didn't know why she'd lied. Maybe because she didn't want word of the phone number getting back to Howie. She didn't want him to feel . . . hurt? Maybe. It seemed like a stupid thing to do.

But she found she wasn't inclined to tell either Ryan or Tyler the truth. Whether it was because she didn't want Howie to get his feelings hurt, or because for the first time she felt a bit uncomfortable thinking about Howie's interest in her, she just knew she didn't want to say anything.

But it was no big deal.

Their radio crackled to life. "Rescue Twenty-eight, do you read?"

Dia jumped into the truck and grabbed the handset. "This is Rescue Twenty-eight; go ahead."

"We have a call on a code one-forty, animal bite, alligator on back porch attacked unsuspecting woman walking out her door." She gave them the street address and the cross street, and added, "Police and Animal Control are dispatched, proceed code three."

"Shit," Dia said.

Ryan drove, Dia took the passenger seat, and Tyler rode in the jump seat.

"Bets on how big the alligator is?" he asked.

"Five feet, nose to tip of tail," Ryan said. "Bigger than that and she wouldn't be able to call for help."

"We don't know that she did call for help. Might have been a neighbor who saw what was going on. Or a family member."

"Might have been, but I'm just guessing it wasn't," Ryan said.

Tyler said, "I'm saying six feet, nose to tip of tail. That's big enough to do some damage. This won't be critical, though. Today is going to consist entirely of crap calls."

"You predicting that?" Dia asked. "Is this the Big One speaking, or Tyler with his brain on iPod?"

"Straight Big One," he said. "This is pure gut feeling."

"Good, then," Ryan said. "We could use a calm day."

"I *hate* your gut feelings, oh Big One." Dia sighed. "But back to the alligator. That leaves me with either seven feet, which is nearly big enough to drag her back to the canal, or four feet or smaller, which would be pretty unlikely to go after an adult woman, I'd think."

"Goddamned dinosaurs are evil. I don't think they care how big you are," Ryan said. "They scare the shit out of me."

Dia closed her eyes. "Either of you guys ever check your stoop for alligators before you step out your door?"

Ryan laughed. "Are you kidding? I just walk out the door. I have a flight of stairs to walk down from my crappy little room, and if an alligator ever climbed all the way up them, I figure he deserves to eat me. He worked hard enough for the privilege."

From the back, Tyler said, "I never even think about it."

The siren screamed, cars moved out of the way—or didn't, depending on the age, alertness, and asshole factor of the driver in question—and Dia sat there considering bad ways to start a day. Having an alligator attack when you stepped out the door seemed to her like a pretty bad one. "So what do you do if you walk outside to check your mail or something and a gator charges you? How the hell do you deal with that?"

All three of them were quiet. Dia couldn't think of anything to say. Apparently neither could the other two.

"They can run thirty-five miles an hour in short sprints," Tyler eventually said into the silence. "And their jaws are strong closing, but so weak opening that if they're closed, you can hold them shut with one hand."

Dia and Ryan exchanged glances, and Ryan said, "Maybe so, dude, but would you want to be in a position to try?"

"I'm just hoping this one is already dead and out of the way when we get there," Dia said. "I'll deal with drunks and druggies and guys with knives and guns, but I draw the line at alligator wrestling."

The other two laughed.

"That would be a lot funnier if it wasn't true." Ryan turned on the cross street they'd been given, and pointed down to two police cars, an Animal Control truck, and a small crowd of men and women standing on the sidewalk and in the street, all of whom turned and began jumping up and down, pointing to a house on the right and waving their arms.

"Well, look at that," Dia said. "Group ambulance boogie, more than eight people, nobody running toward the house. I say the alligator is four feet long or under, it got hold of the woman's clothes, and she doesn't have a scratch on her. And that at this point, somebody has trapped it under some form of furniture."

"I want to change my bet," Tyler said.

"I'm holding steady with mine," Ryan said.

They pulled into a neighbor's driveway and got out.

Dia lugged her paramedic kit, while Ryan and Tyler took the stretcher just in case.

From the back of the house they could hear running feet, screaming, thumpings, thwacking noises, and heavy objects being moved.

"Doesn't sound like they have everything under control yet," Tyler said. "We could . . . ah . . . wait in the truck."

Ryan and Dia looked at each other, and Dia said, "And miss watching the fun? Are you nuts?"

She broke into a trot and loped around the corner.

The scene was pretty much what she'd imagined. There was a woman up on the beams of a very nice solid-wood pergola. She was screaming, and there was a lot of blood on the concrete, but Dia couldn't see where she was doing any bleeding at the moment. Well, maybe she'd cut herself climbing onto her pergola—which, considering the woman's size, indicated a significant triumph of fear over gravity. And Dia wouldn't lose any betting points for a climbing injury.

On the ground there was one lean, mean young alligator about four feet long whipping his head around and charging at the cops and the one Animal Control officer who'd responded to the scene. The Animal Control officer was attempting to get a loop around the gator's nose, and not having much luck with it. Little bastard was fast.

The cops were wielding everything from deck chairs to a stray baseball bat one had picked up, and attempting to corral the gator toward the Animal Control officer's loop.

Everyone was trying to stay out of the way of the gator's jaws and tail, though.

"You guys'll be ready to take that act on the road any day now," Ryan said.

A sweating, exasperated cop glared over at Ryan and said, "Grab a chair, shithead. There's enough fun here for everyone."

Dia called to the woman, "Ma'am, where are you hurt?" She had to yell twice, because the first time the alligator charged one of the cops just as Dia shouted, and the woman shrieked.

She heard the second time, though.

The woman called back, "I'm not hurt. Well, I have some scrapes on my legs from climbing, but I'm fine."

"Who's bleeding, then?" Dia asked. She immediately wished she hadn't, because the woman's face crumpled and she burst into tears. "That monster ate Bobby!"

Dia, Tyler, and Ryan exchanged horrified glances. The gator wasn't huge. A kid would have to be awfully small. . . .

"Her Chihuahua," one of the cops said, before the EMTs had a chance to get too worked up. "The gator grabbed the dog as they came out the door. She went after the gator and tried to save the dog; the gator didn't take that too well."

The loss of a beloved pet was heartbreaking, and Dia sympathized. She was, however, relieved Bobby hadn't been a child.

"Doesn't look like they need us here," Ryan said.

Dia raised a hand. "Just wait. They haven't got the damned thing taped and tied yet. Once it's in the Animal Control officer's truck, we'll leave. But I don't want to pull out of here and then have somebody get hurt." She leaned on the stretcher on the opposite side from Ryan and said, "Besides, this is like an episode of *Crocodile Hunter.* And we get to watch it live. What's your hurry?"

Ryan gave her a little grin. "Just didn't want to miss anything big."

"If we hear anything big go out, we'll put ourselves back into action," she said.

She, Ryan, and Tyler shared a deep and abiding love of running the big calls, leaping into action in life-and-death situations and winning. They also, however, shared a loathing for the junk calls that made up easily fifty percent of their runs. "Look at it this way," she said. "This is about the time that Mrs. Stofosa usually calls in about the snake in her stomach. We're on a call, so someone else is going to have to get her."

Ryan considered that for a moment, and his grin spread into a beatific smile. "So true. So very true."

Mrs. Stofosa was a 911 regular. She called three or four times a week complaining of chest pain radiating to her back and left arm, shortness of breath, and vomiting. These were symptoms that EMS couldn't ignore, in spite of the fact that one hundred percent of the time—so far—when the rescue squad arrived, Mrs. Stofosa's complaint mysteriously transformed itself into her demand that the paramedic remove the snake that had lodged itself in her stomach, and take her to the hospital, because she had to go to the toilet and the python that lived in her own toilet would reach up and grab her and eat her if she sat down.

Mrs. Stofosa invariably had a nasty case of constipation. She clearly never dared have a bowel movement at home. She insisted she never used the toilet for anything—because of the python.

Once upon a time, Mrs. Stofosa would have lived in an asylum. Mental health hospitals didn't have many permanent residents anymore, though, so Mrs. Stofosa had been mainstreamed. Her several trips a week to the hospital to get enemas cost taxpayers hundreds of thousands of dollars a year, and left the old woman in a miserable situation—she wasn't able to take care of herself, she was always dehydrated and poorly fed, she lived in horrible conditions, and Dia wondered how anybody's best interests had been served by taking her out of the psychiatric hospital where she'd once been a cared-for resident and leaving her to fend for herself.

Mrs. Stofosa was just one of an army of people Dia saw semiregularly, had come to know by name, and had come to pity. Dia still didn't enjoy getting those calls, though. Every one of them she took meant that she was tied up for nearly an hour, during which time someone who needed her more might die because she wasn't available.

The cops at last managed to herd the gator in a direction where the Animal Control officer could reach him. They taped its jaws shut, wrapped its legs to its body, and put it in the Animal Control officer's truck. It would be released into the wild.

Dia checked the woman's leg, but it was scratched, not cut. All the blood came from the pet. She asked if the woman could have a friend come over; she was obviously distraught from the loss of her dog, and from the scare of having an alligator in her yard. But she refused Dia's offer to take her to an ER.

"I'm tougher than I look," she said, and Dia believed her. It had taken a determined woman to get up on top of that pergola—and a pretty agile one to get back down again. She might have been large, but she sure as hell wasn't soft. The woman said, "And I got things to do. I didn't survive all these years in this place, through all the things I've been through, to let a mess like this send me to the hospital. When I go to a hospital, it's going to be because something is wrong with me." She glared down her sloping backyard to the canal that ran behind it. "I'm going to get me some men out here to put a damned fence around this yard," she said. "And then I'm going to go get me another dog."

Dia had to admire that. She was looking at someone who shed her tears, then fixed her problem and moved on—Dia could see herself being like that when she got older. She *hoped* she was like that.

"Good luck," Dia told her. Then she turned to her crew. "All right, guys," she said, "let's go put ourselves back in play."

They returned to the ambulance and Dia called them in; Dispatch didn't have anything for them at the moment. She turned to Ryan and Tyler. "Gentlemen, I believe I won that bet."

Chapter 5

Brig and Stan worked their way through the hospitals that housed injured survivors of the previous day's wreck. It was grim going; they went from victim to victim, and from those able to talk they got stories of having no warning, of the eighteen-wheeler ahead suddenly careening sideways and going over on its side. Of shock, disbelief, heartbreaking despair.

They walked out of one room, and Brig heard a soft snapping sound. He looked over to find Stan staring down at a ballpoint pen that he'd snapped in half in his hand, and at the ink he had all over his palm.

"Didn't mean to do that," Stan said. His voice was soft and controlled; Stan rarely lost his temper, though when he did the effect was astonishing.

"What happened?"

"We have to get this asshole."

Brig said, "We will."

"That a promise?"

"A prediction. I'm not saying we'll have an easy time doing it. But my gut says he's going to give us something we can use."

Stan looked at the smear of ink on his palm, and tipped his head toward the men's room door they were passing. "Hope you're right. Gimme a minute, okay?"

Brig paced while he waited, running the little bit of evidence they had through his mind. He couldn't think of a motive for the traffic accidents. Some of them happened where there were plenty of bystanders, so the killer would be able to appreciate his work. Some of them, though, would pose massive logistical problems for a killer who wanted to be on hand to observe what happened.

The payoff seemed to Brig to be the key to this thing; whatever bang the killer got out of the violence he'd wrought.

What sort of bang would he get from setting up wrecks like the one on I-95? Did he have a rooftop perch in back of one of the barrier walls? Did he have a hiding place on the accident side of the barrier, where he could later disguise himself as either a victim or a rescuer? Where he could get in close to enjoy the devastation he'd wrought?

Maybe he passed himself off as a victim, Brig thought. Because rescuers came and went.

Except, of course, for cops. Cops came and stayed.

Brig closed his eyes against that thought. A state trooper's car could sit in the median all day, with the driver waiting for the perfect opportunity to put down one of his bombs on the highway during an instant when no one in either direction would see him. Then he could put himself in the perfect position to set the bomb off, and to respond to the call when it came. He wouldn't need to miss a thing.

Stan came out.

"Ugly theory just crossed my mind."

"Oh?"

"What do you think of someone in the Highway Patrol as our bomber?"

They walked toward the elevators, Stan silent, clearly considering the possibilities.

"Works for the highway stuff. Not too well for the ones we've had in town."

Brig said, "Right. In town, a cop works better."

"Maybe someone impersonating a police officer?"

The elevator door opened, and both stepped in. "Maybe."

Stan said, "I don't like taking our thoughts in that direction."

"Hell, neither do I. I offer it as a possibility only. Would suck not to consider all the possibilities."

"Fireman? Wouldn't be the first time a fireman set his own fires."

"No, it wouldn't. I thought of EMTs, too. With fire and rescue, though, there's always the possibility that they won't get called to the accident. Something else could hit that takes priority. I don't see our guy being willing to miss the payoff, whatever it is. Most of these haven't made the news. So that doesn't seem like a good route for him to get his jones."

The doors opened again at the next stop, and two nurses got on.

No one said anything until they got off two floors below.

Stan picked up right where they'd left off. "The guy who's staging these things isn't into wet work. These are all hands-off killings where he isn't looking into anyone's eyes while they die. I think, though, that he has to know he's going to get to see them. Because otherwise he has no reason to do them."

"It sounds like a possibility."

Stan sighed. "Which tips us either toward some variety of cop, or some variety of guy on his day off."

"No. It doesn't leave us with a lot more than we started with, actually. The possibility exists that we're completely off base here, and that this is something other than what it looks like." Brig considered the other things it could be as the doors opened again on the ground floor, and he and Stan exited while a crowd pushed past them to get in.

He looked around. The lobby had that corporate office, decorator feel, with mauve and teal furniture and dramatically uplit plants and burlap-padded walls to keep everything nice and quiet. It had that omnipresent hospital disinfectant reek that Brig hated, too. He tried to imagine working all day, every day, in that place, and felt his gut tighten. Hospitals gave him a bad case of claustrophobia.

"So," Stan said, "was the hot little redhead the paramedic who got your attention?"

Brig gave him a sidelong look. "No. And I'm not discussing that. But why do you ask?"

"She was really cute. If you're not in the picture, well . . ."

"Mmm," Brig said.

Stan laughed. "I want to know, man. I saw you scribbling a note on the back of one of your cards, but I didn't see who got the card." A wicked smile slid across his face. "Or was it the handsome blond guy with the big blue eyes who was staring at you like you were dessert?"

Brig said, "Neither. And you're a shitbag, you know that?"

"I do know that. So you thought the *Amazon* was hot?"

"Damn, you're an annoying bastard, Chang. But, yeah, I did. She's pretty. And she looked competent." He shrugged. "Not that it matters."

"Unless, of course, she calls you, right?"

Brig didn't say anything else as they walked out to Stan's unmarked.

* * *

"You want to go to supper?" Ryan asked. "I think everyone is going to shower and then meet up at TGI Friday's tonight."

"I'm going to take a rain check," Dia said. "Between the alligator this morning and the naked guy dancing in the median and Drug Boy and Dirt Girl, I've had more weirdness for one day than my brain can handle. I'm going to pick up some groceries, and go home, and make myself a nice salad, I think."

"Sounds dull," Tyler said.

"After today, it sounds like an improvement."

"Kelly's promised to bring Sam," Ryan said. "She's hoping we can all meet him."

Dia grabbed her bag from her locker and rifled through it for her car keys. "The elusive Sam. God. It's almost worth going, just in case. But . . . I'm too exhausted to meet someone important for the first time. You know what I mean?"

"I do," Ryan said. "See you tomorrow, then."

"Bright and early."

She got home a little past eight, much later than she should have. They'd ended up tied into that last call. Dirt Girl had to be peeled out of twelve layers of clothes just so Dia could find a vein; she'd been combative and hallucinating; she'd required restraints, and Dia was going to have a whole series of interesting bruises obtained while putting her in them. The ambulance had ended up smelling of blood and shit and an inescapable, clinging, yellow body odor that suggested Dirt Girl hadn't bathed since Kennedy was president.

Even restrained, the woman kept trying to bite.

The hospital where they took her knew her—she'd evidently been a huge fan of psychedelics in the sixties and early seventies, and had moved on to whoring for her drugs through the late eighties. According to them, she somehow managed to clean up in the nineties. But then paranoid schizophrenia and years of damage had taken her down for the count, and for the last five years she'd been an ever-deteriorating disaster on legs.

Dia had a hard time being sympathetic. The woman's chart had been five inches thick, and according to the nurse who took their report and admitted the patient, it was one of ten. Most of the bad that had happened to her, she'd brought down on herself.

It was different with people who were just in the way of a runaway train. Dia lived for helping them. The biting, screaming, kicking, thrashing, swearing Dirt Girl, though, was another matter. Not all of God's little children deserved the same sympathy.

She pulled into her drive and checked before getting out of her car. Single women living alone had to take an extra degree of care, and she wasn't about to assume everything was okay.

But no one was hiding in the shrubs, or around her in other yards.

She opened her garage door, pulled in, and closed it quickly behind her. Then she grabbed two bags of groceries, locked the car and headed into the house.

She tossed her keys and her purse on the kitchen counter, quickly put the groceries away, and headed into the living room, on her way to her bedroom to change.

Someone had shoved an envelope under her front door.

It was big, and kind of fancy—cream stationery with a small silver band along the back. She lifted it and turned it over. It had nothing on the front. She held it up to the light, but could not see anything through the heavy paper.

She got a knife and carefully opened the envelope. Inside was a single folded sheet of stationery that matched the envelope, and on it were the words, *Thank you. I love you for what you did for me.*

Dia stared at the note. The words seemed harmless enough, but the fact that they were typed and had been printed by a computer seemed ominous to her. Wrong, somehow. As was the fact that the note hadn't been signed. And the writer's unnerving use of the word "love."

The flowers and the note could both be explained if the sender was shy, or had poor social skills. Sort of.

But Dia wasn't in the mood to assume that the situation was safe.

Skin crawling, heart racing, she placed the envelope and note on her kitchen table. Then she went through her half of the little duplex, making sure every window was fastened and that both doors were locked and barred.

Then she stood there, trying to think of the sane thing to do.

Call the police? They weren't going to be too impressed by flowers and a thank-you note.

Call her friends? They'd suggest that she call the police.

Dia fished into her bag and pulled out Detective Hafferty's business card, and first tried him at work.

"He's not in right now," a man said. "You want to leave a message?" Dia gave the man her number, and asked him to note that the call was not concerning information about the wreck Brig was investigating.

Then she tried his home number, and when she didn't get him there, left a brief message. "Wanted to ask your advice about something," she said. "This isn't wreck-related, but it is important. Well, it isn't important to you. . . . Please call me back when you get this."

Then she hung up. She didn't feel much like eating

anymore. She took a shower, came out to the bare, cleaned mirror, missed Mac's note a little and half regretted washing it off, and went to bed, where she lay for a long time, trying to get herself calmed down enough to fall asleep.

Chapter 6

Brig got home late, and didn't check his messages until the next morning.

When he did, he heard a female voice on the phone. Pretty voice, sexy. She identified herself as Dia, and his heart rate picked up. He'd thought it sounded like her, but he didn't want to hope.

And then she said she wasn't calling about the accident, and he grinned.

He was running a little behind, but he wrote down Dia's phone number, called her back, and got her machine. Of course.

People never actually talked to each other on the phone anymore, did they? They just left messages.

He waited through her recorded greeting, which was short and to the point. He was relieved it wasn't cutesy or stupid. And when he got the tone, he said, "Dia, this is Brig returning your call. You have my work number and my home number, but here's my cell number, in case I'm not at either of the others. In fact, just call my cell—I always have it." He left his number and hung up. And then he copied her number to a separate piece of paper, and stuck that in his shirt pocket. If he didn't hear from her, he'd try her again later in the day.

He was still grinning as he headed off to work.

*   *   *

Dia worked straight through to the next Friday in an exhausted daze. She ended up covering for the paramedic who had her truck on day shift when she was off. She worked her scheduled shifts and picked up days for Terry Blankenship, who was out with something influenza-like. Which meant Dia missed two scheduled days off.

The squad was nonstop, which didn't help. Everyone on days was averaging just over one call per hour, which meant, in practical terms, that no one had time to catch a breath; an ambulance had no more than finished one patient than it was sent on another call. She was working with her crew, and then with Terry's crew. She was taking everything from attempted suicides to women delivering babies to trauma to cardiac emergencies to drownings and near-drownings, and she went from work to home to sleep and straight back to work again. She knew she'd eaten at some point, she could remember a few times that she managed to hit a bathroom, but it all turned into one incredibly long day.

Dia dragged herself home on Friday night so exhausted that she couldn't even think. Terry had finally made it back, so she had two full days in which she could relax, and the first thing she did when she got home was to drop onto her couch and stare at the ceiling.

Quiet. Everything was quiet: She didn't have the scanner on, the sound of traffic outside was muted and alien, and all she could hear over the hum of the air conditioner was her own breath going in and out.

She lay on the couch, in street clothes with her shoes still on, because she'd showered at work, and the stillness seeped into her. Eventually, little by little, her mind slowed down. It had been running like a hamster on a wheel for days, but either the hamster had finally gotten tired up there and fallen asleep, or else he'd died. She was remarkably short on thoughts, which was a beautiful thing.

And then she had two, in quick succession.

The first was that she hadn't had any more notes or gifts or anything from the person who claimed she saved his—or her—life.

The second, tied tightly to thoughts of a possible stalker, was that Brig had never called her back.

Which made him a bit of a jerk, didn't it?

Well—okay, maybe it didn't. It was entirely possible that he'd had a week like hers. It was equally possible that something had happened that had prevented him from hearing her message in the first place. Maybe he wasn't ignoring her; maybe he'd never known she wanted to talk to him.

She closed her eyes. That was the trouble with calling people. It was entirely impossible to know what had gone wrong.

She'd evidently overreacted to the note and the flowers, though, so the fact that he hadn't gotten back with her wasn't critical. It would have been nice to see him, she thought. But she might have read too much into his level of personal interest, too.

She closed her eyes and let it all wash away. He wasn't her type anyway. She was too interested in him, and she didn't need to go in that direction.

She breathed in, and held her breath, and then slowly breathed out. With every exhalation, she pushed worries and tensions away. She relaxed her body. She imagined warmth, and sunlight, and every muscle she had turning into jelly.

The phone rang.

She opened her eyes and reached over her head to the end table, where the phone sat.

"Hello?"

Ryan said, "You're still on for diving Sunday, right?"

"Sunday. Yeah, I can do Sunday. Tomorrow, though, I'm not doing anything but sleep."

Ryan laughed. "You worked pretty hard this week."

"I shouldn't complain," Dia told him. "You pull so many extra shifts, I don't know how you make it to a day off."

"I need the money," he said. "And construction never works out all that well for me. They need me when I can't be there, or I need them when they aren't there."

"I know." Dia closed her eyes again. "Dude, I'd love to talk, but I really need to sleep."

"Sleep," Ryan said. "I'll see you Sunday."

She yawned. "Sounds good."

She'd no more than hung up the phone than it rang again. "What'd you forget?" she said by way of greeting.

"Is this Dia Courvant?"

Different voice entirely. Deep, sexy . . . a goose-bumps voice.

"May I ask who's calling?" she said.

"This is Detective Brig Hafferty."

She sat up, suddenly awake all over. "Oh. Hi. Yes, this is Dia. If you were work, I was going to say I was dead, but . . . funny . . . I was just thinking about you, wondering if you got my message."

"I've been trying to get in touch with you all week."

She frowned. "You have?"

"I must have left a dozen messages on your machine."

Now she was puzzled. "There hasn't been one. Well, not one from you, anyway. There have been a few from work, but that's all."

"So your machine is working?"

"Well . . . yes."

"Anyone else besides you have access to your answering machine?"

"No. It's just me here."

The other end of the line was quiet for a long time. Then Brig sighed. "So there are three possibilities. One, I called, but for some reason my calls, and only my calls, didn't record. Or from your perspective, I didn't call before but am now claiming I did. *I* know that's not true—I've called the number you gave me and left two or three messages a day since you called me."

"Did I give you the wrong number?" Dia said. She was mostly just thinking out loud, but he answered her anyway.

"No. I had the right number. Your voice gave the answering message. Yesterday I was concerned enough that when I still hadn't heard from you I phoned the station, but you were out on a call, and your captain told me he couldn't be sure you would get my message because everything had been so frantic."

Dia found that odd. "I'm surprised you didn't give up."

Brig said, "When you left your message, you sounded afraid. I would have liked to think that you had just called to talk, but every time I listened to your message, I became more convinced that something was wrong, and that you actually *needed* to talk to me."

"I had something going on," Dia told him. "It isn't a problem anymore, though."

"Oka-a-a-ay."

"I would have answered if the messages had been there," Dia said. "But it isn't that big a deal, Brig. Really. When I actually had enough downtime to realize that you hadn't called me back, which was about five minutes ago, I just figured your week had ended up as bad as mine."

"It might have been," Brig said. "But the fact that you got other messages, but not those that I left, bothers me." His voice was reasonable, but a little bit worried as well. She found that oddly flattering. "For a good reason. What if the messages went through, and your machine recorded them, but somewhere between when I left them and when you were available to answer them, someone else removed them?"

His words shocked her. "No one could do that."

"Can you check your messages from another phone?"

"Of course."

"Can you delete individual messages, and leave others?"

"Sure."

"Then so could anyone else who obtained access to your password. It happens," Brig said. "But usually not for happy reasons."

Dia realized she'd moved to the edge of the couch and her pulse had picked up. "That's . . . completely paranoid." No one had any reason to tamper with her messages, or to selectively remove some of them.

"The other possibilities are that I never called you and am now lying, or that you got the messages and are now lying. How likely are those possibilities?"

Dia considered. Brig was calling her now, and was concerned; he'd sounded quite worried when she first answered his call. She had to believe that he was telling her the truth and that he had called before. She *knew* the messages hadn't been there, but she also believed him when he said he'd left them.

She sat for a moment considering how best to frame her problem so that she didn't blow it out of proportion or misrepresent it. "When I called you, it was because I'd had a couple of odd things happen, and I wanted some practical advice."

"Define 'odd.'"

Dia realized right then that she missed telephones with cords. She could have used a nice cord to twist between her fingers. She wanted to have something to do with her hands, and she had nothing.

"Someone left me an anonymous bouquet of flowers last Saturday. And last Sunday, when I got home from work I found an envelope shoved under my door. Both of them claimed to be thank-yous from someone whose life I'd saved."

There was no humor in Brig's voice as he said, "That ever happen to you before?"

"No." Dia dropped a throw pillow on her lap and started twisting the fringe between her fingers. "No. Not ever. I've always been very careful to guard access to my address. I don't socialize with patients. I don't give out any personal information about myself, either, and none of the people I work with would ever give out information about me. So I don't receive thank-yous—which is fine. I don't want them. But I don't deal with visits from some of my scariest patients, either."

"You have any idea who might be leaving things?"

"None whatsoever. I've saved a lot of people's lives. I have no idea which one of them might choose to look for me."

Brig said, "Personal information is available to people in a lot of ways now. It might be that you're easy to find for someone with access to some of these databases."

Dia said, "Someone might know where I am. But I haven't made it easy."

Brig said, "Do you still have the note? Or the flowers?"

"I saved both. But there hasn't been anything else this week."

"Unless the fact that your messages were erased was related. If it was related, then there's been something every day."

Dia could hear her heart thudding faster. She stared at

the telephone, thinking about the flowers and the note. About the queasy feeling she'd gotten when they showed up. Something had been wrong. Something was still wrong.

"Are you still there?" Brig asked.

"I'm still here. I'm just having a little problem breathing."

"You're probably fine. For your own peace of mind, though, would you like for me to come over and take a look at what's going on?"

Dia looked around the cozy little front room, still decorated with family pictures of her and Mac, with stacks of her books and his movies. She thought about someone watching her in this little place that had been her home for almost six years. She had regular enough habits that she would probably be easy to stalk. Someone who wanted to know where she lived had only to find out where she worked, then follow her home. It wouldn't take a detective. All it would take was someone who could competently navigate South Florida traffic—and while the competence requirement weeded out nearly everyone on the road, in a county that was closing on two million inhabitants, that still left a lot of drivers who could get the job done.

And as tired as she usually was when she got off work, she wouldn't even notice being tailed. She'd never considered the possibility that anyone might want to stalk her.

She didn't know anyone, really, except for the people at work.

But a lot of people she didn't know, knew her.

She'd saved a lot of lives. She lost a lot, too.

"I'd . . . I'd appreciate that," she told him.

"Then I'll be over. Where do you live?"

She gave him her address. She decided to take

another shower, just to try to wake herself up. The one at work had been pretty unsatisfying. Standing in steaming water would be a stress reliever, too. She had her doors locked, her windows closed and locked. She'd be quick—just in and soak for five or ten minutes, and then back out again.

He told her he'd need at least twenty minutes to get to her, and probably half an hour. She had time.

She stood in the shower, water pounding on her back, head hanging down, and focused on breathing: deep, slow breaths that brought her racing heartbeat back down to a sane speed.

The missing calls were a fluke—some stupid electronic thing that had happened between her phone and his. They were nothing important. Brig would come, check things out, and he and she would both see that everything was fine. He'd look at the card in the flowers and the note from under the door and tell her they were no big deal.

Nobody had any reason to want to stalk her. She had no enemies. She hardly even had people she didn't like. She had saved a lot of people's lives, but people you saved didn't come back to haunt you. And the ones you lost didn't, either, except in dreams.

Their friends, their families, though . . .

The shower wasn't helping. She wasn't calming down. She was just realizing how much bigger her circle of contacts was than it seemed. She started to understand how many people might have reason to know her whom she had never known beyond a name, a face, and an injury or disease. How many people might hate her for being unable to work a miracle, to save the life of someone they loved. Or . . . consider Howie and the man he'd saved. The wife had wanted that man dead. Had been happy that he was dying. How many lives had

Dia succeeded in saving, only to make an enemy of the person who wanted them dead?

Gunshot wounds. Knifings. The guy with the ice pick in his skull. Battered wives, battered husbands.

No good deed goes unpunished, someone had once told her.

She couldn't remember who; she couldn't remember when. She knew she'd been appalled by the cynicism of that remark. But there could be a lot of people in Broward County who had reason to want to hurt her, just because of what she did, who she was, whom she had helped.

The water started to get cold, and she realized she'd been in there for a long time. She turned it off and stepped out of the shower, toweled off, turned toward the mirror.

Mac's message, written in steam four years before, was gone. But in its place, in the same block printing, was a new message.

KILL YOU

Chapter 7

Brig found her sitting on her front stoop, her hair wet and tangled, her arms wrapped around herself. She was dressed in a sweatshirt and jeans, and the temperature had to be over ninety in the shade, but he could see her shivering. She looked pale.

She looked scared.

He got out of the car and studied her neighborhood. She lived in a little duplex, and the area was run-down. It was a typical transitional neighborhood: racially integrated, full of old cars and weedy yards and boarded windows interspersed with mowed yards and painted houses that belonged to the folks who were still trying. Twenty years earlier the place had been developer-fresh, bright with promise, full of new starter duplexes and older couples with empty nests and young couples dreaming of families. In ten more years it would be an area police toured warily, that gave more than its share of calls to the county emergency rescue and more than its share of criminals to the police. Right then, right there, it was fading fast. It would have some guy dealing nearby, it would have a couple of girls turning tricks from one of the duplexes, and it would have a lot of families down on their luck crowding together in the tiny homes, making do. Not too many nest-eggers, not too many hopeful young couples. Not anymore.

And it wasn't the sort of place where neighbors would watch out for one another.

He walked up the drive. "You don't look so good."

"Someone has been inside my house," she said.

His heart skipped a beat. He didn't let it show. "How do you know?"

"There was a message written on my mirror. In the steam, you know?"

"Okay . . ." He waited.

"It said, 'Kill you.' "

He took a deep breath. "Yeah, that's bad. Let's go take a look."

She rose. He liked her height. She was a few inches shorter than him, but only a few. She appealed to him on all sorts of levels, actually. Still damp from a shower, smelling of soap and shampoo, she connected to some very visceral, very sexual images that he really needed to back away from.

She took him into her bathroom, which was tiny. He looked at the mirror. "I don't see anything."

"It only shows up with steam. I didn't think this would clear so fast."

She closed the bathroom door and turned on the shower. Leaning in that way, messing with the knobs, she showed off the curve of a long, smooth back that moved to a rounded, full ass. The sweatshirt slid up enough that he could catch just a flash of skin.

He turned away and calculated his overtime for the last week, because his body was noticing her in ways he wasn't prepared to deal with.

"I don't have that much hot water right now, probably," she said. "If this doesn't work, we'll have to wait and try again."

"That's fine," he told her. "I'll stick around for a while. I want to see the note you got, too. And the flowers."

She nodded.

They watched the steam curling over the top of the glass shower enclosure. Brig turned to study the mirror. It didn't take a lot of steam to start seeing letters. Not a lot to see that the mirror really did say, *KILL YOU.*

He turned to her, and saw that she had tears running down her cheeks. She saw that he saw it. "You need to see any more?" she asked.

"No. That's clear enough."

She turned off the water. Then she pushed past him, and his body wanted to grab and hold on, to pull her close.

He handed the problem over to his mind, which still remembered things like alimony payments and having all his favorite belongings go walking out the door as someone else's stuff. He kept his hands to himself and followed her into the narrow hall. "It's bad," he said. "But not unfixable." He took a deep breath. "To protect yourself, you're going to have to make some changes in the way you live your life."

She nodded. "I know. I have friends who will help me. I'm going to show you the things this guy left before. And while you're looking at them, I'm going to have my friends come over."

He walked behind her into her microscopic eat-in kitchen, intrigued by her response. It wasn't the usual one.

Dia pointed Brig to the counter, where some dying flowers and a fancy envelope lay. "I've only touched the top left corner of the envelope and the message inside," she said. "Same for the note stuck into the flowers. I don't suppose the basket the flowers came in would be too good for holding fingerprints, but mine would be all over that, anyway. I wasn't thinking when I picked it up."

"You were thinking later," he said. "You did fine."

"I'm going to call my friends," she said. "I'll have them come over. And you can tell us all what we need to do."

"All right," he said.

He studied the notes. They were just a little off, not quite the right wording for thank-you notes, missing the name that would make them safe. Any name would have done, really. He considered the fact that if the sender wanted to lull her into a false sense of security, he could have written "Bob" or "John" or even "Jennifer" on the notes. In her career, Dia had probably saved more than a few Bobs or Johns or Jennifers—she would have assumed everything was on the level, and while it might have made her uncomfortable, she would not have been left wary and frightened.

Scaring her, then, was part of this guy's game. Like the writing in the shower.

That was intended to be a frightening thing. No message was there when she walked in; one appeared in the steam when she got out, when she was naked and helpless.

That was ugly.

They were dealing with a game player. An asshole who thought he was cute. And smart. He would think he was too smart to be caught. Brig didn't like guys like that.

"Thanks, Kelly. And . . . sorry Sam couldn't make it," Dia said behind him. "Tell everyone else, would you? I'll see you guys in a few."

She turned to Brig. "They're on their way."

"Who all is coming?"

"The crew from my ambulance—and one of the other day-shift crews."

"Not people you have any problem with?"

"People I trust my life to. My second family. Along with being EMTs or paramedics, we dive together. We're all qualified rescue divers; we team up to keep our hours and certifications current. We've gone mountain climbing and skiing together. We watch each other's backs every day."

"Okay, then. I have friends like that, too."

She nodded.

He looked at her. She was a lot of things he wanted in a woman, even though he didn't want another woman. He admired what she did; he liked her air of competence; he didn't like seeing her scared.

That was bringing out parts of him that he didn't want to deal with.

He was getting protective. He wanted to go into warrior mode, to keep her safe.

Brig said, "Show me through this place. Let me get an idea of what sort of security problems you have."

She showed him around. She'd done a decent enough basic job of keeping the place safe. The windows were double-hung, and she'd pinned them. She had little magnets on the sides that allowed her to pull the pins out in an emergency. She'd gotten decent locks for her doors—they were both dead-bolted. The locks showed no signs of tampering.

"You have a blind spot in your backyard," he said, looking out her back window.

"I know. The neighbors put up a privacy fence. I hate it—all I have back there at night now are shadows."

"You're going to need to get a spotlight for back there."

"I can do that."

Her bell rang. She hurried over, peeked out, and opened it. One of the guys he'd seen at the station walked in, looking worried. He hugged her and said, "You okay?"

"I'm all right," she told him, and turned. "Ryan, you know Detective Hafferty," she said. "Brig, this is Ryan Williams. One of my crew, and a crack EMT." They shook hands.

Brig remembered the tall, sandy-haired guy. "You made good time," he said.

Ryan nodded. "That's what friends are for."

A handful of people showed up in quick succession after that. Brig met Kelly Beam, whom Stan had found so attractive, and Howard Nash, and Tyler Frakes, and an odd duck introduced only as Sherm.

"Evidence suggests Dia's being stalked," Brig said when Dia and her friends were crowded into seats in her living room. He stood watching them, seeing the anger and the worry in their faces. "She's had her life threatened."

All of them reacted with immediate dismay. Ryan said, "She *what?*"

"There was a message written on my mirror when I got out of the shower tonight," Dia said. "It said, um . . ." She took a deep breath. "It said, 'Kill you.'"

They all stared at one another. Kelly, sitting next to Dia, said, "Oh, Dia, that's awful."

"I've gotten flowers and a card recently," Dia said. "Both were anonymous. And scary. And someone has tampered with my answering machine—erasing certain messages. But the message in the shower . . . that was the first time that there was a definite threat. Someone has been in here."

Brig watched them. He didn't trust anyone in situations like this, but there wasn't one of them who reacted in a suspicious manner to what she'd said. They were all surprised, or one of them was one hell of an actor.

"So," Brig said, "what we need is for you to think of anyone who might have reason to want to hurt her.

Along with that, Dia's going to have to make some changes in her lifestyle. She's going to need to watch where she's going at all times. Get a gun and learn how to use it. Maybe get a dog, or else a trusted roommate. Change the way she goes to and from work every day. She needs to start by making her house hard to target, and then she needs to make herself hard to target. She says you can help her do some of the things she needs to do."

Dia's friend Kelly turned to her and said, "Dia, he wants you to turn your life upside down. To put yourself in a cage. You can't do that. You can't give in to this guy, Dia. You can't change your whole life because of him. If you do that, he wins."

And there it was. The line Brig heard out of the mouth of just about every woman who was dealing with a stalker. "I can't give up my aerobics class, even if he does know I go there. If I do that, he'll win." Or, "I can't put bars on my windows. If I live in a cage, he'll win."

An unfortunate number of women with those objections turned into women whose murders he ended up investigating when they discovered the hard way that a restraining order was, in fact, a worthless piece of paper for anyone but the detective who was deciding who made the most likely murder suspect.

He started to respond, but Dia beat him to it. Vehemently. "Are you *nuts?* Kelly, have you lost your *mind?* If I'm *dead,* he wins. I'll do anything I goddamned have to to just to keep that from happening. I'll change my locks, change my routines, change my living arrangements; I don't care. My objective is to still be alive and in one piece when they catch this guy—or woman, whatever—and lock him . . . her . . . it . . . away."

Brig would have hugged Dia right there, had it not been totally unprofessional. And a bad idea personally.

Kelly looked nonplussed.

Dia seemed as startled by her friend's question as Kelly had been by Dia's answer.

Kelly said, "We're all about saving lives. You're talking about doing things that could hurt someone, Dia. I mean, getting a big watchdog. You know what those things do to people; we've worked on the people they did it to. You get a gun, you're going to have to . . . what? You're going to shoot someone? You? You're going to kill somebody if you have to?" She shook her head. "You couldn't do that. It would go against everything you've made your life about."

Dia stood up. "You want to look at it that way, you can. I don't. I've made my life about helping people, but that doesn't mean I intend to be a free shot for someone who has made his life about hurting people. I don't see all lives as having equal value, Kelly. I think that good people who are doing good things have more of a right to live than criminals and killers. If it comes down to one or the other, I'm voting with the good people. And if somebody is going to die and the good person in the equation happens to be me, then I'm all in favor of killing the bad person. By myself, if I have to. I'm not going to be an easy victim for anyone."

The men in the room began to applaud.

Kelly looked around at them, her face turning red. "You'd kill someone?" she said, looking from one man to the next. "You'd take another human being's life?"

"Not for fun," Howie said. "I'd never go out looking to kill someone. Not ever. But if someone came looking to kill me, you're damned right I'd kill him if I could."

She looked to Ryan.

Ryan shrugged. "In a heartbeat. I like living."

Blond, quiet Sherm said, "Me, too. Wouldn't even blink."

Kelly looked at Brig and said, "Well, of course you'd kill him. It's your job to kill people."

Brig stared at her in disbelief. "I'm a homicide detective. It's my job to find out who killed other people. I'm one of the good guys, sweetheart."

She made a face and looked to Tyler, the last of the men. Tyler said, "I wouldn't be happy about it, and I'd see if I could get away first. Or maybe if I could reason with him. But if he didn't give me any choice, I'd fight for my life."

With that attitude, in a fight for his life, Brig thought, Tyler was going to be toast. The last thing an assault victim dared to be thinking about when someone was trying to kill him was whether or not he was going to hurt his attacker. But Brig didn't say anything.

Dia turned to Kelly. "I'm afraid to ask whether you'd rather walk in here and find me dead on the floor, or some stranger I killed."

"You know I don't want you to die."

"But you wouldn't lift a finger to save me."

"I didn't say that."

"Sure you did. That's exactly what you said. If you wouldn't kill someone to save your own life, you sure as hell aren't going to jump in to protect mine."

Kelly's mouth opened and closed, but no sound came out.

"It isn't what *you'd* do that's the issue here anyway, Kelly. Nobody is after you. Nobody has threatened to kill you. The issue is, are you willing to help me do what I have to do?"

Kelly looked like she was about to cry. She said, "You know I'd help you. There are just different kinds of help."

Dia shrugged and turned her attention to Brig. "What do you suggest?"

"New locks. Handgun plus training. An alarm system. A roommate you trust, or if you can't find one, a dog." He looked around the place. "You don't have a lot of room for a dog in here, and you'd need a pretty big one. And your hours could make a dog a problem, too."

He studied the pictures on the mantel. "Any chance that guy's your stalker?"

"My husband?" Dia turned to look where he was pointing, then shook her head. "He died four years ago. On the job."

And Brig felt his foot wedging itself into his mouth. *Yeah. Ask the widow if her dead husband is stalking her. Nice.*

Without warning, he was freezing. Standing there in the warm room, he felt like someone had dumped ice water on him.

The reaction sent a shudder slithering its way down his spine, and for just a moment déjà vu hit him as he remembered one case he'd worked on where that was exactly what had been happening. The dead husband hadn't been nearly as dead as advertised, while no one had believed the wife, who'd been in terrible danger.

What were the odds?

He said, "Dia, can I talk to you someplace private? Just for a minute? And then we'll get back to this." He was studying those photographs, and something about them was making his hair stand on end. It defied logic, reason, the facts as he knew them. But he suddenly couldn't get that other case out of his mind.

She followed him into the kitchen, and he said, "Bear with me, because I know this is going to sound like a stupid question, but . . . can you absolutely, positively guarantee that your husband is dead?"

She stared at him like he'd lost his mind. "Yes. Why?"

Brig said, "A couple years ago, a friend of mine met

this girl who was getting harassing calls from her ex, who happened to be in a coma at the time. When he died—and the FBI had proof that he was dead—he kept harassing her, and he came after her. And she almost died, and a couple other people did die, before we figured out what was going on with her."

Dia looked down at the floor. "Okay. I can see why you asked, then. I know Mac is dead. I was first responder on the scene when the ambulance he was riding jump seat in swerved to miss a car that jammed on the brakes. The ambulance rolled down an embankment and into a concrete-slab wall that buckled and speared into the ambulance. There was barely enough left of the guys in front to scrape into coffins. Mac was thrown clear partway through the roll, though. I don't know why he didn't have his belt on; he might have been setting up supplies for the call they were answering. He did that sometimes."

She took a deep breath and looked up at Brig. "Anyway, he was thrown out the back partway through the roll, and the ambulance rolled over him, and . . ." She closed her eyes. "I found him in pieces."

From one bedroom, music suddenly blared. "Bad Moon Rising," the Creedence Clearwater Revival version. It was so loud it shook the walls.

Any color Dia had in her face drained out right then. He watched her knuckles go white, watched her head whip around in the direction of the bedroom. She left him standing there, bewildered, and bolted for the bedroom.

He followed.

She had a nice little PC set up in there, flat-screen monitor, printer, big-ass cable modem. The screen had some sort of psychedelic swirling pattern going across it, and it was playing Creedence so loud his eardrums felt like they were going to burst.

She turned the speakers down, then grabbed the mouse and the keyboard and started clicking through things. "It was set to play this song. Only this song. It doesn't make any sense. I haven't been able to listen to 'Bad Moon Rising' in four years."

Brig waited for an explanation.

She turned. "We were EMTs together, Mac and I. Before we got married, we were on the same crew. And 'Bad Moon Rising' was our run-to song. When we were running hot to a big call, that was the song we had playing. After we got married, we moved to different crews, of course. He still used that song. And it was playing—loud—when they rolled the ambulance and died. It was still playing when I found them."

She closed her eyes. Brig heard a throat clearing behind him, and turned to find her friends crowded together in the hall. "Nobody came in here," Kelly said. "We were all sitting in the living room waiting for you two to come back."

Dia stood up. "I suppose I can expect other things like this. For a day or two, anyway, until we shake everything down." She looked at all of them, back straight, chin up, defiant. "This is like the message that was written on the mirror. It's something the stalker set up. To scare me. To show me that he was here, that he could get close to me." Her voice was flat and angry. "And Mac's song was set up in here—evidently set up to go off when I was resting, or in the shower, or whatever the bastard thought I was going to be doing right about now." She turned to Brig. "Do you have any ideas of other surprises I might have to look out for? Should one of the guys go out and check my brake lines? Should I make sure the place hasn't been rigged so that my bed will blow up when I get in it?"

So she was the sort who got mad when she got scared. He liked that in a woman. It worked.

He smiled at her. "You're one of the good ones."

Howie laughed and said, "You can't be hitting on my sweetheart right in front of me." And then he stopped himself and glanced at Dia. "That wasn't the brightest thing I've ever said, considering the circumstances, was it?"

Kelly said, "He's checking all of you out anyway."

Everyone in the room looked at her.

"Come on. He'd be nuts not to. A stalker isn't always someone close to the victim, but he is enough times that you guys would have been the first ones he considered."

Dia happened to be looking right at Kelly when Brig said, "Actually, we'll be investigating you, too, Kelly."

And Kelly's eyes went round.

"Me?"

"Not all stalkers are men," Brig said. "Not all women who are stalkers choose men as their targets. I can't afford to make assumptions here, since Dia doesn't have any clue who might be after her."

"It isn't *me*," Kelly said. Her cheeks flushed bright red, and she looked from one of the men she worked with to the next. "I swear to God, it isn't me."

Brig was taken aback by her vehement response.

Kelly turned to stare straight at him. "You're going to find out . . . things . . . that might look suspicious. About me, that is. They aren't."

"You want to talk to me in private before all my information comes back?" he asked her. "Maybe ride down to the station with me and make a statement?"

"It's nothing like that," she said. "It's . . . I wish I hadn't said anything."

Her friends were staring at her, eyebrows raised, and then glancing at one another.

Brig decided not to push the issue for the moment. He nodded. "Everyone out in the living room," he said. "You've had a death threat with clear breaking and entering. Consider it reported—I'll cover the paperwork on it. I'll get a forensics guy over here to pull fingerprints. We'll need sets from everyone here to eliminate, if nothing else."

"Ours are all on record," Ryan said. "We had to be printed and have background checks before we could be hired."

That helped. If her friends were in the system, they'd be a lot easier to eliminate as suspects. He called work, quickly explained the situation, and when people were on the way, said, "All right. While we're waiting, let's figure this thing out."

Dia made a point of turning the computer all the way off.

In the living room, Howie said, "I can go over her car. I was a motorhead when I was a kid. I still work on my own cars. I'll just go out there tonight and make sure it looks okay. And then she can lock it in her garage."

Brig nodded. "I have a friend who can come out and replace your locks. I'll ask him to give you my discount."

Ryan said, "I can install the security system for you— and one of the guys I work construction with has an in with an electronics firm that does top-notch systems. He'll be able to get it for me for cost, and since you won't have to pay labor, you'll only have to pay"— he mentally counted her windows and doors—"probably about three hundred bucks. That's a huge savings."

Dia looked at them. "Thanks, guys."

Sherm said, "I can come by and follow you to work mornings. And back home at night. I don't live that far from you."

Ryan said, "We don't all work the same days—but some of us are working with her every day. Why don't we set it up so that whoever works with her that day follows her home?"

Brig said, "That sounds like a workable plan."

Everyone nodded.

Kelly was fiddling with the fringe on a throw pillow. She said, "Dia? My lease on my studio apartment is up next month. I'd suggest renewing and having you move in with me, but two of us wouldn't fit in that place. I barely do. But if you don't want to go the dog route, I'll move in with you here. Split half the rent and utilities, or if you're buying this place, work out a reasonable monthly amount. That way you wouldn't be alone."

Brig thought a good German shepherd would be a hell of a lot handier than Kelly in a pinch, but at the same time, Kelly wouldn't have to be walked or left in the tiny backyard. She was unlikely to destroy the house in Dia's absence.

Dia said, "You're sure?"

Kelly said, "I may not be much use in a fight. But I'll be here, someone who can watch your back. We work pretty much the same hours. I'm quiet, I'm neat, and I don't sing in the shower."

"I do," Dia said.

Brig tried not to imagine that. It was the sort of thing he didn't actually want to know.

Well, he did. Actually.

But it wasn't good for him to know it.

Chapter 8

Forensics came and went. Dia's friends worked out their schedules and plans, offered their encouragement and comfort, and then they went home. Brig hung back; he said he needed to talk to her privately before he left.

She was about to fall over. She hadn't had dinner, she hadn't slept, the week had been long and stressful, and the evening was, if anything, turning out to be even longer and more stressful than the whole preceding week. She leaned against the door after she closed and locked it, and exhaled.

"You look beat," Brig said.

"This whole week has been one unending nightmare."

"If you want to sit at the counter, I'll cook you something," he said. "Or order delivery."

"I think I'm too tired to eat."

"I've been there," he said, ushering her toward one of the bar stools that sat behind her counter. "The big question is, though, are you going to be able to sleep?"

Dia hadn't even considered that.

Her house had been broken into by someone who hadn't left any marks of his passage. If he'd gotten in once, he could get in again—at least until she put new locks on the doors and checked into bars for the windows and got her alarm system in place. At the moment, she wasn't a lot safer than she would have been sleeping in the street.

"I might not be able to sleep," she admitted. "Tired as I am, being alone in this house tonight, I'm going to jump at every noise. Or I *might* fall asleep." She shivered. "That would be even scarier."

He nodded. "Thought so. Would you feel better having me stand guard?"

She was startled. "You mean . . . what? Stand guard how? You'd walk around outside the house all night to keep anyone else from coming in? That's nuts."

He shook his head and grinned at her. "Nothing quite that dramatic. I figured I could leave my unmarked, which is clearly a cop car, parked in your drive. That should be sufficient deterrent, but if it isn't, no matter. I can sit in a chair and talk to you until you fall asleep, and then stretch out on the couch and watch something on television. That way it'll be clear that someone other than you is here. That might make your stalker unhappier than he already is—but my concern is that you stay safe tonight."

"You think there's that much danger?"

"I have no way of judging when this guy is going to act directly against you, but he's escalated awfully fast. From leaving things outside your home at the beginning of the week to finding a way inside today—or maybe earlier than today, depending on how he got access to your phone messages—it suggests that something has changed for him, that he's been watching you or making plans about you for some time. He was able to get into your house without leaving any sign of how he did it. He was able to tamper with your belongings, edit your phone messages, set up a personal song to play on your computer at a time that he knew you would be here."

As if it had been cued, "Bad Moon Rising" started blaring through the house again, so loudly Dia knew the people in the other half of the duplex would be disturbed.

It couldn't be. She'd turned the damned computer all the way off.

But there it was.

She swore and bolted toward the computer, but Brig grabbed her. He pushed past her, yelling, "Stay behind me." She realized he had his gun drawn.

He opened the door while standing to one side of it and keeping her back, went in fast, and immediately yelled, "All clear."

The music died with a sudden click.

She went in to find him standing there, looking from the window to the closet with a frown on his face, the yanked computer plug still in the hand that wasn't holding the gun.

"You saw me turn the computer off," she said.

"Yes."

"You saw me close this door. It was still closed when you came in here."

He nodded.

"There isn't any way to have a computer that's turned all the way off turn itself back on, is there? I mean, if the power is off, any programming that has been done on a computer is dead, right? No hacker can operate some virus or back door or whatever on a dead computer, right?"

"I don't know," Brig said. "I know enough about computers to be able to find what I need on them. I'm familiar with the programs we use at work; I use the Internet. Computers aren't something I have any real interest in outside of work. I don't know what someone who is an actual computer genius could do with one—or what he could get one to do."

Dia stared at the computer, and the feeling that she was being watched became so strong she started to feel the room closing in on her. She shivered and looked, saw only Brig.

But she was so cold.

Brig said, "A computer genius setting your computer up to do the unlikely isn't the only explanation, though."

Dia turned to him. "Don't tell me you'd suggest a ghost."

"No," he said. "I wouldn't. I would suggest that we did not keep everyone in your home this evening in sight at all times. You and I spoke privately in the kitchen; from there, we couldn't see if anyone got up and headed for the bathroom and detoured into the bedroom along the way." She saw his shoulders tense. He said, "It could be something else, too, but first we need to know about the people you were with."

Dia was shaking her head. "They're my friends."

Brig held up a hand. "I hate to say this, but you don't know that. We think we know people. We don't. I want you to consider anyone you work with who might have a grudge against you. Might be obsessed with you—" He stopped. "Your face changed. You just thought of something."

"Howie has played at having a crush on me for a couple of years. It isn't anything serious, though. He dates all the time, brings the girls he's dating by the station so he can show off. He's just one of those guys who feels it's his duty in life to flirt with any breathing woman. He hits on the ninety-year-olds—and they giggle and flirt and love him. It's just the way he is."

"Mmmm." Brig walked to the bedroom closet and stepped inside. A tiny flashlight materialized in his hand, and he started knocking on the closet walls.

"You're saying that *isn't* the way he is? You don't know him. What are you doing?"

"Checking for a false wall. It happens. Not often, but when it does, you can have access you know nothing about. These walls are fine, though. Solid."

He came back out. "I want to go through the rest of the house—make sure you don't have breaches in the walls or ceiling that you might not know about. We're also going to check doors and windows to make sure the locks work correctly and haven't been made to simply look as if they work." He sighed. "We're going to call each of your friends tonight to ask them if anyone left the living room while we were in the kitchen. If they did, we want to know who, and when, and at what time, and if the person who noticed him leaving saw where he went."

Dia frowned. "This seems . . . paranoid."

"It is paranoid. But your computer just turned itself back on and started playing a song that you link to your dead husband, and specifically to his death. I don't see where we have a lot of places to go that *don't* include paranoia."

Dia had nothing to say to that.

Brig said, "And then I'm going to suggest that, wherever you sleep tonight, I be right there with you. The business with the computer has me spooked."

Dia glanced at him sidelong. He was so serious. So businesslike. And what she was feeling toward him at that moment wasn't businesslike at all. She shouldn't say anything. She knew she shouldn't—but the fact was that she'd never been good at not saying things, and the stresses of the day, and the week, and the night, and her exhaustion and her fear, were not making her any better at not saying the things she knew she shouldn't.

"I'm going to ask a stupid question, and this is probably

a dreadful time for it. But . . . when you gave me your phone number—your home phone number, that is—was it because you were interested in me? Or was it because . . . of something else?"

He leaned against a wall and studied her—long, lean, with his thumbs hooked into the pockets of his jeans, with his white cotton button-down shirt snug across the hint of hard muscles. His sleeves were rolled up, and she realized how much she liked the muscles in his forearms. His tapered wrists. His big hands.

He grinned just a little. "You have interesting timing. I'm doing my all-out damnedest to maintain a professional distance here, seeing as how I've invited myself into your home and then pretty much insisted on taking up residence in your bedroom while you're in there. And seeing how my presence there is supposed to be protective. And then you go and point out the chink in my armor." He stood and held the door open for her. "After you," he said, and she walked out of the spare bedroom and into the long, narrow hall. She stopped.

He pointed to the kitchen and said, "I'm still hungry, and we can talk while we eat, if you don't mind."

"I don't mind," she said.

He followed her into the kitchen. She was still so tired she hurt, but now she was awake in interesting ways, too. She had the feeling she wasn't going to get much sleep that night, and suddenly that didn't seem like such a bad thing.

"You're not my type, you know," she said, digging around in the freezer for a couple of good steaks. She found two boneless rib eyes that she could put on her countertop grill still frozen. They wouldn't be as great as broiled steaks, but they wouldn't have to be defrosted, either.

He laughed. "I'm not?"

"Well, you are. You're exactly my type. I knew it the first time I saw you—that you were a risk taker, that you were willing to go out on the edge. You have that look— you've done some dangerous things, and you liked it." She put the steaks on the counter and set up the grill.

"I'll make a salad and steam some vegetables if you want to do the steaks," he said. "And you're my type— only I'm out of the game. No more relationships, no more reefs, no more shipwrecks in my life." He glanced at what she had pulled out of the freezer. "Those are nice steaks."

"How do you like yours?"

"Medium-rare."

She grinned. "Yeah. Me too."

"So if I'm exactly your type," he said, pulling salad fixings out of the fridge, "how does that make me not your type?"

"It's a long story. It has to do with me and Mac, and how we pushed each other into some pretty hairy situations, just because neither of us was willing to be the one who said, 'No, that's too dangerous.' It's about how we were so much alike that we ended up fighting, and how we were so much alike that we knew how to really hurt each other when we did fight. We bled. A lot. Hard."

"Okay. You two manage to make up?"

"Oh, making up was lots of fun. I think sometimes we fought just so we could make up afterward."

"Yeah. See . . . I never had that with my ex-wife. She was very cool, very distant. Logical. We didn't fight. I got mad and she'd just vanish, right in the middle of the room. She wouldn't talk, she wouldn't fight back, she wouldn't ever say what she was thinking. She'd just look at me like I was making a fool of myself or embarrassing her, and that just pissed me off more. Apparently what she was thinking when she wasn't fighting back was that she didn't like being a cop's wife very much. She liked getting a cop's alimony a whole lot more."

"That sounds miserable."

"It was. She's remarried now and making some other man unhappy, and meanwhile, I'm finally a free man. I promised myself I was going to stay that way." He looked over at Dia. "Loud fighting with someone you love doesn't sound like such a bad thing to me."

Dia slid the steaks, salted, peppered, and lightly seasoned, into the little grill, and pressed the lid down as tightly as the frozen steaks would permit. She turned to Brig. "So you're going to stay a free man. And you're not the man I'm looking for, so we can just be friends, and all the pressure is off."

"What are you looking for?"

"Someone who is calm, anchored, not too adventurous. Mature. Someone who doesn't live for risk, who isn't driven by adrenaline and danger."

"A bookkeeper."

"Basically."

Brig laughed. "You'd be bored out of your skull in a day."

"You think?"

"You ever play golf?"

Dia rolled her eyes. "I went with some friends once. It was like watching grass grow."

"Right. Imagine being married to the golf course. Everything very neat, perfectly manicured, calm, sedate. No running, no shouting, no swinging from the trees."

Dia found herself laughing. She held up a hand. "Okay. Maybe not a bookkeeper. But . . . someone with stable hours, a job that doesn't entail getting shot at, someone with his feet on the ground."

"We have a saying where I'm from," he said, and for

just a moment, Dia could hear him emphasizing that drawl she caught hints of when he was speaking. "'If you keep your feet on the ground, you can't ride the horse.'"

"They say that where you come from, huh? That'd be someplace out west, I guess?"

"Montana. Too many years ago now."

"Well, as sayings go, it's not a bad one. Only maybe I don't want to ride the horse."

"Sure you do. It's what you live for. Same as me."

He started to turn his attention back to the salad.

She said, "I rode the horse, and I kept getting bucked off. It hurt. And then the horse died doing what horses do. And I don't want another horse." She turned the oven on broil. "I just know that neither one of us was willing to be the grown-up. Sometimes one of you has to be the grown-up."

Brig dropped the vegetables in the steamer and turned to face her. "Is that right?"

"It seems like it should be."

He took a step toward her, and her breath caught in her throat. "I can be a grown-up," he said, and his voice went soft and dangerous.

She licked her lips and took a step toward him. "That's not what I meant by acting like an adult."

He pulled her into his arms and kissed her.

She damn near went limp. His body was so hard, so strong. She felt like she could melt right into him, almost as if she'd turned to liquid. It had been there all along—that pull between them. Bad pull—like breathing in something addictive and moving closer to get more. Circling, circling, holding back out of sheer willpower, and then at the last minute, giving in.

He was all wrong for her. He was exactly what she was never going to do again. He was a drug; she was a junkie. He was all the things she craved, all the things she knew would hurt her, bruise her, and eventually break her heart.

And yet she kissed him back, and slid a hand along his chest, feeling the heat, the power, the lines of sleek muscle. Her brain might have been complaining about her behavior before she kissed him—about the way she was dancing around risks and letting herself be close— but with his touch, it had shut up.

Drug—he was a drug, and drugs were bad.

She wrapped her arms around him and slid her hands over his ass. And . . . *Oh, God.* Good *drug. More of that.* She wanted more, much more, of that.

He cupped her breast with one hand, and her breath came so quickly she thought she might faint. It had been so long since anyone had touched her, and her body cried out for more. She groaned and slid her hands up his back, across his shoulders—so broad, so strong—up his neck, into his hair. Coarse hair, cut short, thick.

He'd slid a hand under her shirt, undid the back-close bra she wore, and slipped both hands to the front to stroke and caress her breasts. His thumbs kneaded small circles into her nipples, and she whimpered.

So long, it had been so long, and she had missed this so much. The frank hunger, the blatant heat, the sheer physical craving.

Her drug, her drug, he was her drug.

His lips slid over hers, his tongue probed her mouth, they clutched and clung, and she opened her eyes, trailed her hands down to the button fly of his jeans, and started unbuttoning.

Hard. He was hard everywhere, and when she had him free of his jeans, free of his boxers, she stroked him and was rewarded with the growl he made, and the gasp as she grasped the length of him and slid her hand from base to tip and back.

"Clearly we're both grown-ups," he muttered in her ear.

"This isn't being grown-up. This is just being bad." She bit the side of his neck, and felt his body tighten and pull her closer in response. "But we could be . . . badder."

"What did you have in mind?"

"The kitchen counter is clear."

"Yeah. It is." He bent down, pulled his jeans up enough to find his wallet in the back pocket, and pulled the wallet out. He had an aluminum foil packet in there.

She arched an eyebrow. "In your *wallet?* How clichéd."

"I was best man at the wedding of a friend of mine. Name was Alan. He was a doctor, great guy, married a wonderful woman. He gave me that before he walked down the aisle."

"Well, you were wise to hang onto it. Or its brethren."

"Still the original," he muttered. "It's been two years. I was beginning to lose faith." He gave her a wicked grin. And slid the condom on, and pulled her pants down.

She kicked her jeans and underwear into the corner. He tugged her shirt and bra off, and for a moment just stared at her.

"Take *your* shirt off," she said, "or you're losing buttons. My hands aren't steady."

His fingers worked their way down the placket, but she was pretty sure she still heard buttons clattering over the linoleum. He pulled the shirt off and it sailed across the room to drape itself over the dinette like a drunken tablecloth.

"Pants, too. I want to see you naked."

He lost the pants with blinding speed.

He was gorgeous. Hard-bodied, scarred, with curls of dark hair across his chest and belly. Flat, lean muscles.

Her lips trembled. It had been so long since she felt that hunger. It had been so long since she'd wanted anything the way she wanted that moment: without care for the consequences, without thought of the future.

She was ready. Right then, right there. She leaned her hips against the kitchen counter and pulled him toward her and took him into her. Her body flushed with heat; her mind went away.

Impaled on him, filled with him, she locked her legs around his waist and tightened.

He groaned. "Yes," he said. "Like that."

"Ride me," she whispered. "Hard."

He nearly withdrew from her, plunged into her hard. And again. Again.

Her hands dug into his shoulders, fingers flexing. Her toes curled. Her back arched, her head went back, and she gasped, "Harder. Harder. Break me."

He crashed into her, made her blood sing and her bones ache and her muscles turn to fire. She hooked his ass with her heels and pulled him in even harder, made him fight to get back out.

She was lost in the haze of him. Of heat and delicious tightness and driving lust, of the full, hard thrust of him pistoning into her.

Her drug, her drug. Bad for her, no doubt about it, that she would be so reckless, so heedless, so hungry. Her eyes fogged over; the world ceased to be anything but him in her and the distant rush of her blood in her ears. She cried out, thrashed, her head flinging from side to side, her body an alien thing lost in ecstasy.

He was right there with her, hanging onto her, whispering in her ear, "Yes, my God, yes."

He moved her to the floor—just picked her up with him still in her and knelt, lowering her to the linoleum. He put his hands on either side of her shoulders, and then he waited, still inside her. "Look at me, Dia. Look at me."

Her legs were still locked around his waist. Her fingernails scrabbled across the floor, searching for something to dig into. Her back arched and trembled; she was lost in little earthquakes. Shivering, she managed to open her eyes. To actually see him. He kissed her on the lips, lightly, and said, "Stay with me."

And began to move in her again.

She kept her eyes on his, forced them to stay open even as it became too much, as him inside of her overwhelmed her again and her body arched and the scream came unbidden to her lips.

"Stay with me," he said, and drove into her harder, pounded into her. She was the beach; he, the storm-driven sea. Her palms went flat on the floor; her muscles locked. Her eyes were fighting her, trying to close on their own; she struggled to keep them on him, to look into his eyes. But because she did, she saw the wildness in his own face, the feral grin as the last wave took him, too. His head went back, his teeth bared, and he drove deeper into her, and deeper. His body locked as tight as hers.

He pulsed into her; she wrapped tight around him.

And then she was liquid again.

He hung over her, braced on his arms, his hands planted beside her shoulders. Their bodies still tangled together, he stared into her eyes. He was searching for something, trying to see through her. But she was so lost in the wonder of him that she could not begin to imagine what.

Chapter 9

Brig was shaken. He got them off the floor as quickly as he could, got Dia dressed, pulled his own jeans back on, and rescued the steaks from the grill before they went from well-done to inedible.

He hadn't expected that. Any of it. He'd fantasized about it—his brain turned to sex as often as the next guy's, and he figured maybe even a bit more, since he'd been a long time without.

But that hadn't been sex.

Well, yeah, it had. But it had been sex mixed in with something so compelling, so mesmerizing, so insane, that he couldn't even find a word to describe it. She'd taken him somewhere he'd never been before.

And there she was, dishing the salad into bowls, quiet. Not saying a single word. She had her back to him, like maybe she couldn't even bear to look at him.

He found himself wondering about his predecessor. Brig was well rid of his ex-wife; he'd sometimes wondered if the average inflatable woman wouldn't have been a lot more fun and a lot fewer headaches than her. But clearly Dia's feelings about her dead husband were a lot more complicated.

Maybe what she and Brig had done together hadn't

been anything spectacular to her. Maybe that had just been . . . well . . . scratching an itch.

They'd already set the terms, anyway. She was looking for someone he wasn't, and he wasn't looking for anyone at all. So why was he letting it bother him?

He had other things to think about.

But he had to ask.

"You okay?"

"I'll let you know when I get my knees back," she said.

She didn't sound upset. Just dreamy.

Okay. He was all right with dreamy. It suggested that he'd done a decent job of representing the home team. She hadn't acted bored, but then when she didn't say anything after it was over, he discovered he was nervous. He wouldn't have minded applause. A rave review. Maybe just a hug.

She turned with the salad bowls in one hand and he saw the tiny curve of a smile on her face. "I wasn't expecting that."

"No," he said, once again conscious of breathing. He grinned back at her. "Not even a little."

"Which isn't to say I didn't think about it," she said.

He laughed and put the plates on her counter, and slid one of the not-quite-crunchy steaks on each one. "I have, too. I'd guess it's something a lot of men who meet you think about." He shook his head. "But . . . wow."

She pulled steak knives and forks out of her silverware drawer. He realized he was noting the location, so he could remember it for next time. Only, thinking rationally, he had to think that having a next time would be a terrible idea.

She poured drinks, then walked around the counter to sit on one of the bar stools. He took the other one, and was immediately conscious of her nearness.

She glanced at him sidelong, smiled again—that

private smile—and dug into the steak. "Tough," she said after a minute.

"Sorry."

"I'm not. That was worth it." She shook her head. "But, boy, that wasn't . . ." And then she chuckled. "Hell, I can't even say that it wasn't what I intended. Because it was. And I don't regret it a bit. I can't say I think it was a very good idea."

"Idea? That would seem to imply that one of the two of us was thinking. I suggest that would be a false representation of the events."

She laughed a little and nodded. And they subsided into silence. Eating. Thinking.

"How do you suppose he did the trick with the computer?" Dia asked. "Really."

"I don't know. Went in and turned it on and set it up before he left. Or somehow broke in while we were otherwise occupied. You have an attic?"

"No—angled ceilings in all the rooms. I have a little storage shed outside."

"First thing in the morning, I need to take a look at that."

"Okay." She pushed the plate back. She'd eaten her salad, her vegetables, and the few bites of the steak that were least brown. "I need to go to bed."

"I know you do. And your friends will be over tomorrow."

"I don't know when. What if one of them . . . did the thing with the computer, or did all . . . everything?"

"That's all right. I'll take a personal day tomorrow and stay here instead. And I'll keep an eye on them. If they don't know they're suspects, maybe the one who did something will give himself away."

"It isn't them," Dia said.

"It might not be. But the possibility that it is one of

them provides the least convoluted explanation to what happened."

She yawned. She stretched. And he thought, *I get to spend the night with her.*

"C'mon," he said. "Let's get you to bed before you fall over."

"The mess—" she started to protest.

"Will still be here in the morning. Messes are pretty thoughtful that way; they never wander off when you aren't looking. And you need sleep more than you need a spotless kitchen."

He got her up on her feet and aimed her toward the bedroom. She went, though she went slowly.

She had a great butt. He admired it all the way down the long, narrow hall.

When he started to leave the room while she changed, she said, "Stay. Chasing you out of the bedroom now would seem awfully silly."

Truly a woman after his own heart.

She went into the bathroom to brush her teeth and wash her face and otherwise get ready for sleep.

He heard the water running in the sink. And then running. And running. And then she yelled, "Could you come in here?" in a tone of voice that made his heart hammer.

Brig ran in. The mirror was steamed over. In the steam, he could make out faint words.

WATCHING YOU

She was standing there, dressed in little cotton shorts and a soft cotton T, and she was staring at the words as if they might reveal the secrets of the universe.

"So one way or the other, he's been in the house since you got here," she said.

"It looks that way." He put a hand on her shoulder. "Breathe. You're going to be okay. We're taking care of this tomorrow. We'll make sure that we get this place locked up tight; we'll keep you safe. All right?"

She nodded. She turned the water off, grabbed a towel, and started to wipe off the mirror.

"Don't. If he didn't leave fingerprints with that last one, he might have with this one. I'll call forensics back. Mirrors are a nearly perfect surface for fingerprints."

She wrapped her arms around herself, and he ushered her out of the bathroom and back into the master bedroom. "Bedtime," he said. "Way past bedtime, even. But we're not spending the night here. I'm too tired to drive home, but there's a hotel two blocks from here. I'm paying." He stared around the place, frowning. "I have just one call to make, and when my guy gets here, we're out of here."

He called the home of a colleague from forensics.

Billy answered on the second ring.

"It's Brig, and I have something interesting for you."

"No, you don't," Billy said. "It's Saturday night, I'm off, and your idea of 'interesting' always involves serious decomposition."

"This isn't a case, precisely. I'm handling it personally for now. And there's no decomposition, I swear."

"Really?"

"This is a . . . personal thing. I want to make sure this girl's taken care of. I'm over at her house, and she had a death threat written in steam on her bathroom mirror, and a computer that turned itself on and started playing a song from a very bad moment in her past while I was here. I'm wondering if you could take a look for me—see if you can come up with some hows and whos. Fingerprints, DNA, little tiny bits of goodness that I didn't see."

"And I'll be around live people?"

"Like I said, this isn't my case, it isn't my department, it isn't my thing. I'm just helping a friend."

"Didn't know you had any."

"Thanks, dick-socks. You're a sweetheart, too. Going to give you her address; I'll meet you here. As soon as you get what you need we're going to leave, so plan to be speedy."

"Any details I should know?"

"She has a stalker problem, and I'm trying to assess her level of danger. She can't go with a restraining order, because she has no clue who might be stalking her."

"That's different. Usually they know."

"Like I said—she's covered her bases with us, but we need to know who to go after. I'm just digging around for her."

On the other end of the phone, Billy was silent for just a bit too long. Then he chuckled. "Okay. That's what you're doing."

The cop would be a problem.

Larry stared at the pictures of Dia that lined the wall of his workroom. The bitch had failed him again.

The Chinese had a proverb that he had always felt applied to the two of them: Whoever saved a life, the Chinese believed, was responsible for that life until he died.

Dia had saved him. And then she had abdicated her responsibility to him. She never came to see him after the accident, never let herself get to know him, never cared at all that he was still breathing.

And yet, every action he had taken after the moment in which she won him back to life, he had taken only because she had paved the way for him.

She should have gotten to know him. She would have come to understand him if she had. She would have seen him for the man he was, brilliant and misunderstood, compassionate and driven to greatness. She would have loved him, eventually. He had been willing to give her time to mourn her husband. She'd had time, yet when at last she moved on, she'd moved to the cop.

Had she come to him, had she finally seen him, that would have made all the wrong her husband had done him right.

She'd had a thousand chances—ten thousand chances. Larry had kept close to her. He had put himself in her hands over and over again, and had given her every opportunity to step up and claim her responsibility. And at every chance she had turned away, rejected him, failed him. She looked at him and never even saw him.

His latex-gloved fingers worked their way over a new type of bomb casing, carefully bundling in the wires for the radio-controlled components. Learning to build bombs was a time-consuming and risky process; learning to build them well, a never-ending art and discipline. He had, in the years since he was sent away to that special school for troubled teens, become a master of discipline.

There, he had first studied the Tao. There he had learned that life was about balance. Walk equally in the paths of light and dark, do not presume that some event is lucky or unlucky, but simply accept it as it is. Seek the middle road; strive not to push the universe into either constant darkness, or constant light.

Save a life, take a life.

Maintain the balance.

He had spent years pursuing and then winning the trust of people who could help him, teach him, mentor him—always making sure that they had no idea who they were helping. He had studied, struggled, mastered . . . and then moved on, always with the single goal in mind:

Pursue balance, make things right.

Dia was an unbalancing force. He intended to correct that, one way or another. She wasn't entirely out of chances. Yet.

The lights were flashing again, slicing at crazy angles through utter blackness.

There was no road. There was only the rolled and crushed ambulance. The rolled and crushed men inside it. Mac, thrown free, but not clear.

He lay there, shattered and torn, watching her as she walked toward him. Watching.

She looked for anger in his face, that she had been with another man. She looked for hurt or betrayal.

But all she saw was fear.

His lips were moving. She couldn't hear what he said. She tried to make it out, tried to get down on hands and knees and hear what he was saying, certain that if she just got closer, she could make sense of it.

But from him, she got no sound at all.

His lips moved.

"I can't hear you," she screamed. "I can't hear you."

He raised an arm, pointed with a finger. She didn't let herself look at the arm—what she knew was too horrible. She turned instead to the car where lay the one man she would be able to save from the wreck. She knew he was there, simply because that was where he'd been before. She couldn't see the lone survivor, however. Or the car. She started walking toward it, knowing what she would find when she got there.

And then, somehow, the red and white lights flashing through the dark reached the car.

She hurried toward it, knowing she didn't have time.

On the rear window of the car, still intact somehow, someone had written, WATCHING YOU. In blood.

The man in the car turned to look at her. He grinned

at her, his face covered in blood, and then turned all the way around so she could look him full in the face. He was no longer the hugely overweight man she had rescued time and again in her dreams and once in real life. He was gaunt. Emaciated. His face was bones. He was nothing but a skeleton, she realized, with a few ragged patches of skin hanging on his bones. But he had living eyes, and they gleamed. She knew she was supposed to save him, but she couldn't save him.

And then he burst from the car and lunged at her, and wrapped his bony fingers around her throat.

Dia woke screaming.

Someone grabbed her, and she screamed louder, and started to fight.

"Hey! Ow! You're okay! You're safe, Dia! You were just dream— *Ow!* Dreaming!"

And then Dia recognized Brig's voice. She stopped fighting, and he let go of her—and hanging right at the edge of the bed as she was, and tangled in the covers, she fell off. Hit her head on the hotel room nightstand.

She swore.

A light switched on, and a face peered warily over the edge. "You okay? Know where you are and . . . everything?"

Brig's right eye looked a little red and swollen.

"Nightmare," she said. "I've been having variations of this same one a lot lately."

"Must be a bad one. After that scream, I'll be lucky to fall asleep again before next week."

She climbed up into the bed and lay down beside him. He wore his boxers, and she found herself admiring how wonderful he looked, and trying not to imagine getting him out of the boxers again.

"Want to talk about it?"

"Sure. I guess. Well . . . not really, but . . ." She sighed. "I was back at the accident—the one that killed Mac. And he was . . . all torn up. Like he was when I found him. He was dead, and I knew he was dead, but he was still trying to tell me something. Only I couldn't hear him."

"Ugh."

"It was bad, but then it got worse. I saw the wrecked car off to one side, just like I had in real life. And I went over to it. Because there was nothing I could do for Mac or the other two members of the crew, you know. Because I was in shock, and the only thing I could think of was to work the scene, see if there was someone I could save."

"This was in real life? Or in the dream?" Brig asked.

"Both."

"Okay." He rolled over on one side to look at her.

Dia wished he hadn't. The nightmare would have been easier to talk about if they'd both been in the dark and she couldn't see his face.

"So anyway. I got to the car, and I could see someone in there—at least when the lights from the ambulance flashed just right. Only this time, instead of a bloody guy, there was a skeleton. With eyes. It turned to grin at me, and I backed away, because skeletons . . . well, they're already dead, right?"

"You kind of hope so."

Dia laughed a little. "Well, yeah. But when I backed away, this skeleton came tearing out of the car and grabbed me around the throat." She sighed. "It sounds lame and stupid when I tell it. But being there, it was scary as hell. Anyway, that was when I screamed and woke up."

"And elbowed me in the eye, and kneed me in the belly—I'm so glad your aim was off, by the way."

"I'm sorry. Nightmare made that the response to go with, you know?"

"That and everything that's happened to you in the last week." He looked over at her and grinned. "You have a nice sense of self-preservation. Good moves, even sleeping."

She laughed. "I really am sorry I hurt you. And glad I didn't hurt you any more than that."

"Me, too." He flopped onto his back and stared at the ceiling. "So . . . you keep having this dream, huh? What do you think it means?"

"It's a nightmare. I don't think it means anything."

"Nah. You can't look at it that way. If you only had it once, I'd say it was just a dream. But if you keep having it, your subconscious is probably trying to tell you something."

Dia was no big believer in the deeper meanings of dreams. But she decided to humor him. A detective dream interpreter. Go figure.

She said, "Mostly the dream just repeats what was there in real life. Only dead silent. The ambulance lights still work—they illuminate the scene in bursts. The guys in the ambulance are dead. No hope for either of them. Mac is dead, too. Completely unsalvageable."

"You're an EMT. Tell me why you didn't try to save him."

She closed her eyes tightly and said, "His right arm was off at the shoulder. His head had been almost severed from his body. He'd bled out. It was . . . hopeless."

"Right," he said. She glanced over at him and saw the expression of pain on his face. That was the question people asked and invariably wished they hadn't. "Yeah. That had to be hell."

"Not my best moment," she said.

"Let's keep going, though. You say he's talking to you in the dream?"

"His mouth is moving, and he's trying to tell me something, but there's no sound. The dream is completely silent. This is where it has changed. Years ago, right after it happened, there was sound."

"What did you hear in real life?"

"'Bad Moon Rising.' Over and over and over."

"Who else knows that?"

"The guys I work with. The ones who were with our station back then, anyway. It isn't something I've talked about to anyone since."

"So. You and your crew got the call, you got there, you and whoever else saw all of this."

She shook her head. "That's not how it happened. I wasn't actually on duty that night, but I had the scanner on, and I heard the call go out. It sounded like a big one, and some of us respond to those even if we're off duty. I jumped in my car and took off—I was only a minute or two behind Mac and his crew. Not close enough to see what happened, but close enough to be the first to pick up the pieces."

Brig was silent for a long time. "So . . . until last night, when your computer went off, none of the people in that room knew about 'Bad Moon Rising'?"

Dia said, "Kelly knew. Neither Ryan nor Tyler knew. Howie didn't know." She paused. "Oh! *Howie didn't know!* So he can't have been the one who did that."

"Well, let's not say can't. But it does make him seem less likely. How about the other guy?"

"You mean Sherm." Dia closed her eyes. "He was there, but he'd just joined."

"So if the computer setup was done by one of your friends, it was most likely Kelly or possibly Sherm."

"Not Kelly. She's been my friend since I started in the EMS."

"You can't seriously be considering rooming with her."

"I trust her."

"She isn't reliable, and she's hiding something."

"I trust her anyway."

Brig started to say more, and then stopped. He paused for a moment, then said, "I'll make sure we do her background check first. And then there's Sherm."

"Sherm has shown absolutely no interest in anyone, including me, ever. He lives and breathes EMS; it is his obsession. He's a good EMT, and getting ready to go to medical school to become an ER specialist. He lives the life of a monk; he studies all the time."

Brig said, "If we're being realistic, we could probably eliminate Sherm as a candidate, then. If he isn't collecting his own cadavers to help his chances in medical school, anyway."

Dia rolled over on her side and stared at Brig. "Eeuww. Is that really necessary?"

He grinned at her, and her stomach tightened and her pulse picked up. He should never, ever smile. It made him delectable, and she did not want him to be delectable. He said. "We have to air all the possibilities. Some will be easier to eliminate than others. We should be able to eliminate Sherm as a cadaver collector by wrangling an invite to his house and checking out his fridge."

"Then I can take him off the suspect roster right now," Dia said. "He keeps vegetarian fare in his fridge. We hate to go over to his apartment—and it is a one-bedroom apartment the size of a postage stamp, made smaller because medical books are everywhere—because he never has anything good to eat. We've *all* been through his fridge. It's pitiful."

Brig laughed, but then his face went serious again. "How about Kelly, then?"

"Kelly is a doll. She doesn't even want to hurt the bad guys. You heard her last night."

"That's her public face. The private one might be different."

Dia shook her head. "She's a certified rescue diver. She works EMS. She spends her entire life helping people. She's been my shopping buddy and my diving buddy, and when Mac died, hers was the shoulder I cried on."

"You're a paramedic, though. She isn't."

"She's going for the test again. She gets panicked when she has to intubate." Dia said, "Even on a dummy, intubation is terrifying when you're suddenly the one in charge of the code. Your hands get shaking, and when you slide the blade in and look for the vocal cords, your mind just goes blank." She got out of bed, suddenly full of nervous energy, and stood beside him. "It's worse the first time you do it on a real person. You know then that it's life or death, and if you screw up, the person you're trying to save is going to die because of you. Right then, right there, because if you haven't secured the airway, you've lost the code." She shrugged and took a deep breath. "She and I talk about it. I've run her through simulations a bunch of times. And we've been practicing together. I think she'll get it. She's already nailed the written. She just has to get through the practical."

"Doesn't sound like someone who would want to hurt you. Or kill you."

"No."

Brig patted the side of the bed. "Join me. It's cozy in here, and we still haven't dealt with the other part of the dream."

"The guy I rescued?"

"Right."

Dia got back in the bed, but she stayed sitting. She felt once again like someone was watching her. She was cold, and her skin prickled. I felt like someone was staring at the back of her neck. She couldn't think of any reason why she abruptly felt so strange, or so scared. She was with a guy who could take care of whatever came at her. Who was there to do just that.

She said, "There isn't much to say about him. In real life, he was a bloody mess. I secured his C-spine and got him out of his car; he stopped breathing not long after that. I did the usual stuff. I ran and grabbed the paramedic kit from the back of the overturned ambulance. It was still secured to the stretcher, overhead because the truck was upside down. Then I tubed him, breathed him, put pressure on the wounds while his heart was still beating. Managed to get an IV started. And then the follow-up ambulance came, and the guys took care of him. And me."

"You ever see him again?"

"No."

"Did you know him?"

"No. I found out his name later. Sinclair Forbes. I heard he wanted to meet me. To thank me for saving his life. But I was torn up about Mac, and I didn't want to meet anyone who had any connection with that night. Especially not the guy who caused the accident by slamming on his brakes. Not even if he did stop to keep from hitting a kid." The room seemed to get colder.

She shivered, and Brig said, "I'm freezing, too. Hotel air conditioners are bad, but this is ridiculous."

"I thought it was just me."

"Not just you."

She pulled the covers higher and moved close enough to him that his warmth fended off some of the iciness in the air.

"Okay. So. Sinclair Forbes. What do you know about him?"

"Nothing except that he was a young white male, and that he was a wreck when I found him. He had an open fracture of the femur, and crushed ribs on the left side of his chest that had punctured his left lung. Lacerations in his scalp from hitting the windshield. Probably smashed his face up a little bit."

"Probably?"

Dia turned to Brig. "It was pitch-black out. The ambulance lights were angled away from the car, so they weren't helping me much. His face was covered in blood, so he looked like hell."

"Would you recognize him if you saw him?"

"I wouldn't even recognize a picture of him taken the day after the accident. Mac was lying down the berm, in pieces. I didn't see the guy I worked on. Not at all. Not as a person. All I saw was a bunch of injuries that I could treat, because I couldn't stand to just do nothing, and I couldn't do anything to save the people I cared about."

Brig put an arm around her. "That makes sense."

He was quiet for a long time. "It's odd that the skeleton that was standing in for Forbes attacked you."

"It was just a stupid dream."

"It might have been," Brig agreed. "But it might have been something more. I'm serious about the business with repeating dreams. I haven't had them often, but when I have, it's been because I noticed something at the time that I didn't realize until later—a piece of a puzzle in a case I was working on that I'd managed to ignore, or something that a witness said to me that didn't fit with what I knew was the truth."

"So you've had some experience with nightmares like this."

"I spend all day every day trying to figure out who killed all sorts of people, from little kids to sweet suburban housewives to crack whores to pimps to decent, hardworking dads. All I see in my dreams are dead people. They're everywhere, all the time, talking to me. It does not make for restful sleep."

"Doesn't sound like."

Brig said, "So, since in your dream the skeleton of Sinclair Forbes attacked you, and since you refused the opportunity to let him thank you back when he asked, I'm going to spend a little bit of personal time tracking down Sinclair Forbes, just to see what he's been up to lately. He did live, didn't he?"

"Last I heard was when he asked to meet me."

"Right."

She was quiet for a long time. An image flashed into her mind, and suddenly her skin started to crawl. "Written in blood on the car," she said.

"What?"

"I just remembered. 'Watching you.' It was written in blood on the back window of the car. Just like in the bathroom. It's probably . . . well, just my mind thinking everything scary into the same nightmare," Dia told him.

"It probably is. But this is worth checking out. You have someone who has gone to a great deal of trouble to thank you for saving his life. And something about the fact that you turned down an opportunity to meet this guy, coupled with the fact that in your nightmares he's attacking you, makes me think that your subconscious has made a connection. Probably not anything to it. But I'll still check it out."

The room was suddenly warmer. Comfortable, instead of freezing. It felt like someone had just turned off winter, and spring had slipped into its place.

"This room is strange," Brig said. "Funky air conditioner."

"So you got warmer, too?"

"All at once. So abruptly that I couldn't help noticing."

"I don't know what's going on. It's annoying, though." Dia shrugged. "Anyway, I was just going to say that the dream was weird, but what you said made sense. The bad feelings I had in the dream the first time, back right after the accident happened, were all about Mac and the fact that I couldn't save him. This time all the fear in the dream has come from the guy in the car. He's turned scary."

"Some part of your subconscious might have recognized him from the accident scene, and then you might have seen him around somewhere. The threats have triggered the nightmares again."

"You think?"

Brig laughed. "I don't know. I'm a cop. All I know is when I start having repeater nightmares, they're trying to tell me something."

And then he leaned over and kissed the side of her forehead. Only what he'd evidently meant to be a casual kiss didn't stop there.

Because she rolled into him, and the kisses wandered down the side of her face, and down her neck, and to one breast that managed somehow to appear from under her shirt and the sheets.

She groaned. "Oh, God, you're good at that," she whispered.

And slid under him with a neat shift of her hips, rolling him onto her.

He was hard. Ready.

And she realized that she was ready, too.

She started to slide down his boxers.

He stopped kissing her.

"What?" she asked.

"Um. I don't have any more condoms," he said. "I just had that one."

"Shit," she said. "Really?"

"My buddy only gave me one. I mostly kept that for the novelty value. You don't have any?"

"I haven't been with anybody since Mac. I got rid of his stuff after a while, and . . . we weren't using condoms. And . . ."

"Short answer, then, is no."

"Short answer is no," she agreed.

"Shit."

She closed her eyes. He was still on top of her. Hot and muscular, hard and ready. She wanted him. She wanted all of him, right then, and she knew he was all wrong for her, and in spite of that she just didn't care.

But she needed to care.

Because he *was* all wrong for her.

It wasn't that Brig was a Mac replay. She'd already discovered that Brig was nothing like Mac.

Dia and Mac had been best buddies, competitors, confidantes. They'd liked each other immediately, they'd worked well as a team, they'd believed in each other, they'd seen themselves as each other's kindred spirit. They'd managed to be honest with each other, which was a big deal. They'd come to love each other in that first year, and then they'd gotten married, and Dia didn't regret the marriage. She regretted the way it had ended, and she still missed Mac. They'd had only three years from first hello to last good-bye. Four years later, he still mattered to her.

But she had never felt the sort of all-encompassing physical obsession with another human being—any human being—that she already felt for Brig. She had never in her life been overwhelmed with desire. She'd never just *wanted,* with the raw, mindless, starving want that she felt with her legs wrapped around Brig's thighs, with her hands braced on his shoulders.

She'd hear women say they could "just eat him up," when talking about a man, and she'd always thought the saying was stupid. She'd never experienced anything that made her feel that way, and she didn't believe anyone else had, either.

And now she knew she'd been wrong. All along, she thought she knew the whole deal, how everything worked—and she didn't realize she'd never even sat down at the big table to play.

She didn't need mindless obsession. She didn't need stupid lust. She didn't need Brig, and all the pain he could bring to her life. She wanted him. No doubt about that. She wanted the hell out of him.

But she didn't need him.

That was what she had to focus on, because just letting her face brush against his neck, she wanted to bite him. Just breathing him in, she wanted to toss him across the bed, climb on top of him, and ride him till they exploded.

Her cell phone rang.

Thank God her cell phone rang. "That's going to be some of the guys," she said, scrambling out of bed and digging for her purse to answer it.

Brig looked over at the hotel clock. "It's seven o'clock in the morning on their day off. What the hell are they thinking?"

"This is a late start to the day for us."

"Yeah. Me, too. But not on my damned day off."

"Is it your day off?" Dia asked.

"Fuck." He glanced at her. "Pardon my French. It will be as soon as I call in. I can't believe I forgot to do that." Brig swung out of the bed and pulled on jeans and shirt, muttering under his breath. "Go ahead and tell them we'll be there in a minute," he said. "I'll take you home and you can get them started. Once they're going and know not to let you out of their sight for a minute, I'll go home and change. I'll call Stan and tell him I'm not coming in today—I have a ton of personal time banked. And I'll let him know to look into Sinclair Forbes."

"You're going to follow up on that? Because of a dream? Really?"

"I've had weirder hunches pay off. It's worth a look. And if we come up empty, no harm done. We've just eliminated one person who isn't after you."

"The more of them, the better."

Chapter 10

When they arrived at her house, Brig noted the surprise on the faces of Ryan and Tyler, the early-bird bell ringers, who'd brought two enormous boxes of doughnuts with them. Evidently she'd forgotten to mention that he would be with her.

"I stood guard last night," he said, letting them in. "Her damned computer went off again after you guys left. Same song."

They both looked genuinely shocked. They both went the same degree of pale, and exchanged looks, and Ryan said, "But we *saw* her turn the computer off."

"You did," Brig said. "And I did. And yet, after everyone was gone and I was getting ready to leave, it started blaring that same song again." He thought he ought to claim that he'd been getting ready to leave. He didn't think advertising their sudden collision into relationship territory was a good idea, considering that she had a stalker who would be likely to take such news badly.

"That's why she stayed at the hotel," Ryan said.

"Couldn't even think the house was safe after all that," Brig agreed.

"So . . ." Tyler said. "So . . . the guy who's stalking her got into the house? While you were here?"

Ryan said nothing. He was just shaking his head.

"I'm not sure what happened." He was watching Ryan. "What are you thinking, Ryan?"

"I'm thinking that this business is weird, and scary, and it doesn't make sense. If the guy is watching the place, why the hell would he break in while people are here? That's a dangerous game."

Tyler nodded. "He must be crazy."

"Yeah," Ryan said. He looked worried. "Crazy. Schizo. That's . . . terrifying."

Brig smiled a little at their reactions. This clearly wasn't something they'd dealt with on a personal level before. "The actions of stalkers *don't* make sense. A logical person would realize that his attentions were not wanted and walk away. Common sense and stalking are unrelated to each other." He sighed. "Don't assume this guy is crazy, though, or out of touch with reality. He may be completely rational, function well in society, and just have an agenda that doesn't make sense from our perspectives."

Ryan said, "Well, we have things that should help stop this crap. We picked up new locks for her on the way here. Also alarm system components; I asked the supplier I've dealt with before which security system he'd want for his own family, and he picked a really expensive one. But he did give us a good deal on it. Locks, too."

"Let's see what you got," Brig said.

Dia's friends weren't kidding. They'd come in with top-of-the-line locks and dead bolts and a superb alarm system. "Good deal," he said. "Though maybe you should have checked with her about the cost."

Tyler grinned. "We decided to take up a collection last night after we left. Between the five of us, we covered a lot of this. Ryan floated the rest on a credit card."

"I have one I don't ever use," he said, looking a bit

embarrassed. "It's just for emergencies. And to me, this seemed like an emergency. We'll get the rest of the guys in the station in on this, and that'll cover most of the cost. She can owe me whatever's left after that. If it's anything—and it probably won't be—it won't be much."

Brig nodded. That was the way they did things in Homicide, too. It was all about family. You took care of your own.

Dia came in and dropped her bag on the floor. She saw the table, cruised over to it, opened the box of doughnuts and grinned hugely. "Jelly filled *and* cream filled. Guys," she said, "you're so great."

Brig did a careful once-through on the house. When he was finished, he said, "I'm heading out now. I have a couple things to take care of, but I'll be back as soon as I can." He turned back to Dia. "Stay with your friends. Catch a little sleep on the couch if you can. Call me if anything— and I mean *anything*—strange happens."

"Right," she said.

All the way home he kept thinking about Dia's nightmare, and the writing on the mirror, and the music from the computer coming on by itself, and about her. He couldn't kid himself that he was standing on the edge of a slippery slope with her; he'd already careened down that slope, over the cliff at the bottom, and was falling headlong into an abyss that would take him who knew where.

He was sure he didn't want to find himself tied up in another relationship.

(Wasn't he?)

He was confident that he could face her and let her know that he'd been serious when he said she was his type, but he wasn't looking.

(Only the second he thought that, he knew it was a lie.)

He was, in fact, confused, bewildered, convinced that last night he had made a huge, serious, stupid mistake. And yet he was still mind-blowingly turned on by just the thought of her.

She'd been amazing.

Maybe, he thought, he could convince her that the two of them ought to have a lot of sex but no commitment.

He wanted to think he knew himself well enough to accept that he could have a purely superficial relationship with a woman. That he could, like any number of his friends and colleagues, turn off his brain and run on testosterone. He was pretty sure that if he dated the women they dated—shallow bitches who lived for boob jobs, manicures, and the latest shoes from . . . well, from whatever Italian foot fetishist it was they all seemed to worship—he'd have no problem staying just for the sex. The problem was that, though those women were eye candy and he appreciated the curves, the second they opened their mouths he lost interest. He didn't give a shit about actors, he could not humanly care less about who did the best lip collagen, and he despised the shallowness of women who would date a dick who drove a Beemer on the off chance that they might get to be Mrs. Dick and live in the land of the big AmEx card until divorce and a massive payoff left them set for life.

He'd had one of those—had acquired her when he'd been young and dumb, and she'd been naive enough to think that a South Florida cop in real life lived anything like Sonny Crockett of *Miami Vice,* which she'd evidently watched as a young teen and believed implicitly. When he didn't get the Ferrari, the sailboat, the speedboat, and the remarkable amount of free time the cops on that show somehow managed, her enchantment with him wore off fast. Then it was three years of married misery, and an equal span of divorced misery.

Finally she married her own Beemer guy. She got all the surgery she'd dreamed of, and became the plastic Barbie doll she'd always wanted to be.

While he was left to rejoice in being single.

Well, it wasn't all that much fun—not the way he did it. But the women who would put out for dinner at an expensive restaurant weren't women he could stand, and the women who didn't care about all the things his ex had worshiped weren't women he could, with a clear conscience, bang and abandon.

That was all it was with Dia, he assured himself. He was having a case of conscience. He'd taken her to bed, she was nothing like his ex, and he was afraid that she'd be hurt when he dumped her.

He wanted to think that was what it was. Conscience.

Of course, last night he'd wanted to think that he was the master of self-control, too, and that in offering to guard the place for one night before Dia's friends had the chance to install new locks and a security system for her, he was acting out of an altruistic concern for a good woman in a bad place. The things he wanted to think about himself and the things he was starting to think were miles and miles apart.

He could just be another opportunistic asshole on the make.

He didn't want to be tied down. However, clearly he didn't want to bail out on her in the same twenty-four-hour period in which he'd slept with her. That would be reprehensible.

He wondered if forty-eight hours was too quick, decided it was, considered seventy-two, decided that, also, was far too cold, and concluded that he'd figure his exit strategy after he'd completed a seventy-two-hour cooling-off period.

Feeling in control again, he called Stan.

"Where the hell are you?" Stan asked by way of greeting.

"Yeah. Always good to hear from you, too. I'm taking a personal day. But I have someone I'd like for you to track down. His name is Sinclair Forbes, and he was in a multivehicle accident about four years ago that ended with the deaths of three people. One of them was named Mac Courvant."

"Spell the names," Stan said, and Brig spelled them out for him. Stan read back the information, and said, "So what exactly am I looking for?"

"First, a current address for Forbes. Any background you can find on him. Any criminal history. Basically, any damned thing that you can dig up. This is a fishing expedition; I'll be up-front with you. I have nothing except a gut twinge to suggest that this guy is anything but an upstanding citizen."

"All right. Care to give me the cause of your gut twinge?"

"Not at the moment," Brig said.

"*In*-teresting," Stan said.

"Not too. If it pans out, I'll tell you where it came from. At the moment it's just kind of flaky, and I want you to respect me in the morning."

And Stan laughed. "Too late for that."

"While you're at it, see if anything pings on the following people, who are all coworkers of hers. Sherman Stoltz, Howard Nash, Ryan Williams, Kelly Beam, and Tyler Frakes. They're all EMTs at Station Thirty-one, in Coral Springs."

"Wow. What the hell are you digging up?" And then he burst out laughing. "No. Never mind. You dog. You're after the tall Amazonian babe. The one with the wicked smile."

Brig paused. "You saw a wicked smile?"

"When you weren't looking at her, she looked at you like . . . like . . . my latest girlfriend looks at that specialty chocolate in the Sawgrass Mall."

Brig closed his eyes and rested his forehead against the palm of his hand. "Thanks *so* much. I really needed that image," he growled.

"Wanna know an ancient Chinese secret?" Stan asked.

"If I did, I'd ask someone who might know one."

"If you got laid, you'd be *so* much more pleasant to work with."

"And that's why you have no future as a Chinese wise man," Brig said.

He hung up.

Brig showered, shaved, got the basic necessities of hygiene out of the way, and wistfully looked at his unslept-in bed, which called to him seductively.

He was tired. His right eye hinted at bruising—Dia had really hauled off and walloped him in her sleep. He thought he wouldn't care much to see what she could do awake.

He looked at the bed some more. He already *knew* what she could do when she was awake.

He wanted her to do it again.

He was not going to pick up condoms on the way to her place. He was going to make a clean break; seventy-two hours of restraint, followed by taking the necessary steps to resume his freedom.

Dammit.

Chapter 11

The guys were great. Mostly great. Aside from talking about the floater. She was really tired of hearing the floater replays, but she didn't complain, even if listening did make the doughnuts less appetizing.

Thanks to her friends—and a willingness to get in and help with the work herself—Dia had all new locks and most of a new security system in place before Brig got back.

She was so glad to see him, though. It wasn't that the floater talk upset her. It had just been her call. She and Ryan and Tyler had to pull the floater—a dead body that had been in the water long enough for decomposition to release enough gases to bring it to the surface—out of a canal that week, and haul it to the morgue in their truck. She could still catch whiffs of the smell. Or maybe she kept imagining it. But that smell wasn't something that left the nose quickly. She figured it burrowed straight into the smell receptors and the brain and clung there, warning everyone, *Caution. This could be you.*

When Brig did show up, he gave her the most bizarre, indescribable look she'd ever seen, and took off to check the house again, to make sure the guys were doing the work right.

Ryan finished the last wiring touches on the security

system. He said, "I'm going to show you how this works. And give you the current pass number. You change it, okay? When everybody is out of here, the first thing you do is you set the system to a number nobody else knows, but that you'll remember. And you don't write it down, and you don't tell anyone what it is. All right?"

Dia nodded.

He showed her where the sensors were in the windows, where they were in the doors, how an intruder couldn't break the circuit without setting off the alarm, and how to get in and out of the house once the alarm had been set.

"You don't have anyone monitoring this, though," he told her, "so you're going to have to be prepared to deal with intruders yourself. You know how to do that?"

"Dial nine-one-one."

"No, if you're alone in the house, that's not your plan of defense. You know this, Dia. You've seen the women who called nine-one-one and then waited for the police to come rescue them. Even when the cops are only a couple minutes away, that's all it takes to beat the shit out of them, kill them, abduct them. . . ."

Dia sighed. He was right.

"Brig talked to you about getting a gun last night."

"I think he mentioned it in passing. I didn't really give it much thought."

"*Give* it thought." He rested a hand on her shoulder and stared into her eyes. He looked worried. "If you don't get a gun, get some other form of personal safety device. Make sure you have that with you at all times. Whatever you get, make sure you know how to use it. You call nine-one-one when you have your weapon in your hand. Not before."

She nodded.

Ryan frowned at her. "You know this stuff, Dia. You don't get to flake out just because it's you it's happening to this time. Right?"

She gave him a small, faint smile. "Right."

Kelly came over to Dia's side. "Stop spooking her, Ryan. She isn't going to be alone. I'm going to be here."

Ryan said, "You aren't going to be here every minute of every day. She has to know what to do when she's alone."

Kelly gave him a hard look, and Dia laughed. "He's not a pacifist, either, Kel."

"You have the alarm system now. You'll be fine."

Brig came out of the spare bedroom. "All done," Ryan called to him.

"Nice—that was fast."

"Lot of practice with this," Ryan said. "Places this small are pretty simple."

"We're done, then?" Tyler asked. He'd just come out of the bathroom, and Dia saw that Brig was watching him with interest.

Ryan said, "New locks and security are in. Kelly said she's going to start packing the day after tomorrow, so Dia only has two more nights alone in here."

Brig was watching Kelly talking to Dia about her moving plans when his phone rang. It was Stan. "What you got?"

"Pay dirt like you wouldn't believe."

He lowered his voice. "Kelly Beam?"

"No, though interesting you should mention her. I checked her first, just like you asked. She's a lesbian. In a longtime, way-undercover relationship with some doctor out in Westgate. Nothing criminal, though."

"Ah," Brig said.

"Tyler Frakes has more speeding tickets than sense,

but is otherwise clear. Williams has had a couple of lead-foot issues, too, but nothing recently. Stoltz is an upstanding citizen. Howard Nash had a patient try to sue him for sexual harassment about five years ago, but it turned out that the woman was known to be malignantly litigious, and that she'd said the same things about three other EMTs who had responded to her calls in the past six months. And there was no way a jury was believing her."

"Unlovely?"

"As a dog's rectum."

"Then what *did* you come up with?"

"Your fishing expedition yielded gold of the sort that makes me wonder how the hell it fell in our laps."

Since Stan didn't know what Brig wanted the information for, Brig found Stan's response bewildering.

"Sinclair Forbes is the son of state senator Elisa Keyes Forbes and orange-grove tycoon Peter Forbes. Thanks to their wealth and fame, information about their lone son, which should have disappeared into sealed juvie records, was in fact a tabloid spectacle for about three months. Young Sinclair Lawrence Forbes was . . . wait for it . . . causing traffic accidents. He had a number of different tricks he used, from dropping cats from overhanging trees onto windshields to mining sections of road with homemade caltrops that caused tire blowouts."

"No."

"Oh, yes," Stan said, sounding smug. "But there's more. Oh, so very much more."

Brig said, "Don't keep me in suspense, you bitch."

"Never. Sinclair Forbes was caught, and turned into authorities, by his best friend from age eight—a Boy Scout who went on to be an Eagle Scout and a Purple Heart–decorated US Air Force PJ."

"Mac Courvant?"

"None other. And it still gets better. Sinclair Lawrence Forbes, the trust-fund kiddie with money to burn, was the sole survivor of the accident that caused the death of his onetime best friend and, incidentally, two others. And the kid Forbes claimed had actually caused the accident by riding across the road on his bicycle in the dark? Was never found."

Brig's heart was racing—this was, once again, validation for his habit of following up on unlikely leads and gut instincts. Forbes felt right, just as he had when Dia first mentioned him. However, he had to maintain objectivity. He said, "That's not unusual. A lot of parents will cover up for their kid in a heartbeat if they think he did something that will get him in trouble with the law. Lie, hide evidence, hide the kid."

"Oh, sure. But . . . follow this. I'm getting a revenge motive here. Decorated war hero Mac Courvant was responsible for Forbes's being sent to three years of high school in one of those private, pricey 'troubled kids' programs. Forbes did not take well to confinement, according to a teacher I called who remembered him. So Courvant *dies* in a car accident in which Forbes was the only survivor. And in an ultimate sick twist of fate, Courvant's widow saves the life of the man who may have murdered her husband."

Yeah, Brig thought. *Yeah.* Weirdly, that fit with Dia's nightmare.

He told Stan, "There's more." He felt both sick and excited at the same time—the same feeling he got when a case broke open for him. "Our widow turns down an opportunity to meet the man whose life she saved. She stays with her unit, becomes a paramedic like her dead husband, and four years later, at the point where she starts working auto accidents that were set by a killer, someone abruptly and anonymously thanks her for saving his life, then starts stalking her and threatens to kill her."

"You're shitting me."

Brig shook his head, disbelieving this piece of luck he'd fallen into. "I had no idea there might be a tie-in between the cases, but I'm not. I'm here with her, trying to figure out how her house was broken into last night, while all her friends and I were here, no less."

Stan was quiet for a long moment. And then he said, "She's seen something. Maybe she doesn't know it, but she's seen something that would allow her to tie Sinclair Forbes to these accidents."

"Yeah," Brig said. "Yeah . . . yeah . . . he saw her there and she saw him—and he thought she recognized him. Or . . . something. He's sure she can connect him to this, and that's why, out of nowhere, he's coming after her. But we know who he is."

"The problem," Stan said, "is that we don't know *where* he is. He disappeared shortly after he recovered from the car accident. Fell right off the face of the earth."

The hairs on the back of Brig's neck stood up, and his stomach knotted, and suddenly he was freezing. Icy cold, scared cold, with his heart racing and his nerves tingling and his mouth dry.

He said, "I'm going to have to go. I need to talk with her. Fast. I knew she was in trouble, but this is worse than I'd ever imagined."

"Bring her down to the station. Let's get her statement. Let's find out exactly what it is that she does know."

Brig stood in the bathroom for a moment, shivering, imagining Dia on the night her husband died, fighting in the dark, in shock, to save the life of the man who'd murdered her husband. Because she was a good woman. An extraordinary woman. A woman who had saved the life of the man who was now coming after her to kill her.

Chapter 12

Brig came out of the bathroom looking like he'd seen a ghost. Dia frowned. "Something wrong?"

"I need to take you down to the station with me. Stan thinks he has a line on the guy who's stalking you. It isn't good, and I want you out of here while we figure out how we're going to deal with this."

She stared at him. "I don't care who it is, Brig. It doesn't matter to me. I'll deal with it."

"It's more complicated than that."

She looked over at Kelly, who had been hanging around with her after the guys had left, just to see what Brig wanted them all to do.

Kelly said, "You want me to come too? I'm her best friend."

Brig shook his head. "I think making sure we can reach you will be enough."

Kelly nodded at him. "Pager. Cell phone. Car radio. I'm totally plugged in."

"Okay, then," he said. "You ready?"

Dia said, "I need to change the combination on my alarm keypad. I haven't done that yet."

"Do it later."

"Ryan told me to do it immediately, so that if anything else happened, he and the other guys would be in the clear. He wants me to be the only person who knows it, until Kelly moves in."

"He and the other guys are already in the clear," Brig said. "But go ahead. Change it, make sure you remember what it is, and then we'll go."

Dia nodded. She opened the handbook that had come with the alarm system, and carefully followed directions that Ryan had circled for her. Then she punched in the date that she and Mac had met. It was one she would never forget, and she was comfortable that no one else would know it. And it was something she wouldn't have to write down anywhere.

When she was done, she ushered the other two out the front door, set the alarm, and closed and locked the place.

Kelly said, "I'm going to be another two days packing. But I'm going diving with the guys tomorrow. Are you still in?"

"I'm still in," Dia said. "I have to get my dive hours. And tonight I should be able to sleep, anyway. Between the new locks, the new alarm system, and someone guarding the house, I don't see how anything could happen to keep me up all night."

"The guys told me to let you know that they'll be by around six thirty."

"In the *morning?*" Brig, who'd been standing impatiently by his Crown Vic, waiting for them to finish talking, looked from one to the other in disbelief. "You're going to be out the door that early in the morning on your day off? What's *wrong* with you people?"

Dia laughed. "We have the bug. It's a wicked, wicked bug. We. Save. Lives."

"Yeah," he said, but he wasn't smiling. "You do."

Kelly's look to Dia asked, *What's wrong with him?*

Dia shrugged. "See you at the dock?"

"I'll be there. Sam flaked out on me, so I'll be coming alone again."

"That'll work. We'll have pairs, right?"

"We're good. We have it all figured out."

In the car, driving her to the police station, Brig was uncommunicative.

"Okay," Dia said at last. "You were great earlier. Good mood, positive outlook—whatever you want to call it. And now you're gloom and doom and darkness. What the hell happened?"

"I got some bad news."

"What kind of bad news?"

"It was about you. About your past, and Mac, and a number of other things. I don't want to go over it in the car. Stan's still tracking down a few pieces of info, and I want him to be able to give you the supporting details as we go over all of this with you."

"All right." She crossed her arms over her chest, closed her eyes, and leaned back in what was, she discovered, a very comfortable seat.

And got an elbow in the ribs. "Wake up. We're here."

She was at the downtown Fort Lauderdale station. That was a long trip at the best of times, due to the area's heavy traffic and endless stoplights. "How long have I been asleep?"

"I wasn't counting," he said. He came around and opened the door for her, and led her into the busy station, up back stairs, down a wide, well-lit corridor, and into an open room filled with cubicles.

"This isn't how I would have pictured your office," she said. "I was seeing an old-fashioned room with concrete-block walls painted some sort of industrial green, with a battered desk and a wooden chair. This is so . . . modern."

"You would have liked our station in Helena," he

said. "It was a little closer to your imagination. I had a window there."

"You'll have to tell me how you ended up here," she said.

"Maybe someday." She realized he was looking not at her, but over her shoulder, and he didn't look happy. She turned and found his partner, Stan, coming into the large cubicle.

Stan carried a plastic-covered ring binder, a yellow legal notepad covered with what was either very bad handwriting or very good hieroglyphics, and three cans of Pepsi, all unopened.

"Have a seat," Brig said, and pulled out a well-cushioned office chair for her. He didn't go to sit behind his desk. Instead he pulled up a chair beside hers. Stan did the same. They were both making an effort to be . . . what? Not cops. Not distant. They were using the same techniques she used when she wanted to comfort a victim.

Their bad news, she was suddenly afraid, was going to be very bad indeed. But she couldn't imagine what it could be.

"I'm just going to double-check a few facts first," Stan said. "You saved the life of a man named Sinclair Lawrence Forbes four years ago, more or less, at the site of an accident involving him and three EMTs in an ambulance. He was the sole survivor."

"Yes," Dia said.

"How well did you know Sinclair Forbes?"

She frowned and glanced at Brig. "I'd never met him. I told you that. I'd never seen him before; I've never seen him since."

"You're sure of that?"

"Well . . ." She thought about it. "No. I mean, I wouldn't recognize him if you stood him right in front of me. It was dark, he was covered in blood, and I was in shock."

"You're sure you wouldn't recognize him?"

"Positive."

"What can you tell me about what you remember of him?"

"He was overweight. Obese—probably about three hundred pounds. I think that was part of why he was hurt so badly in the accident. He had his seat belt on, but he was wearing it too high. It didn't stop him the way it should have, and he was in an older car that didn't have an air bag. He took a brutal hit to the chest with the steering wheel when he went into it." She paused, remembering. "I had a hell of a time getting him out of the car."

"Okay. So . . . aside from that, what do you have? Something useful, some memory of something that could help us recognize this guy when we see him."

"He was white, he was overweight, he was covered with blood. I don't know his eye color, his hair color, whether his nose was big or small, what he was wearing, what sort of tattoos he might have had. Nothing. I'm not kidding on this. Why?"

"Had you ever heard his name before that night?" Stan asked her.

Dia was exasperated, and sounded it when she replied. "No, dammit! Why? Why is this guy I was in contact with for maybe fifteen minutes one night so damned important?"

"He was your husband's best friend from the time they were about eight until they were freshmen in high school."

Dia sat there in complete silence for a long time, trying to fit that into anything she had ever heard Mac say, anything that anyone else might have said—Mac's family, his friends, the guys whom he occasionally ran into who'd been PJs with him in the air force. It didn't fit.

"He never said the guy's name once. We weren't married all that long, but we'd worked together for a year before that, too, and Mac was a talker. He loved to tell stories. He had a bunch about him and his parents, and about his brothers and sisters, and about living down by the beach before this place filled up—about how much fun it was. Scouting . . . he talked about Scouting all the time. He eventually made Eagle Scout, you know. He would have said *something* about a guy who was supposedly his best friend."

Brig said, "He probably wouldn't have. He's the person who found out that his best friend was causing traffic accidents. There hadn't been any fatalities when Mac turned Forbes in, but there had been some serious injuries. It was because of Mac that Forbes was sent away to one of those schools for troubled teens."

Dia shuddered as the full weight of that information rolled over her.

She put it all together, one horrible piece at a time. First, that Forbes set accidents, and had a reason to hate Mac. Second, that Mac had died in an accident where only Forbes had survived. Third, that someone was creating accidents again. Fourth, that she had been at the sites of some of those accidents.

He'd seen her. That had to be it. He'd seen her, and recognized her.

And then she put together the last piece. The piece where she'd saved the life of the man who had probably murdered her husband.

"Oh, my God," she whispered. "Mac."

Her fists clenched tight, her short nails digging into the palms of her hands. She bit the inside of her lip and closed her eyes tight. It was the day he'd died all over again, and she was on her hands and knees in the flashing light, looking at what was left of him, knowing there was nothing in the world she could do that would save him. And then looking up the berm, and seeing the other car rammed into a big old poinciana, half-buried under the spreading branches.

Seeing a man not moving in that car. Watching herself run up that hill again.

And saving the man. Doing all the right things, in all the right ways. Saving his life, when if there had been justice, if there had been anything right and fair in the universe, she wouldn't have seen his car until it was too late. Until he was dead.

Her husband and her colleagues—her friends—hadn't died in an accident. They'd been killed. Murdered. And she'd rescued their murderer.

She felt tears burning the back of her throat. She blinked them back; she would not let herself cry. She was angry. She was angry, and she had a right to be angry. She had a right to rip someone apart.

The man who had done this to her husband. Her friends. Sinclair Forbes.

"Where is he?" she said. She didn't open her eyes. She didn't dare. She could still feel the tears, and she wasn't going to give that bastard any more of her tears. He'd tied her in knots for a year with what he'd done to Mac—with everything he had stolen from her. He'd changed her whole life. Her husband's murderer was stalking her, trying to terrorize her, threatening to kill her? Mac's killer, hunting her. It took a couple minutes for her to get that new ground under her feet, and while she was fighting for balance, she got even angrier.

"Where is he? I want him found, I want to tear him into ribbons with my bare hands, I want to see him strung up and shot."

"That's the idea," Brig said. "That's what we want. Stan found a couple of old pictures of him. We want you to take a look at them and see if you've seen anyone who looks like him anywhere lately. It could be *anywhere,* remember, because he's been stalking you."

She looked at the pictures he showed her. A fat, pale teenager with short-cropped, nondescript brown hair, wearing glasses, an Izod shirt, a pair of pleated khaki pants, standing in an expensively groomed yard beside a pricey foreign car.

She squinted, trying to make out more details of his face. The picture was too small.

She turned to the next one. It was older—a head-and-shoulders school shot, a still-heavy young man in a cap and gown, not smiling. He had acne. He looked unhappy.

And that was it.

She turned to Brig and Stan. "I might have seen him, but he could be almost anyone. Look at him. He's half the male population. There aren't any better pictures of his face, or anything more recent?"

"We're looking," Stan said. "We'll be checking with family members, but we're not expecting much cooperation there—his family is rich and connected, and his parents were quite good at stonewalling before, where he was concerned. His mother is a state representative. Both parents have friends who are judges. All in all, unless we have something solid on him to start with, we don't expect much help with search warrants or subpoenas. And to complicate things, odds are that he's changed his name since he went into hiding."

"What do I need to do?"

"You're already doing most of it," Brig said. "The little security cameras over your doors will catch him if he tries to come in either way again. We can use any picture you get from that to push for subpoenas, search warrants, and other goodies. But first we need that. If anything shows up in your house again, like writing on your mirror, or your music playing on its own, you let one of us know. Don't touch anything. This is tied in to an active murder investigation now, and you're a witness. You just became part of our case, and you are one hell of a lucky break for us—we can make sure your neighborhood gets extra patrols; we can have people start looking for this guy." Brig said, "You can buy a good handgun and I'll take you to the range and teach you how to shoot it."

Dia nodded. "Okay."

"Keep doors and windows closed and locked at all times, don't open your door until you've identified the person on the other side of it, take a different route to work every day, keep your car in your garage and your garage locked so that you can be confident that it hasn't been tampered with. Remove any easy access routes to you. Stay with people you know. Don't take stupid chances."

She stood up. "I need to get out of here," she told Brig. The muscles in her legs were twitching and aching. It was her stress reaction—she needed to walk: hard, fast, a lot. Get a good long hall where she could pace, or go out on a track and run in circles until she dropped from exhaustion. She needed some space. The cubicle around her kept getting smaller, and the constant racket of other voices talking on phones and to other people, calling back and forth; the drumming of feet on tile; the ringing of phones and the clatter of keys on keyboards; people with music going, none of it the same . . .

Too much. "I have to walk," she said, and pushed past both of them as the big room closed tighter and tighter around her.

She headed out in the hall and saw portly white men wearing glasses everywhere she looked. Stocky men, chunky men, fat men. There were lean ones, too, but they faded into the background.

Sinclair Lawrence Forbes, spoiled rich kid who had somehow become friends with Mac Courvant, skinny middle-class kid. Who had done something that had destroyed their friendship. Who had sought revenge. Who had gone back to doing what he liked to do after Mac was dead, and then who had suddenly decided to come after her.

Had it been sudden? Or had this been part of his plan all along?

She knew this was just a theory, that Sinclair Forbes was a suspect but not definitely guilty. There might be no connection between him and Mac's death. It might have been a freak accident, just like everyone had said—with the past ties between the two of them something that no one, not even Forbes, knew had existed. He might not have known Mac died in that accident.

She bet he did. But . . .

What if he were innocent? What if he'd been rehabilitated? What if he had gone on to live a decent life, had hit his brakes to keep from running over a kid on a bike, and had been creamed from behind by an ambulance racing to a call? What if, after he regained consciousness, he discovered that one of the people killed in the wreck had been his best friend, back before that best friend turned Forbes in for a few stupid, childish pranks? What if Forbes realized that, if he admitted to anyone that he and Mac had a connection—or if anyone accidentally stumbled across that connection—his life was going to turn into hell? That people were going to look at his past and assume that he'd set up the accident to kill his onetime friend?

He would do exactly the same thing he had done. He would fall off the face of the map. Not because he was guilty, but because he was innocent.

She didn't think he was. She was no big believer in coincidence, serendipity, or happenstance. They hadn't been a part of her life, and she found it unlikely that they had been a part of Forbes's life.

But she had to entertain the possibility. She had to look for Forbes. But not *just* Forbes. The person out there hunting her could still be anyone.

The long corridor was mostly empty, and she walked fast—up one end of it, turn, and back. Brig snagged her arm on her way past the detectives' room.

"Hey. You all right?"

"No," she said. "Maybe Mac was murdered. That's big. Maybe the man causing those horrible accidents is the man stalking me, in which case I have to assume that he won't hesitate to kill me. Maybe I'll spend all my time looking out for Forbes and the real stalker will walk right up to me and slit my throat because I was looking for the wrong person." She started walking again, and he followed along. "It isn't that I resent being careful; for the most part, I did that anyway. It's just that I don't want to take all these precautions and still miss the most important one."

"What's the most important one?"

"I don't know," she said. "You don't know. Nobody knows. But the most important precaution might be the one no one has figured out I need to take."

Brig put an arm around her waist. "You have a lot of people willing to watch out for you."

"I know."

"I'm going to be one of them," he said.

She looked sidelong at him and suddenly grinned. "Decided that, have you?"

He pulled out that easy Montana drawl and said, "Yes, ma'am. I *have* decided that."

"We'll see how that goes."

Chapter 13

Brig bedded on the couch at Dia's place, just as he'd promised himself. He'd taken the first shower, just to make sure there weren't any steamy surprises on the mirror. There weren't.

She'd headed in, and he listened to the water running, and running. And to her humming.

He smiled a little. That humming was sort of endearing—she couldn't carry a tune in a wheelbarrow with training wheels, much less a bucket, but he thought that was sort of cute. And intriguing. He stretched out and listened, wondering what song it was she was massacring so badly. If she'd give him a few words, he might hope to guess; as it was, that song was guaranteed anonymity.

He wasn't going to abandon her. He'd spend the next night, too—and then Kelly would move in, and he could gracefully exit from her life a little bit at a time.

She was his best link to his most likely suspect, so his exit would have to be a gradual thing. He wouldn't hurry it along. He'd just made sure he would be on the couch when she came out, and since she wanted the same thing he wanted, she'd get the message. They were going to be friends.

He'd do what he could to keep her safe. He took care

of his friends. And she was a smart, sensible woman anyway. She was doing what she could to keep herself safe. He'd taken her to a good gun shop, introduced her to the owner—an ex-cop—tried a couple of different weapons, and found the one that fit her and suited her. And then she bought it and the two of them stood in the indoor shooting range and she practiced for nearly two hours.

When she was done, she complained a little that her arms ached. But she could hit the target at center mass every time from standing and sitting positions from most distances. He assured her that they'd come back a few more times and he'd work with her, and she would be a good enough shot to be a cop.

Then he'd taken her home and gone over weapon safety and weapon cleaning and weapon storage. She'd listened. She'd paid attention. She would, he thought, be able to fieldstrip and reassemble her weapon blindfolded in just a couple of days, if he suggested that this was something she needed to be able to do.

She was doing everything right.

He settled more deeply into the couch. Almost everything right. Was she trying to hum "Only the Good Die Young"? If she was, Billy Joel had good cause to sue.

He chuckled, content to think of her as a quirky friend. That way, she—and that song—could remain a mystery.

Dia was taking too long in the shower, and she knew it. But she dreaded the possible awkwardness of going into her room and discovering that Brig was in there. Her body was saying all sorts of things about how it wanted him there. Her mind, however, had gotten the upper hand once again. She'd spent most of the day with the man, and the emphasis on guns and shooting and stalkers and people in danger and people dying reminded her that she did not want every day of her life to be some variant on that day.

A calm man. A settled man. That was what she needed. Not what she wanted, maybe. But people wanted ice cream and potato chips and cookies and fried chicken instead of steamed vegetables and raw carrot juice, too, didn't they? People always wanted what was bad for them a lot more than they wanted what they needed.

She'd get over this.

She realized she was humming the same song, over and over. *Blue moooon,* she sang in her thoughts. *You saw me standing . . . alone. . . .*

As soon as she realized it, she stopped herself, because that was a bad, bad song for a woman who needed to be thinking independent thoughts. She needed some kick-ass rock-and-roll I-don't-need-nobody anthem to loop through her head, instead of that heartsick lament.

She got out of the shower, toweling off as she did.

And was hit by freezing, bone-chilling cold. Was something wrong with her air conditioner, too? It was like being back in the hotel again—only worse. Good God, her skin was goose bumps all over and her teeth were chattering, and her heart was running like a racehorse.

She wrapped the towel around herself, shuddering. And looked at the mirror.

It said, *YOU CA . . .*

She realized that a line was appearing next to the *A,* though. As she watched, it formed itself, haltingly, into:

N . . .

' . . .

T . . .

The invisible hand paused.

Dia's heart stopped in her chest. She tried to make a noise, but no noise would come out of her throat. She tried to move, but her feet were cemented to the floor.

H . . .

I . . .

D . . .

E . . .

She could hear her teeth clacking together.

Brig. He was on the couch. He could . . .

He could . . .

The cold vanished. One instant the air felt like Antarctica on a bad day; the next, the bathroom was South Florida steamy.

Her muscles unlocked and she sagged to the floor, still shivering, with tears running down her cheeks, and clogging her throat, and blurring her vision.

She blinked them away and wiped at her face with a corner of the towel.

And looked up at the mirror.

The message was still there.

YOU CAN'T HIDE

She'd seen it being written. Not for a minute did she think there was some way that Forbes had managed to rig an invisible hand to write her a message just as she was stepping out of the shower. Not for a minute.

But she couldn't accept what she'd seen. She couldn't face what it meant.

And she couldn't tell Brig.

It was too impossible. It was too much.

She sat there shuddering, trying to put the pieces together. The nightmares in which Mac, who had been murdered, tried to tell her something. The scary cold spots in the house, her feelings of being watched.

Brig was out there. All she had to do was scream, and he'd come running, and she could show him the words written in steam. She could explain that she watched them being written, and he already knew nothing had been there before, because he'd taken the first shower.

She wrapped her arms around her legs, pulling her knees to her chest. What if it was Mac? What the hell was she supposed to do about that?

When Mac first died, she would have given anything to have had a sign that some part of him was still around, caring about her. She went to the shirts on his side of the closet and shoved her face into them and inhaled, because some of them still smelled like him. It was something to hold on to.

But she'd had nothing of him then but the nightmares, and back then, he hadn't been trying to talk to her in her dreams. He'd just been dead, lying on the manicured berm. Dead and pale and still.

And what was he now, if he was in her bathroom writing her messages? She'd been ready to move on with her life. In a lot of ways she had; in a few ways she was still waiting to meet the right someone. And she'd had a clear field—she'd been free to move when she was ready. No complications, no ties, no confusion, because there wasn't a much clearer ending to a relationship than having one of the two participants be dead.

And now all of a sudden he wasn't all the way dead anymore. He was sort of back in her life, sort of back in the little house the two of them had shared. She'd loved him when he'd died, and the memory of him held a huge place in her heart. She would never deny that. But it was four years later, and she was a different woman than she'd been back then. And he hadn't come back enough that she could touch him, hold him, talk to him, or have a meal with him. Not enough that she could figure out whether he was the right man for her any-more. Not enough that she could have any control or any say in the process of his being back.

No. Just enough that she could feel him watching her, that she could get frozen and spooked by his presence, that he could leave her warnings on the mirror. That she could think that she didn't want him there, and that she could know she couldn't do a thing about it.

Brig banged on the bathroom door that Dia was lean-ing on, and she yelped. "You okay in there?" he yelled.

She stared at the mirror. At the message on it. There were more questions in that message than she wanted to answer. She didn't want to talk about this; she didn't want to make sense of it; she didn't want to do anything but forget what she'd seen.

She stood up, careful not to make any noise. She padded silently to the toilet and flushed it. "Your stom-ach upset, too?" she yelled. "I'll hurry." She flipped on the bathroom fan, and used the towel she'd had wrapped around her to wipe down the bathroom mirror, erasing the message there. "Just let me air the place out a little and I'll get out of your way." She reached under the counter, fished out a can of Lysol spray, and spritzed it into the air, then pulled on the pajamas she'd brought in with her—an ugly cotton shirt-and-pants set in a hideous chartreuse-purple-and-brown plaid that her mother had given her for her birthday a year ago. She'd never worn them. But they seemed to say, *Don't touch me; I'm poisonous or rabid or possibly insane, and sex with me could be hazardous to your health.*

She opened the door to find him standing there. "Mostly safe in there, I think. I ate something that just isn't sitting right," she said, and left the fan running.

"I'm . . . fine," he said, faltering a bit as he caught sight of her pajamas. "I just got worried about you because you were in there and quiet for so long." He was trying not to stare at those pajamas.

If anyone knew about the birth-control properties of hideous cotton, it would be her mother, Dia thought.

"Good night," she said. She figured that if her smile looked unconvincing, Brig would write it off to her stomach ailment. "I have to get to bed; tomorrow is going to start pretty early."

He was frowning, managing to look both thoughtful and delectable as he did it. "Right," he said. He glanced past her into the bathroom, and back to her. "Have a good night."

He didn't walk away, though. Dia stood in the bathroom doorway, the forced smile on her face feeling increasingly false. "Thank you for staying until Kelly can move in," she said. "I . . . really appreciate not being alone. And you didn't have to do this, but I'm glad you did."

He just nodded. "I was happy to be able to help." And then, sounding a little stiff himself, he said, "I'm sorry your life got tangled up in my case."

She shrugged. "Things happen."

At last he shifted to the right, and she slipped by him and into her room. She closed the door. She didn't lock it, though she thought about it; there wasn't much sense in having him in the house to protect her if she put barriers between the two of them.

And then she curled up in her bed and lay staring at the ceiling. Dia hated herself right at that moment. She lay under her covers, fighting back tears, twisting and turning in the bed.

She could have admitted what she'd seen in the bathroom.

But admitting it would have made it real. As it was, she could tell herself that she hadn't seen anything—not really—that stress and nightmares and lack of sleep were playing with her mind, that she'd made streaks on the mirror into some sort of message that hadn't actually been there.

She didn't want to believe part of Mac had come back, because if he had, then what?

Mac was dead. She wasn't going to get to hold him, or kiss him, or make love with him again. Nor fight with him. Nor compete with him over who had the most critical rescues in a day, or the most successful codes, or the fastest trip up a cliff face, or the deepest dive. Was she supposed to still be his wife if his ghost was watching over her? She couldn't be a ghost's wife. She couldn't accept that Mac hadn't gone on to wherever the dead went. Into nothingness, or heaven, or some summerland, or . . . wherever. He *needed* to be wherever the dead belonged, and not lurking around her house, even if he was trying to help her. And she had no proof he was trying to help her. His messages had been vague. And threatening. How much help was a ghost who didn't just save everyone a lot of time and write, *Forbes did it* on the mirror?

And if he was around, had he been around all the time? Had he been there the first year, when she almost couldn't breathe from missing him so much? Why hadn't he done something to comfort her when she needed him, instead of complicating her life now that she was okay again?

What did she owe him?

What *did* she owe Mac, really?

What?

There was a guy out on her couch who made her feel like she'd never felt before, and even if he was all wrong for her, it was still amazing that she could feel that way. She wanted to feel that way a whole lot more; she wanted the goose bumps and the butterflies and the racing pulse and the wild, fantastic, consuming day-dreams of her and Brig doing thrilling, hot, sweaty things to each other.

No. *Not* Brig. Some *other* guy. The *right* guy.

But she wanted those feelings.

And what she had lying in her bed at that moment was guilt, because she'd had sex with Brig on her kitchen counter—and floor, she reminded herself—and her four-years-dead husband might have been watching. Might have felt cheated on.

How the hell was she supposed to deal with that?

She managed to calm her thoughts down. She counted, and breathed in, and breathed out. Slowly. Slowly.

Slowly.

She was already away from Mac, from the ambulance, and from the dead EMTs crushed inside. She was already on her knees on the ground, intubating the C-spined, immobilized victim whose name she hadn't even had time to check out. She was at his head, looking into his throat, getting a clear view of his vocal cords with the little light on the end of her endotracheal blade. She had a tube in her right hand. With a deft, dart-throwing motion, she slid it down the victim's throat, into his airway, and inflated the bulb that would hold the tube in place, then compressed the bag that would squeeze air into his lungs and listened at his chest for breath sounds.

She couldn't hear anything. Not a single sound. She couldn't hear "Bad Moon Rising," though she knew it was still playing loudly. She couldn't hear the night sounds, the sounds of nearby traffic passing over busier roads. She couldn't hear herself breathing; she couldn't hear the sharp clicks as, frustrated, she tapped a fingernail against the stethoscope diaphragm.

"He's close to you."

She recoiled from the voice.

Mac was behind her. Right behind her. She couldn't feel his breath on the back of her neck, because he wasn't breathing. She knew he was dead. Still dead. She didn't turn around to look at him, because she was afraid of what she would see.

"He's close to you."

"Who?"

"He's close to you."

She whipped to her feet, turned around. And Mac wasn't there. Nothing was there. "Who, dammit!"

"He's close to you."

She screamed, and someone

shouted, "Hey!"

She froze. She opened her eyes just enough to see that a large male form *was* close to her. Hovering right over her, in fact. She bunched her legs up to her chest and kicked upward and outward, landing a solid hit in his midsection, lifting him off the floor and kicking him across the bedroom, where he hit the wall and slid down it.

She rolled up in the bed and tried to remember where the gun she'd just bought was, and recalled that it was in the lockbox in her nightstand, on the side closest to her would-be attacker.

"Fuck," Brig gasped from the floor. His voice squeaked when he talked. "Why the hell did you do that?"

Brig. Not an unknown assailant, not Sinclair Forbes, not the ghost of Mac suddenly made flesh and with vengeance in mind.

She'd just launched *Brig* into the wall. *Oops* was probably not the right thing to say to him. "You were close to me," Dia told him instead, and knew as the words came out of her mouth how stupid that sounded.

Still half caught up in her nightmare, she stared at him. "You were close to me, and Mac was telling me, 'He's close to you.' It's what he's been saying all along, every night I've had that damned nightmare. It's what his lips were sounding out before I could hear him talking to me, but tonight I heard him for the first time, and realized that's what he'd been saying all along, and then I woke up and there you were. Close. To me."

Brig was rubbing his chest. "Yeah. That makes a whole lot of sense." He got up carefully and limped out of the room, clearly pissed off.

Dia stared after him.

"I was *asleep!*" she shouted down the hall. "I don't wake up well."

"That's an understatement."

She heard knocking on the front door, and Brig answering it, grumbling. "She's fine," he snarled to a muttered question. "She just woke up screaming from a nightmare a minute ago, and I ran in to check on her, and she kicked the living shit out of me. I'm going to have footprints on my ribs for a month."

"I was *asleep!*" Dia yelled. "*Asleep.* You don't wake people up by *yelling* at them when they're asleep! When they're clearly having nightmares." She grabbed her robe and wrapped it around her, and stomped out to the living room. Ignoring Tyler and Ryan, who were staring at her, she glared at Brig. "I'm sorry I kicked you. I really am. But you should be glad I can take care of myself."

Tyler and Ryan looked from her to him as he said, "Your couch is uncomfortable, I hardly slept at all, and now I think I have broken ribs. So much for my do-good impulses."

Ryan kept sneaking glances at Dia, and he looked like he was fighting back laughter.

"What?" she snarled at him.

He did laugh, then, waving both hands placatingly. "*Nice* jammies, Dia. You break those out just for company?"

Right. She was in the mama-jamas in front of people she worked with. *Shit.* This would not be the last time she heard about them.

Of course, both Tyler and Ryan were already dressed in scruffy T-shirts and swim trunks. And at her house. Which meant she was running late.

Dia never ran late.

"We're going to give you a lift to the docks, remember?" Tyler said. And then, accusingly, "*You're* not ready."

"I forgot to set my alarm," she said. "Wait for me. It'll take me five minutes." She held up one hand, fingers spread. "Five. I have my gear ready to go; my kit's right in the front of the garage. Grab it for me, okay?"

Tyler sighed and went out to get it, while Ryan stayed behind. Brig was staring down at his chest, which did have a couple of round, heel-shaped red spots on it. "Dude," she heard Ryan say, "what the hell did she hit you with?"

"Just her feet," Brig answered. "It was like being kicked by a Buick."

She felt guilty about that. She hoped she hadn't done him any damage. She had to admit her work on the inclined press at the gym was paying off, though. She'd been pushing four hundred pounds of iron up that incline for the past few months, because working out and staying in shape allowed her to do the heavy lifting her job required. Because of that, launching Brig across the room with her legs had been remarkably easy. He couldn't have weighed more than two hundred . . . maybe two hundred twenty pounds. Tops.

Dia ran back to the bedroom, threw on a bathing suit with shorts and a T-shirt over it, darted into the bathroom just long enough to brush her teeth, and then hurried back to the living room, hopping on one foot as she tugged the heel strap of a sandal up over her right heel.

"Ready," she said.

"Diving watch?" Ryan asked her, looking at her bare wrist.

"In my kit."

He glanced at his own watch. "Three minutes. That's fast."

Tyler was already back in the living room. "Your stuff's in the back of the van. You ready now?"

"We getting something to eat on the way?"

"Yeah."

"Then I'm ready now." Dia looked over at Brig. "I would never have kicked you like that if I'd been awake. I'm sorry."

"Yeah," he said. "I know. Sorry I . . . scared you. I guess."

"You going in to work?"

He looked at her with an expression of mild annoyance. "As opposed to sitting in here and babysitting your well-protected house while you're out having fun? Yes, I'm going to work."

She didn't like having him unhappy with her. She looked at him, and she wanted to run over and throw her arms around him and shove her face against his chest.

But she had to face reality. He was as much a workaholic as she was. She was getting in dive hours on her day off; he admitted that he worked from before he was even supposed to be in the building until after he was supposed to leave, and took work home with him. He was, he'd told her, a one-dimensional man.

She wished she didn't understand that so well.

She set the alarms. Glanced at the tiny camera over her front door. Everything would be fine, she told herself. No one would be in there waiting for her when she got home.

She climbed into Tyler's van with Ryan and waved to Brig.

Ryan had an old boat he'd gotten from a salvage yard after a hurricane ripped through and sank it. He'd lovingly restored it, and sometimes he talked about living on it, instead of in the room he rented from the hermit. He said if there had just been a way to keep it close enough to the action of his rescue squad, he would have done it in a heartbeat.

Out at their dive location, with the boat cross-anchored, Dia had no trouble imagining why. Awnings covered the decks, and the filtered light, the cool ocean breeze, and the easy rocking and rolling of the boat on the light chop all made it seem like the perfect place to be.

Everyone got out dive gear and did their safety checks. They put on wet suits, tanked up, and teamed up. Dia and Ryan were paired, as were Kelly and Tyler, whose girlfriend had canceled their date, and, he thought, probably dumped him, while Howie had brought a cousin of his who was a paramedic in a station over in North Lauderdale.

Everyone synchronized their dive watches, made final checks on tubing and tank pressure, and then went in.

The cool water was like a kiss; the sounds of their bubbles drifting upward as the six divers dropped gently toward the bottom soothed her, and Dia had no trouble seeing the wreck. Ryan had done a great job of putting them right over it. Of course, it was a well-known wreck and they were just diving it because it was fun and they needed the underwater hours—but still, she was impressed by his navigating skills. And she liked the way he boated a lot better than the way he drove.

She grinned at him. That struck her as funny. Really funny. She had an image of him driving a boat on the road instead of an ambulance, and that seemed just too delicious to ignore. She laughed out loud, and her mouthpiece popped out of her mouth and floated on a tether. "Oops," she said in a wash of bubbles, and reached for it, but it kept eluding her fingers. She wasn't really trying very hard to get it.

Ryan looked at her, and kicked over to her, fear in his eyes. He grabbed the mouthpiece and shoved it into her hand.

She put the mouthpiece back in and took another breath, but it didn't seem to matter, really. Not even a little bit. The mouthpiece was just in her way, and she wanted to tell Ryan the funny thing she'd just imagined about him and the boat on the roads . . .

It popped out of her mouth again, and she didn't even try to catch it.

He seemed so upset. Well, she supposed he had a reason to be. She knew she needed air. She just didn't care if she got it.

He grabbed her and pulled her close, took his own mouthpiece, and put it into her mouth. She inhaled. He shot a water flare down past the other two teams, which had gotten ahead of them. They all turned. He took his mouthpiece back and breathed. Gave it to her, and she breathed.

Something was wrong with her. She should be afraid. She knew she should. She should care about the fact that she wasn't trying to breathe her own air. But knowing she should be afraid was nothing like being afraid.

She grinned at him again, trying to reassure him, because he looked so panicked.

Mouthpiece to her, mouthpiece to him. He was, she realized, hauling her back to the surface, which was going to spoil everybody's fun. Just because she didn't want her mouthpiece.

She didn't want to be a party pooper.

She didn't.

They'd been diving in relative shallows—they reached the surface with only one stop to decompress.

Ryan said, "Tell me your name."

"Dia." She giggled when she said it. He was so serious, and of course she knew her own name.

"The date."

She laughed, lolling on the surface of the water, watching her friends pop out of the sea like otters. "It's Sunday, silly," she told him.

"The *date*," he repeated.

She was sure she knew it, but she couldn't make herself care. She wanted to dive again. She wanted to be an otter—no tanks, no gauges, no mouthpiece, no weight belt, no diving knife or flippers. She wanted to be naked and free, to do underwater ballet and catch fish with her teeth.

She laughed at the image, and realized everyone else was talking about her.

Ryan shut off her tank, which was still bubbling, and had Howie and Tyler and the guy whose name she didn't remember get her up the ladder and back onto his boat.

"I'm fine," she was telling them. "Fine." She started giggling uncontrollably. Some part of her that was watching what she was doing knew that wasn't right.

They were taking her tanks off of her, marking the one she'd been using with a dive marker.

"Someone tampered with her tanks," Ryan said. "That isn't a dive mix. That's something else. She could have died."

Still happy, still giddy and deliciously silly, she realized she was going to throw up.

She flopped to her hands and knees just in time to puke her OJ-and-biscuit breakfast all over the deck.

Things stopped being funny.

Someone cleaned up the mess, and someone else got her to the side so that she could throw up again. It was all faceless, weird, and bewildering for a while.

The first thing she heard that she could focus on was Ryan talking on his radio, calling in to shore. Calling Brig, she realized, telling him they were going to need an ambulance. Tyler and Kelly stayed with her, holding her head when she barfed. The other two guys were going through Ryan's well-stocked emergency kit, putting her on mask O_2 at high volume once the barfing eased up.

Blur . . . it was all a blur. She couldn't make it add up. Couldn't make it make any sense at all.

Brig and Stan were at the dock when the *Lucky Lady* arrived, along with an ambulance and a couple of stringers with cameras and mikes who'd evidently been hanging on their scanners hoping for something juicy. Attempted murder on the high seas was pretty juicy.

Stan gathered up the evidence—her tanks and her diving bag. Brig collected all the witnesses.

He was trying not to think about the fact that Dia could have been dead. The emotions from that slammed into him, and had since he'd taken Ryan's almost-panicked call. The guy had done all right, though. Had gotten her to the surface alive. It was what they trained for, of course, but working on one of your own was a different animal entirely from working on a stranger.

After he told all of them not to go anywhere, he caught up with Dia as two guys were strapping her onto the gurney. She was doped. Her reactions were off, her pupils too wide, her answers erratic. She'd been vomiting, one of the guys said. She looked at him listlessly. "I don't know what's the matter with me," she said. "For a while it all seemed so funny."

"I'm going to follow you guys in," he told the paramedic, and got the name of the hospital where they were taking her. He told Dia, "I'm right behind you."

The paramedics were telling their story to the stringers, who had their cameras going and their mikes out. If it was a busy news day, the story would disappear, which would suit Brig fine. If it was a slow day, though, diving EMTs rescuing a gorgeous paramedic from attempted murder was going to make some very sexy copy. He sighed as he waved Ryan over to his car. It might not even need to be a slow news day to get picked up.

"Ride with me," he said. "We're going to follow her to the hospital. We'll talk on the way in." Ryan didn't quibble. The other divers were with Stan, who would corral the bunch of them down to the station and get separate statements from each.

They'd process the evidence, find out what had been in her tank, and then they'd go over her garage looking for signs of a break-in.

It was a nightmare. She could have been dead.

"You okay?" Ryan asked him.

Brig was right behind the ambulance, lights flashing, no siren going.

"I've been better, to tell you the truth. She was lucky you were there."

"Any of us would have done the same thing. She could have done it, if the victim had been one of us." He shrugged. "I'm glad I was there."

"What happened? I have the basics from your call, but . . . give me details."

"It was fast," Ryan told him. "We did our safety checks; we dove. She hadn't dropped more than seven or eight meters when she started . . . um, I guess . . . swimming funny. I mean, she's a hell of a strong swimmer. Very efficient. And she started getting kind of floppy in her movements. I thought she was just screwing around."

"She doesn't seem to be the sort for that."

Ryan laughed. "You'd be surprised. She's a wicked practical joker when she decides to be. So at first I thought, Okay, what's the game?"

Brig raised his eyebrows. "I'm kind of surprised. But, okay. So, then what?"

"She started laughing. It totally screws with your breathing rhythm. And she lost her mouthpiece, and when I really got scared was when she was sort of flailing around trying to catch it, and she was missing." He shook his head, and all humor vanished from his face. "I grabbed it and shoved it back into her mouth, and she breathed in. She wasn't so far gone that she tried to breathe water, but . . . man. I've been scared before. I've never seen *anything* like that, though. She laughed again, and the mouthpiece popped back out, and I remember thinking that something was wrong with her air. I gave her mine, and we buddy-breathed and I got her back up to the surface, but she just wasn't even there. It wasn't like she was fighting me." He frowned. "If she'd gotten combative, we both would have been in trouble. But she was just hanging there. Smiling. When I got her to the surface she knew who she was, and I'm pretty sure she knew when it was, but she wouldn't tell me. Her pupils were dilated. Her heart rate was elevated. I put her on pure O-two and opened it up in a mask so she could clear whatever it was that was in her tank."

Brig pulled into the ER parking lot right behind the ambulance, grabbed a reserved space, and got out of the car. Ryan followed. "You don't think it was bends, do you?"

"Wrong symptoms," Ryan said. "Except for the vomiting after she'd been up for a while, it was nothing like the bends. She doesn't hurt, for one thing. At all. She's sort of the opposite, in fact. She's very, very happy. Well, she was. The puking eventually seemed to get rid of that."

"Puking," Brig said. "I hate puking."

There were more reporters at the ambulance door, he realized. Or the same ones, but they'd acquired friends.

Slow news day, or sexy story. He didn't know, but he had a funny feeling the story was going to make the noon report.

They didn't crowd around him, though. They were all over Ryan, wanting to know the details. "Give them as little info as you can, get your fifteen minutes of fame," Brig told him. "You don't know anything about a murder attempt, and any questions along that line you refer back to me. Don't mention that you think her tank was tampered with, either. They may have already gathered that from your distress call, but if they didn't, do what you can to make my life less stressful, okay? The less they know, the less the guy who did this knows we know. What little we do know, of course."

Brig hurried into the ER.

He flashed his badge to the doctor, another intern he would see a few times and then never see again, no doubt. The guy had just stepped out of the bay that held Dia.

"How's she doing?"

"She looks all right now. Vital signs are good; we have her on positive-pressure O-two, but won't for much longer. Indications are she was breathing some bad air, and from the symptoms her colleagues described, it might have been something added, rather than just a bad diving mix."

"We're checking her tank for anything that shouldn't have been there," Brig said. "We have reason to believe this was attempted murder."

"We've done toxicology studies on her," the intern said. "If you find anything out of place in her tank, please let us know."

He went in to see her. She was pale and looked exhausted. She smiled when she saw him, though, and his heart felt tight in his chest. "The guys got more out of their dive than I did. They each got part of a rescue."

"How do you feel?"

She laughed softly. "My head is pounding, my eyes feel like they're trying to escape my skull, and I don't think I'm ever going to want to see or taste or smell food again. Other than that? Not so bad."

He pulled up a round metal stool that was tucked under the foot of the stretcher and sat down beside her.

"Who had access to your diving gear?" he asked.

"Either everyone or no one, depending on how you look at the question. The garage is always locked. The door into the garage from the house is always locked, though I've never bothered to have a dead bolt put on it. I keep my gear well maintained, I use it frequently, I know my safety procedures, and in all my years of diving, I've never had a single mishap—neither on my own, nor with someone I was teaching."

"You're an instructor?"

"I'm instructor qualified. I do just enough teaching to maintain my qualification, usually with young EMTs who want to be involved in rescue diving."

"Have you done much rescue diving at work?"

"No. As a paramedic I'm stuck on the surface. Specialist divers get the victims out; I treat them once they're out of the water. But I think it's important to be able to dive. There are a lot of canals around here, and one of these days I may not have a diver at the scene when somebody needs to be rescued. I keep thinking of that woman not long ago who was in her car, under the water, calling nine-one-one from her cell phone. Nobody got to her fast enough to save her."

"That's a lot of training for a skill you don't use. And a lot of risk."

Dia grinned at him. "How often have you shot someone?"

Brig smiled. "Once."

"In how many years?"

He got a little cagey about that—it would make his age obvious, and all of a sudden he didn't want to do that. "Lots."

"But you still go to the range and practice." She smiled. "Knowledge is never wasted."

He laughed. "I get your point."

She closed her eyes and pressed the palms of her hands to her forehead.

And his heart lurched again. "You okay? Do I need to get a doctor?"

"It just hurts," she said. "The nurse is supposed to be coming in here with something for the pain as soon as they get some idea of what happened to me down there. It isn't decompression. I told the doc I sort of remember my air tasting sweet. Just a little. I should have realized that wasn't right, but whatever it was hit me as soon as I inhaled it."

Brig said, "I'll go see how they're coming on that, then." As soon as he was out of earshot, he called Tracy at the lab, who'd promised to run the air sample as soon as it came in.

When he identified himself, she said, "We just got it

a couple minutes ago. All hell has broken loose in here, or I would have called you back. It was nitrous oxide."

Brig thought about that for a moment. "Laughing gas? She had that in her tank?"

"She did indeed. It was mixed about fifty-fifty with her air. The air mix itself would have been good otherwise, and her tank was marked and signed at the place where she had it filled. Signs are that whoever did this blew off about half her air and refilled the tank with medical-grade nitrous." Tracy sighed. "Your friend is damned lucky she couldn't keep her valve in place. If she'd taken too many more hits off of that thing, she would have developed hypoxia and killed her brain cells."

"Define 'killed her brain cells' for me, would you?"

"Think 'vegetable.' All she would have had left was the stuff on the outside."

His legs felt weak.

He walked over to the nurses' station and said, "I got a call in from the lab on the agent that was in Dia Courvant's air. Her doctor around?"

The nurse pointed. He had a chart and was coming out of another bay.

"I got the results back on her tank of air," Brig said. "It was nitrous oxide in there."

The doctor stopped and stared over at Dia, who was holding her head, only partially hidden by the curtain. "Wow. Yeah. That stuff can make someone sick in a hurry. Damn. You know the percentage of the mix?"

"The tech said about fifty-fifty with air."

He stood there with his eyes fixed on the ceiling, lips pursed. "So she was getting only about eight percent oxygen, assuming the rest of the stuff in her tank was good air."

"Lab says it was."

"That's not good. Not good at all. With only eight percent O-two and a heavy dose of nitrous, she could have been very, very dead."

"She's a paramedic—she and her team were diving. She was lucky to be with the right people when that happened."

"She's actually in very good shape now, in spite of her headache. She have family with her or anything? I'm going to give her a scrip and tell her to get it filled and then go home and take it easy for a day or two."

"I'll take her home," Brig said. "She's a friend of mine, and I need to talk to her about this anyway."

Dia leaned back on the broad, comfortable seat of Brig's Crown Vic. "I thought I had my place sufficiently secured."

"I think you do," Brig said. "But you had the tank filled, what—two weeks ago?"

"More or less," she told him. "The date's marked on the side."

"Then Forbes could have done this before you ever even knew you had a stalker."

Dia couldn't make any sense out of that. If he'd already had her murder set up, why bother with the flowers, or the note, or the computer stunts? She paused. Well, she didn't have any proof that he was responsible for the computer stunts. If what her computer was doing was related to what her mirror was doing, she had a little proof that he wasn't.

She looked over at Brig, trying to guess how he would react to her saying, *I think my husband's ghost is writing on my bathroom mirror. And maybe playing with my computer.*

It used to be that she could close her eyes and see Mac's face. That she could think about him being close to her and remember the sound of his voice when she walked into a room. That she could make herself think that when she curled up alone in her bed, she would wake up and find him there again, if only she did some magic little thing; if she believed hard enough, or wished hard enough, or wanted hard enough. But after four years, that was gone.

She could imagine Brig coming around a corner and smiling at her. That was pretty easy.

She could imagine waking up in a bed next to him.

She could imagine feeling safe, and wanted, and loved, and having him be the one who made her feel that way.

"You okay?" he said, glancing over at her.

"It's been a bad day, you know? Few of those in a row, and you start feeling a little unsure of your convictions. Having Kelly move in will be a good thing, I think." She smiled, knowing as she did that she hadn't managed to look too convincing. Having Kelly there would be better than nobody. But having Brig there would just be . . . Well, her gut thought that would be the way to deal with this whole crisis. "I'm going to be fine," she said. "I've done the right things, I'm going to be careful."

"You are," Brig said.

They pulled around the corner, and she saw a box sitting on the front steps. Even from the road it didn't look like a standard shipping box.

Brig said, "Wait here."

He got out of the car, walked to the package on her doorstep, and did not pick it up. Instead he pulled out his cell phone and called someone. He talked for a minute, then turned and walked back to the car and got in. "I believe you and I are going to be sitting in the car for a bit. I've called the bomb squad to come take a look at your box. And once they arrive, we're going to go inside and take a look at your security tape and see what your camera picked up. I believe we may have a winner."

"Really?"

"The card taped to the top of the box says, 'Darling Dia.'"

She shivered. "That sounds like a winner to me." She laid her head back on his seat and wrapped her arms around herself. "So . . . he's trying to kill me twice in the same day? First with the tampered tank, and then with explosives on my front porch?"

Brig said, "Take a deep breath. We're having the bomb squad boys come look at the box because I'm paranoid, not because there's definitely a bomb in it. In fact, there's probably not a bomb in it. There's probably a . . . a negligee, or a book he thinks you'll like, or something of that sort. You can't be sure that he knew you were going to go diving today. If you figure that tank has been sitting in your garage for a couple of weeks, then the odds are that it was a backup plan of his. Right? Most likely he didn't try to kill you *any* times today. Actively, at least."

"That's not much comfort." She wrapped her arms tighter around herself. She felt like she was going to blow apart if she didn't hang on, and she was determined not to flop across the front seat and latch on to him like a sobbing limpet. Not that limpets sobbed, but they did cling, and she wanted to cling—and was pretty close to sobbing.

He sighed. "No. It isn't."

"I didn't *see* anything, dammit. I didn't see him do anything, I don't know him, I wouldn't recognize him in a crowd or a police lineup. Why is he doing this to me?"

"We're going to find that out," Brig said. "You probably have a big piece of the evidence sitting in the VCR attached to your security camera. If we get a little home movie of the guy dropping off that package, and if the package is definitely from him, and not something from a sibling, or a parent, or a neighbor with a crush on you, we can either confirm that Forbes is the one after you, or deny it."

"It doesn't seem very certain."

"At the moment we're working on pure speculation, based on your nightmare and circumstantial evidence. If the man delivering the box is Sinclair Lawrence Forbes, then we have real evidence. We can start putting together warrants and getting the legal wheels rolling. We can't do that based on a nightmare."

"I want this to be over."

He reached across the car and draped an arm around her, and gave her a quick hug. "It will be."

The bomb boys showed up promptly, and equally promptly cleared the package. It wasn't explosives. It was, in fact, a teddy bear. It was filled with nothing but stuffing, and though it was bound for the police department evidence room, it was just a harmless little token. The note in the envelope, on the other hand, was not.

The Chinese say if you save a life, you're responsible for it. But you keep rejecting me.

Dia saw the note and wanted to scream. It was the same handwriting as the other notes. Just looking at it made her skin crawl.

"The bright side is," Brig said as they walked into the house, "that he's back to being frustrated he's on the outside of your door. That's an improvement."

She followed him to the VCR. He popped out the tape, immediately put in another one, and carried it to her television, where Ryan had hooked up another VCR just so they could do playback on the tapes her camera took.

She and Brig sat on the couch, and, in fast-forward, they watched people scurrying by on the sidewalk in front of the house. Dia discovered that the teenage girl down the street actually dragged her little dog right up to the shrubs in front of Dia's door and walked him back and forth there until he left his mess.

"What did I do to her?" Dia wondered. "There's always crap out there, but I just figured it was dogs off their leashes."

There were long blank periods, when the most exciting event happening was a car zipping by on the street.

And then a tremendously fat man in a windbreaker walked into the picture. He wore a ball cap, and he carried the box.

"There," Brig said. Dia caught the grim satisfaction on his face.

The man looked in both directions, wearing a worried expression. Then he walked up to the door, put the box down, hesitated, rang the doorbell, and hurried away.

Brig backed up the tape and moved the picture forward in the tiniest possible increments.

"Damned ball cap," he said. "Hides his eyes. We never get a good look at his eyes."

"I read somewhere that ears are useful for identifying someone."

Brig nodded. "And if the bastard had had a haircut in the last year, we'd be in good shape."

"You have height, weight, mouth, and nose. It's more than you had. It could be him." She sighed. "Well, I mean, obviously it's the stalker, but it could be Forbes."

"I don't know that it's going to give us anything we can use." Brig looked over at her. "I'll log the tape into

Evidence, and see if we can enhance the images and get anything that will positively identify this guy as Forbes."

Dia stood up. "I guess we should have expected that he'd be careful. The cap was probably to make sure neighbors didn't get a good look at him. The long hair—could that be a wig?"

"Could be. Didn't look like one, but it could be."

Dia looked around the inside of the place where she'd lived for the past six years. It had always seemed homey to her, cozy and welcoming and safe. It didn't seem that way anymore. On the outside she had Sinclair Forbes, or perhaps some other freak. On the inside she had nightmares and something that she couldn't explain and didn't want to believe. She was certain of one thing, and that was that she didn't want Brig to leave.

Chapter 14

"Stan," Brig said, "you get anything useful?"

"Everybody had the same story to tell. They hadn't been in the water long at all, she acted strange, Ryan grabbed her and buddy-breathed her to the surface, they got her in to land and called you." A chuckle, and Stan said, "These guys are hard-core, though. I remember being a rookie cop, out there every day ready to save the world. But I don't remember *ever* being as flat ate-up by it as these folks."

"What do you mean?"

"You listen to them talking, you know. People sitting around after they've given their statements, after the pressure is off; they're friends, you expect to hear some stuff about their personal lives, maybe something that could prove useful. But the whole time they were in here, they were talking about a new technique one of them trained on for extracting people from cars, and some certification program they all want to take, and whether Ryan is ready to test for paramedic, and a handful of cases they worked over the past week. Dia is apparently well liked. A number of the stories centered on her and her gift for calm in the center of a storm."

Brig looked over at her. She'd headed into the kitchen

and was rummaging through her freezer, pulling out assorted frozen vegetables and meat packages.

"With reason," he said. "She's pretty steady. Considering someone tried to kill her today, she's holding together remarkably well."

"Probably hasn't completely hit her yet."

"Might not have. We got a picture of the stalker, by the way. It sucks."

"How'd you get it?"

"Her surveillance camera."

"We'll get something off of it. We can do a door-to-door, see if anyone has seen the guy lurking around. Get some nice old lady to keep an eye out and call us if she sees him again."

Brig had looked around the room. When he looked back at Dia, she was leaning on the countertop in the middle of the food she'd pulled out. Her head was on her arms, and her shoulders were shaking. "Gotta go," he said, and didn't even wait to hear what Stan said next.

He just cut off the call, dropped the phone into his pocket, and ran over to her and pulled her close. "Hey," he said. "It's okay."

"It's . . . not okay," she said between sobs. And hiccups.

"It's not *good*. But it's okay. I'm here, I've got you, and I'm going to take care of you." She was warm in his arms, strong and soft and firm. He stroked her hair and rested his face on the top of her head. She still smelled of salt water and sun, and when he closed his eyes, he could feel the two of them standing on a beach somewhere peaceful, alone. He thought that being alone with her would be the most wonderful thing in the world— just the two of them, with no one trying to hurt her, with everything still and safe so that all they had to do was pay attention to each other.

He wanted that. He didn't just want that in the abstract, he realized. He wanted to have a woman in his life again. One who loved him.

He needed someone to hold, to care for; he needed to know he mattered, not in general, but deeply and personally to one other human being on the planet.

That realization hit him hard. It suggested a vulnerability that he didn't want, and that he knew for certain would get in his way.

Dia sobbed and shuddered against his chest.

He kept stroking her hair. "It'll be all right," he whispered, rocking her from side to side as he held her. "All right. It'll be all right."

Her arms were tight around him. As her sobs quieted to sniffles, she whispered, "I believe you."

He tightened his grip on her and picked her up. Her legs wrapped around his waist, her arms over his shoulders; she pressed her face against his neck. He was terribly aware of the clothes between the two of them, and the fact that she was, at that moment, vulnerable from the assaults on her safety and her confidence that she'd faced that day.

He wanted to be protective. He wanted to know that he wasn't taking advantage of her. But his hands were cupping the curves of her bottom, and he could feel the soft, heavy weight of her breasts against his chest. He knew what it felt like to lie atop her, to feel her moving with him, to feel himself inside her. And he wanted that. His body told him it was ready right then, right there.

Something about the kitchen, he thought. So, with her wrapped around him and clinging to him, he carried her into the living room.

She swung her legs down and started kissing him as he neared the couch.

And unbuttoning his shirt.

And undoing the buttons on his jeans. And then she was pushing her hands against his chest, and aiming him closer to the couch.

"You, ah . . . Maybe this isn't such a good time. . . ." He thought of the fact that he had condoms in a bag tucked into the back of the glove compartment of his car, but he hadn't actually bothered to open the box. He was in no condition to traipse out there to get them.

She tugged open a drawer in the coffee table and pulled one out. "I invested," she said. "Thought it would be silly not to have them when I wanted them." She smiled at him—her smile still heartbreakingly wobbly— and gave him a final shove. The couch caught him behind the knees, and he sat down abruptly.

"You're wearing too many clothes, cowboy," she said. "Kick off those jeans and lose the shirt."

"You're still fully dressed," he pointed out.

"Not *my* fault. If somebody isn't doing his job, you don't get to blame me for that." She looked a bit more sure of herself. She stood by his feet, lifted one, pulled off his shoe and then his sock, lifted the other and pulled off that shoe and sock. "Say good-bye to the clothes, cowboy." She tugged off his jeans and his boxers, and he watched them go sailing across the room to hit the opposite wall. He tried not to think about the fact that, in her line of work, she had a fair amount of practice getting men out of their clothes. At least she hadn't used trauma shears on his.

He reached for her shirt, but she moved away.

She stood over him, staring down at him. "Broad daylight," she said, "and you look better in the light than you did in the dark. Wow."

He managed to smile, but he considered the possibility that it came out as a leer instead of a smile. "So move closer. I want to take *your* clothes off."

She shook her head slowly. "I think I'm going to leave them on. You'll be all hot and nekkid, and I'll be prim and dressed. Sort of. Well, I'll be dressed. Not prim." She smiled at him. "Put your head on the pillows. I don't want you lying all the way down."

He said, "You're . . . telling me . . ." He was going to finish that sentence, but he was aroused and curious, and she was watching him with hungry eyes.

"Yeah," she whispered. "I am."

He scooted back on the couch so his head was propped up. He was comfortable enough.

She rolled a condom onto him.

And then she sat astride him, a wicked smile curving across her lips, still wearing everything but her shoes. She had on the T-shirt. Shorts. Bra and underpants, he presumed.

She held herself over him and leaned down and kissed him. He kissed her back, hard, and curved his hands over her hips and tried tugging her shorts down. She said, "Grope. Feel. But don't take them off."

The shorts were soft cotton—stretchy. And a little big on her. Her gaze locked on his, she pulled one leg of the shorts wider and slid him inside them, and then, with a quick, hard move, she sheathed him.

He gasped. He hadn't expected that—not right then. Brig could feel his eyes glazing, his heart pounding, his whole body aching to thrust and grind and push deeper. She didn't let him. She slid up and down him in a slow, steady movement that pulled him right to the edge of control.

She lifted up her shirt and he discovered that she didn't have a bra on. She rubbed her breasts across his chest, and licked her lips, and said, "Now we'll find out if all that time I put in at the gym has paid off."

She tightened her thighs around him, so tight he

thought she was going to snap him in two, and everything inside clamped down. "God," he groaned. "Where the hell have you been all my life?"

"Yeah. More of that, huh?"

Still squeezing him, she moved faster. Her hands locked onto his shoulders and her head tipped back and her eyes shut. He'd been letting her do the work, but suddenly he couldn't stand it anymore. He grabbed her hips and pulled her down faster, shoving up at the same time.

"Oh." Her teeth were clenched, her body tight. "Harder."

He flipped the two of them over so that he was on top, and her legs came up around his neck and dragged him into her. He drove hard, and she dug her hands into the couch cushions and moved against him, matching him move for move.

She screamed, "Harder! Harder!" and he complied, driven by a hunger and a desire and a lust fiercer than anything he had ever felt in his life. They bucked against each other, wrapped around each other, fought like wildcats, tumbled and bit and scratched and finally, at last, fell out of the sky like mated eagles and collapsed into each other with wordless cries.

Afterward he stroked her hair again, and studied her face, and wondered how one human being could become so completely consumed by another. He'd been blindsided. He hadn't been looking; he hadn't been considering; he'd been living the life of a work-driven monk, and out of nowhere she had fallen into his life.

And all he knew for sure was that he would not let anyone or anything hurt her, or hunt her, or tear her away.

He couldn't tell her he loved her. He couldn't confess to her that she had taken him out of his seclusion and changed him, overwritten him with her own hand, made him something that he hadn't been before. She would think he said such things easily, and that he didn't mean them. She would not believe him.

So he wouldn't say them. But he knew.

Dia looked up at Brig, watching the way the sunlight illuminated his face. He had scars. One on his chin that she'd bet he could trace back to childhood. One on his left cheek that looked more recent.

Low on his chest and across part of his abdomen she traced a scar that she recognized only too well as a knife wound. He was a warrior, she thought. She had a thing for warriors, for heroes.

And she could lie to herself all day about how what she needed was some placid, timid man who would keep her feet on the ground and keep her reined in so she didn't go off on risky tangents, but the fact was, she'd found the man she wanted.

She tried to think of what to say to him—to tell him that she wasn't sure she'd been right when she told him what she was looking for in a man. She wanted to find the perfect words to let him know that he made her body sing and her heart race and her blood charge through her veins, and she could just barely wrap her mind around a semicoherent sentence, because he turned all of her to jelly, and that included her mind.

And the doorbell rang.

"You have to be fucking kidding," Brig said. He said it while he was leaping to his feet and into the kitchen, where he made quick work of the condom; then he yanked on pants faster than she had ever seen a human being move, and she thought it was a damned good thing that he had button-fly jeans, because she could see where he could have done himself a world of hurt right then. He pulled on his shirt and had it buttoned into place as he was crossing the floor, and glanced over her way to make sure she was ready.

All she had to do was adjust her clothing a bit. That made things a lot easier.

Brig looked through the peephole and sighed. "Them again," he said.

When he opened it, Kelly bounded through the door, followed by Howie and Tyler and Ryan and Sherman.

They all looked from Brig to Dia. Dia saw Ryan's eyebrow lift slightly, but everyone else seemed oblivious to what they'd just walked into.

"How are you holding up?" Kelly asked.

"Better," Dia said. "I was . . . I've had . . ." And the tears were, all of a sudden, right back with her. "Dammit." She closed her eyes and took a deep breath and clenched her fists tight, and willed the fear and the shakiness away. She swiped at the tears that escaped her with the back of one hand. "Dammit, dammit." She looked up at all of them. "I'm fine. Honestly. I've been shaky, but I'm better; I'm over it. I'm not going to let this get to me."

Kelly grinned at her. "Not quite as convincing as it could be, Dia, but we'll work on that. The guys are going to help me pack my stuff. I have most of it in storage, but I'll be bringing it over as soon as I can. I could sleep on the floor tonight," she offered.

Dia said, "That's not necessary. Brig will be here tonight . . ." She glanced over at him. "Will you? I mean . . ."

"I'll be here tonight," he assured her. "I don't have a cat or a plant or anything that I have to be at my place to take care of."

"Okay. I didn't want to presume." She told Kelly, "Let me get my stuff out of the spare bedroom. You and the guys can bring everything over when you're ready."

"I like the way 'the guys' just got casually tossed in there, Kel," Howie said, laughter in his voice. "Did we volunteer to box up all your belongings and cart them around like a bunch of . . . of . . . pack elephants or something?"

"Yeah, we did," Ryan said. "They just keep us around for our muscles, you know. We are otherwise utterly disposable to them. We should have those shirts that say, 'I may not be smart, but I can lift heavy things.' It's how they see us."

Dia laughed. "We keep you around because you can start IVs."

"No hope for me then, huh?" Brig asked.

Dia looked over at him and felt her cheeks heating up. "There's always hope."

Brig grinned.

Her house stayed full of people for the rest of the afternoon and evening. The guys ordered pizza, and everyone ate. They watched a couple of bad movies on television, and eventually turned the volume down so that they could do their own commentary. Brig, Dia noticed, seemed bemused by the whole thing; he joined in eventually, but she could see that he wasn't used to the sort of family relationship she shared with her friends.

When she saw them out at last, pleading exhaustion, she could almost feel him waiting for the door to close so that he could say something.

"I'm sorry they stayed so long," she said, hoping to fend off criticism. "I could have kicked them out sooner, I know, but I would have felt like a heel for doing it."

"I like them," Brig said. "I was watching you with them, and wishing I had friends like that."

"I'm rarely ever lonely," she said.

"I can't say the same."

She walked over to him and rested a hand on his chest. "I think the only reason you would be lonely is because you wanted to be."

He shrugged. "You could be right. It could be that, lately, I've been getting a lot of mileage out of being lonely. Finding someone you want to not be lonely with is hard—pick the wrong person and you're just lonely with someone else in the room."

Dia nodded.

"I'm not sure I want to be lonely anymore."

She smiled up at him. "I'm not sure an accountant is my dream man anymore."

"Still thinking about it, though?"

"It's way too soon to say one way or the other. That's the sort of decision that needs time."

"Any idea how much time?"

"No. I'm thinking a year or two, though. Why? Are you in a hurry?"

He dragged her over to him and kissed her breathless, then said, "Depends. Do I get to not be lonely with you while you make up your mind?"

"I'm considering the idea."

"Good," he said. "Then let's go not be lonely some more in bed."

Chapter 15

Dia's alarm started bleating at the usual time the next morning. Brig had his arm flung over her, and she was loath to pull away to turn the alarm off.

He didn't wake, though, and she slid back to where she had been, and felt the wonderful weight of him against her. With him there, she felt safe. Protected. Cared for. She hadn't felt that way in a long time, and she liked it.

Of course, he was going to have to get up and go in to work to fight crime and solve murders, and she was going to have to decide how she would be facing her day. She wasn't ready to go back to work. She knew they needed her, but she didn't think she was in any condition to deal with other people's emergencies and traumas. She thought about getting up, taking a shower, and then seeing how she felt. But the idea of even going into her bathroom scared her.

She wished she could afford to move, actually.

She couldn't. Real estate in South Florida was insanely overpriced, and rental rates were commensurate with the current mortgage rate. Well, worse, actually. But either way, she didn't have the money for a down payment on a place, and she didn't have the cash for first, last, and security plus the costs of moving. She managed to stay in the place she had simply because it needed a fair amount of work before the landlord would be able to rent it again. Her landlord hadn't raised the rates on her too much; she figured it was because he knew that when she left, he was going to have to sink a bunch of money into the place to make it rentable to someone else.

But she didn't know how she was going to deal with . . . well . . . she didn't even want to think the word "ghost." She decided on "unexplained occurrences," and acknowledged to herself that she didn't want to deal with them either.

It would be easier when she had a roommate. She'd have someone to talk to, someone to share the bathroom with, someone with whom she could discuss anything untoward that happened in the place.

And of course, someone who would be there with her as a deterrent against her stalker.

Brig would be a better deterrent, Dia thought, wishing she could just keep him with her. It would have been wonderful to nest in the little duplex, just the two of them, hiding away from the world, never having to go anywhere alone.

The domesticity of that thought made Dia squirm. She wasn't ready to be half of a couple again. They could take things slowly. And she could always back out.

"Hey," Brig said. "You're awake."

"My alarm went off."

"You staying home today, then?"

She sighed. "I think so. I can't take the chance that I'd fall apart in the middle of an emergency. Wouldn't be good for me; sure wouldn't be good for whoever it was I was trying to help."

He kissed her forehead. "I think you should stay home

because some lunatic who is creating traffic accidents is trying to get to you. Everything else is secondary."

"Not what my captain will say."

"Probably not," Brig agreed. "But I'm right, and your captain isn't."

Dia grinned over at him. "I wish I knew everything. It would be nice."

He winked at her. "It's useful."

He unwound himself from the bed. "I'm going in, though. I have to go home and shower and shave and change my clothes, and then get to work looking like a man stressed out by his cases, instead of the happy man I am."

"You can't be the happy man at work?"

"Oh, I could," Brig said, tugging on his jeans. "But Stan is a detective, you know. He'd notice something like that. And then he'd grill me until I confessed everything. I'm usually bad cop when we're interrogating someone. But in real life, it isn't that way at all. He's brutal."

Dia laughed. "I wouldn't wish a brutal interrogation on you. So go be Stressed Man, and tell me if you find anything useful."

"I'll call you as soon as I learn anything new. And maybe before that, too." He finished buttoning his shirt. "Just for no good reason, you know."

"That's as good a reason as I need."

She got up and quickly brushed her teeth and saw him to the door. Called in to work and explained that she wasn't coming in because she was still a mess from the day before. Her captain was surprisingly understanding, and offered to let her take the next several days off. She didn't outright turn him down, but having someone trying to kill you wasn't the sort of thing that sick days covered. And there were no paid trying-not-to-be-dead days.

And then she faced the rest of the day in the house alone. By herself.

She trudged into the room that Kelly would occupy. She didn't have that much stuff in there. The computer with its speakers. A couple of boxes full of the sort of things she never used but couldn't quite bring herself to throw away—storage containers and instruction books and paperbacks that she hadn't liked.

She looked at the computer and decided that she didn't want to move that into her bedroom. If—for whatever reason—it started playing "Bad Moon Rising," or anything else, while she was sleeping, she was likely to have a heart attack. But she couldn't very well leave it in the room to bother Kelly.

She balanced her checkbook on it, and played a few games, and listened to music. Surfed the Internet, got e-mail. Nothing that she couldn't do in the living room, she decided.

And then, knowing where she wanted to put it, she stood there with her hands trembling and her heart racing, trying to make herself pick it up. If it started playing while she was carrying it, demonstrating again that it could operate without being plugged in, she was going to drop the damned thing, and then she'd have to do all the checkbook stuff over again. And she had e-mails that she hadn't answered yet.

The phone rang.

She ran out to get it, and the caller ID told her the caller was unknown.

Her heart raced faster.

Could be nothing. Could be some time-share bastard pushing a free vacation. Could be a credit card offer.

Could be her stalker.

She didn't pick up.

The walls around her seemed closer; the space in

which she had to move seemed tighter. She clenched her hands and gritted her teeth.

She had one simple thing she needed to do: clean a room. She had no reason not to succeed at the task. She could move furniture, throw things away, run the vacuum, and Kelly could move in and everything would be fine.

Something scratched across the living room window.

She swore. It was that damned palmetto, wind blowing the spiky leaves across the glass. But she could hear the sound of her own heart beating, and she knew there was no way she was going to take a few more days off so that she could be alone in the house.

So that she could debate whether she really needed to go to the bathroom, or if it could wait. Whether the room was cold or the air conditioner was acting up or whether something she didn't want to face was happening around her.

"Not going to happen," she muttered. "I'm going to move the damned computer, and it'll be fine. Nothing is going to happen. Nothing."

The phone rang again. And this time caller ID pegged the call as being from Brig. She couldn't grab it fast enough.

"We got two pieces of corroborative evidence this morning," Brig said, and his voice sounded pleased and a little bit excited.

"Really?"

"One of your neighbors saw a man coming out of your house a few days ago who looked like the man who delivered the box. Apparently he had a key. Second piece of good news—handwriting analysis of your notes says Forbes and the man who wrote them are one and the same."

She walked over to the couch and sat down. Her

knees were too weak to trust. *"Really?"* she said again. "You're sure?"

"Sure as we can be."

She sagged back into the cushions, grinning. Because if Forbes had definitely been in the house, it had been to tamper with the computer and write on the mirror. He'd left her the song, and the messages.

Not Mac.

Forbes.

And she probably hadn't seen what she thought she saw that night in the bathroom—it had most likely been stress—and if she had seen it, it had not been some weirdly spooky event. It hadn't been Mac's ghost watching her from beyond death. It had been her stalker, and if she didn't know *how* he was doing what he was doing, that was okay. She didn't need to know. She just knew that somewhere, somehow, there was a logical explanation.

"God," she whispered, "that is the best news I've heard since this started."

"It is," Brig agreed. "We finally have the proof we need to go after Forbes. We can positively place him inside your house, we can positively link him to the writing on the mirror, and that means we can positively link him to making death threats against you. Our connections between him and the car wrecks are less certain, but that's all right. We're running his picture now, and we have a reward for information leading to his whereabouts. Stan and I are calling in his parents for questioning, as well as a couple of old friends we've managed to locate. We're going to find this guy. And once we have him in custody, we'll see if we can connect the rest of the case."

She felt warm all over. Warm, happy. Safe. Everything was going to be all right.

"You're wonderful," she told Brig.

"Okay. I'll allow you to say that," he said after a moment. "You can say any good thing about me that pops into your head. I give you my permission."

"You're cute, too."

He snorted. "*Cute* is not a good thing. *Sexy* is a good thing. *Studly* is a good thing. *Powerful, strong,* and *heroic*—those are all good things. Puppies, and kitties, and knickknacks from places with names like Buttons and Bows are *cute*."

"You're also funny," Dia added.

"I'm hanging up the phone now," he told her. And then he laughed. "But only because I hear Stan coming, and I have to maintain my dignity. I'll call you again later. Stay safe."

"I will," she told him.

Because Forbes was locked out, and Mac was only in her nightmares, and everything—everything—made sense again, and she was going to be all right.

After that, she had no trouble getting the room cleared for Kelly, or throwing away the old things in the boxes that she was never going to use, or setting up the computer in her bedroom. So long as she knew how everything worked, and why, her life was safely and securely back on rails.

Larry Forbes—also known as Sinclair Lawrence Forbes—shuddered from a sudden, bone-chilling cold so damp he felt moisture bead on his forehead.

He stood at his kitchen table in the middle of the day. He had his air conditioner on, of course. He always did. It had never, ever made him even chilly. When he was Larry, his massive bulk made him feel like he was melting on even the coolest day.

But at that moment, with his heart racing, he was suddenly freezing. All he could think was that he could not imagine what it was like to be warm. He could not imagine ever being warm again.

He'd been marking down Dia's schedule for the next week, but he set that aside. He needed to go run his hands under hot water, splash hot water on his face, warm himself just a little. He was frightened, and he could not explain—or even imagine—why.

He walked into his bathroom, turned the water on as hot as it would go, and let it run until the steam started rising into the icy air.

It clung to his mirror. He put his face down into it, and closed his eyes, and felt the warmth as if it were . . . a picture of warmth, or a memory of warmth—something tantalizingly near him that he could see, but could not reach.

He raised his head and almost screamed.

In his mirror, he saw words written in the steam.

I SEE YOU

Chapter 16

Brig sat across the table from Sinclair Forbes's mother, State Representative Elisa Keyes Forbes. She was an attractive woman in her mid- to late fifties. Her hair was expensively blond, her face competently lifted, and her figure aerobicized and Palm Beach–dieted and no doubt routinely spa-ed.

He didn't like her. He didn't like her attitude of entitlement, or the fact that she acted like she was entirely too good to be sitting in an interrogation room talking to police about the criminal behavior of her son.

Seated at the table across from Stan and him, she managed to look down her nose at both of them.

"You're mistaken, no doubt."

"The possibility exists," Stan said, staying in character as the soothing cop on her side of the issue. "The evidence is pretty compelling, but at this point a possibility of error does exist."

"No, it doesn't," Brig said, making sure to snarl. "He's threatening to kill this woman, and he already killed her husband. You know as well as I do that we have him dead to rights."

Stan gave the bitch a sympathetic half smile and a tiny little negative shake of his head. "You say your son is a decent man, and I'm sure you're right. No evidence is absolutely one hundred percent."

Brig triggered his cell phone to ring, put it to his ear, and said, "Yeah? . . . Okay. Right . . . I'll be right out." He made sure to glare at Representative Forbes—who insisted on being *called* Representative Forbes, no less— then turned and stalked out of the interrogation room.

He walked over to the closed-circuit monitor and watched Stan say, "I'm sorry about him. Representative Forbes, all we really need is a chance to speak with your son and get this mess straightened out. If you could ask him to come in and talk with us freely, we can stop the APBs and prevent the negative publicity that is going to erupt from this."

She looked thoughtful. "I'd prefer to avoid negative publicity."

Of course you would, Brig thought. *You're coming up on an election year.*

She frowned. "Unfortunately, Detective Chang, while I know where my son is, I can't reach him. After the accident, he told us that he needed some time apart from us—to rebuild his life, to discover who he was. He entered a Taoist monastery that was offering training of a sort that I thought would be very good for him. But it does not permit contact with the outside world."

"So you think he's in a Taoist monastery? Where?"

"The one he entered is in Colorado, but there are branches in other parts of the world, and he may have been sent to any of those branches. His trust-fund money is sent monthly to a bank in the town where the monastery is located, and withdrawn monthly. So I'm assuming that he has not been sent elsewhere—otherwise he would have requested that we send the money to a different bank, I imagine."

"Colorado."

"Yes. Rico, Colorado. The monastery is in the mountains above the town, which I believe is quite small. It's called the Shimmering Cloud Monastery." She sighed. "It is unlikely that the brothers will permit you to speak with him. He has taken a vow of silence, I understand."

Stan said, "He's the primary suspect in a murder investigation. While, if he's been in Colorado for the last four years and can prove it, he has an ironclad alibi, they *will* let us speak to him. Vows or no vows."

Her lips pursed. "Well, I'm sure you know better than I do how these things work," she said, and rose, ready to leave.

Stan hadn't actually told her he was done with her, but he didn't stop her. When she was just past him, halfway to the door, he said, "What can you tell me about Mac Courvant?"

"Nothing good," the bitch said. "My son always looked up to him and admired him, and tried his best to be like Mac. So it always struck me as funny that Mac, who was the leader, was the one who accused Lawrence— always the follower—of instigating the car wrecks. Doesn't it seem much more likely that Mac was the one involved, and that Lawrence was the one he pinned his crimes on? Which is what Lawrence always insisted, but he wasn't the Boy Scout of the pair, was he? So no one believed him."

"You never found it odd that your son was involved in the car accident that killed Mac and two others?"

"Do you realize how badly injured that accident left him?"

"We've talked to the EMT who saved his life; she said that, while he had a number of acute injuries, none of them caused the sort of damage that would have affected him long-term."

"He was psychologically traumatized," Forbes said. "Devastated by the death of the friend who had betrayed him, worried about the child who disappeared. I think it was that trauma that sent him into a monastery and into silence. I'd consider that long-term damage."

Brig thought, *How did Forbes and Courvant end up being friends?*

At almost the same instant, Stan asked her that question.

Forbes said, "Lawrence was a very reserved child. He kept to himself, had his own interests, didn't much like other children. Mac Courvant, on the other hand, was one of those boys who feels that everyone must be part of his group. He made out that he hated to see anyone not have friends; he actually had the nerve to say that to my husband once. He pursued Lawrence to be his friend until finally Lawrence gave in. And then, of course, Mac tried to get my son to join the Scouts, and to go on camping trips and participate in all those activities that his father and I had no wish to let him be a part of. Eventually we suggested to our son that he should be more selective in his friends. Lawrence didn't listen, though. He was far too trusting, and far too much under the spell of that boy. And, of course, my son was the one who ended up getting hurt by his trust."

"I see," Stan said. Brig could see the sympathetic look on his partner's face wearing thin.

Time for him to put an end to this session. Brig walked back into the interrogation room. "More corroborative evidence," he said to Stan. And he gave a cold, hard smile to Forbes's mother. "We've pretty much nailed the lid down on this case, ma'am. Your son is under it. So if you've been aiding and abetting him in his criminal activities, we'll make sure we follow up on that, too. We're going to have you look at a video, ma'am."

The representative looked worried. "What video?"

"A man walking up to a door. We want you to identify the man."

She crossed her arms over her chest. "I don't have to."

"No. You don't," Stan said, and Brig could see that amiable smile returning to his partner's face. "But we would appreciate it if you did. Being able to vindicate your son will certainly put your mind at ease, too."

The arms stayed crossed over the chest; the lips stayed thin and pursed, giving the lie to her carefully hidden age.

Brig walked out and rolled in a television set and a video. He made sure to position it so that both Representative Forbes and the picture on the television would be visible to the hidden camera that was recording their session.

He started the tape back a way from the point where Forbes showed up. The three of them stood watching people walking by, the girl leading her dog into Dia's yard, cars passing.

He slowed it down, still a way before Forbes made his appearance. He wanted her to relax a little. To be bored.

She watched the tape. "You're wasting my time," she said.

"We aren't. You haven't recognized any of the people you've seen so far?"

"No. And I don't appreciate your—"

Sinclair Forbes appeared from around a corner and waddled up the walk, and the color and the expression drained out of her face. She didn't say another word; she didn't breathe.

"Recognize him?" Brig asked, but the question was just a formality.

"He's so . . . fat," she whispered, and he could see shock and dismay on her face.

"So you *do* recognize him," Brig said. "You can see

by the date in the corner how recent that is—and by the palm trees that he isn't anywhere near Rico, Colorado."

She turned to glare at him. "That isn't my son."

"You're sure about that?" Stan asked her.

"Of course I'm sure. You think I wouldn't recognize my own son?"

"We wouldn't want to presume," Brig said, unable to resist the jab.

They had her on record denying that the man in front of her was her son. If they could go on to prove that the man was her son, they had a very good case against her for obstruction of justice, harboring a fugitive, accessory to murder, and a handful of other charges that would make it difficult for her to get reelected—by a competent electorate, anyway. Considering Florida's past voting problems, it might not hamper her too much.

Stan smiled at her and said, "If you're sure about the identity of the man, we don't have anything else we need you for. You can go, Representative Forbes. Thank you for coming down to talk with us. We'll be in touch."

She glared at Brig as she walked by.

Stan and Brig left the interrogation room together, and Brig quickly located the Shimmering Cloud Monastery via the Internet. It offered a physical address and a phone number.

Brig said, "You want to call, or you want me to?"

"I'll call."

Brig leaned back in his chair, grinning. "Five bucks says they never heard of the bastard."

Stan said, "Sorry. I think five bucks is all I have in my wallet today; I'm not losing it on a sucker bet."

Stan called, and Brig listened to Stan's half of the conversation. While he listened, Brig wore on his face the contented smile of a man about to peg a woman for lying outrageously.

And Stan suddenly said, "You *have?*" He turned to stare at Brig. "No. He's the primary suspect in a murder investigation. I'm afraid we're going to have to meet with him. . . . No, we have physical evidence that ties him to the crime, and we will be only too happy to involve your monastery in this case, should you make that necessary."

Stan talked awhile longer, and got the monastery to agree that it would cooperate with the investigation. But when he hung up, he looked shaken. "Forbes is there. Has been there for four years."

Brig said, "That can't be."

"Well, they say he's there, so one of us is going to have to visit the monastery. And you—you bastard— you had dibs on the next travel. I want to know how the hell this works, incidentally—I got to identify a weeks-dead corpse during smog season in Chicago; you got to question a blond bikini-model eyewitness in Bermuda. I got a case with a connection to bodies in a New Jersey landfill; you get a murder suspect living in a charming monastery in a charming small town in the mountains. Who the fuck did you bribe to get your luck, I want to know?"

Brig considered the trip to Rico, Colorado, and decided that, charming town at high altitude with good weather and minimal traffic or not, this was not the time for him to be leaving South Florida. He was watching the case, and far too many other cases, and he wasn't willing to leave Dia alone for any length of time. Mostly the latter. Not the way things were for her. Not with bits of his case not working, and the danger to her coming from directions they still hadn't sufficiently pinned down.

"You can take the travel this time," he told Stan.

Stan stared at him. "I can?"

"You can. I want to stay in town. There are some aspects of this case that I want to be present to keep on top of."

"The lovely, tall girl you're chasing."

"Not chasing."

"Ah. Concerned about. Riiiight. Hey, a day out in Colorado this time of year does not sound like a hardship to me. You deal with her—and cover all the rest of our cases while I'm gone—and I'll see what the hell the story with Forbes is."

"You do that," Brig said. "I call dibs on the next *two* travels as compensation."

"The hell you do. You snooze, you lose."

Brig went back to his notes, the evidence, all the things he and Stan had put together. Details kept bothering him; little things didn't fit, and no matter how hard he tried, he couldn't make them fit.

First, the way that Forbes was keeping track of Dia. Something about that smacked of frequent, easy access to both public and private aspects of her life. The fact that she looked at the guy when he dropped off the package and was confident that she didn't know him, and couldn't remember ever having seen him, sat wrong with Brig. He'd been sure that, when at last they saw the stalker, he would turn out to be someone she knew.

Second, the whole business with her scuba tanks, her close call, and her subsequent rescue. Something there bugged him, too, though he couldn't say what. It just didn't work for him. Was it that it was a damned inefficient way of killing her, especially when she dove with EMTs, when—since the bastard clearly knew a lot about her—he knew she dove with EMTs? Was it the access issue again?

Brig didn't know.

But he took his tape and trudged down three flights of

back stairs to the imaging unit. He knew a guy there who could expedite things for him.

Weezer was in, doing enlargements and refinements on a photograph of a suspect in a convenience-store murder. "Hey, Weez," Brig said, "I have a weird one for you."

"You *are* a weird one," Weez muttered, not looking up.

"Seriously."

"I didn't sound serious to you?"

Brig sighed. "According to a probably reliable source, the suspect from whom I have several recent, locally presented handwriting samples has been locked away in a Taoist monastery in Colorado for the last four years. The mother has seen the videotape and denies that the man is her son. But she was lying, and handwriting analysis says it is. I need to see if I can get some facial comparisons between this guy and previous photos of my suspect."

Weezer looked up. "Okay. Taoist monk is interesting. That's not the usual excuse. Two places at once isn't bad, either. Lemme see what you got."

Brig handed over copies of Forbes's high school graduation and family photos, and the copy of the VCR tape that caught the man delivering the box.

"I'll do it after this. All you want is confirmation that it's the same guy, right?"

"That's all I want."

"Okay. That's not too tough. I can sharpen images, do points for bone structure and placement, and call you back before long."

"If we don't get a match, could you run the photos against a bunch of EMTs and tell me if any of them is my guy?"

Weezer said, "I can do a one-face comparison for you in the next hour. You want me to go fishing with you, it'll have to wait until the weekend. I'm booked so solid my eyes are going to compress into my skull and turn into raisins from looking at all this shit. 'Kay?"

"I'll take whatever you can give me today," Brig said. "And book you for a fishing trip if I end up needing one."

"You get to buy me dinner and take me to a movie, too," Weezer growled. "That's still the going rate for getting screwed, far as I can tell."

Brig laughed and walked back to his desk.

He'd managed to gather up pictures of most of the EMTs in Dia's station. He stared at them: good-looking young men, a couple of older men, two women. Say Forbes really was in that monastery. Any of them could be working with him, delivering things for him, doing bits and pieces of his dirty work. Motive? Money— Forbes had lots of it.

Brig wasn't believing any alibi or trusting any story. Not until he had Forbes in hand, fingerprinted, charged, and locked away. He looked over their personal details again. A couple of them had speeding problems, one had the dismissed complaint about sexual harassment, up the chain of command one of the administrative types had an open issue with the IRS that could come down on him pretty hard.

Nobody had sealed juvenile records, nobody had felonies, the few misdemeanors were all traffic related. They looked clean, and if they weren't clean, they were doing a hell of a job of hiding it.

By comparison, Forbes had the sealed juvie records; a couple of near-misses where he'd been brought in for questioning but then released because of aggressive lawyers; five- and six-year-old neighbor complaints about weird noises and bad smells coming from his apartment; then the wreck, in which he as the lone survivor played the part of upstanding citizen stopping to avoid hitting a kid. And then the disappearance into the monastery.

Brig dug deeper, found the investigating officers' reports on the two incidents of neighbor complaints about noises and smells, and located the complainant's phone number.

Odds were that the person had moved—the apartments were not in a great neighborhood and Brig imagined turnover was pretty high. Still, it was worth a shot.

He called. An older-sounding woman answered.

"This is Detective Hafferty of the Fort Lauderdale Police. I'm trying to reach Louisa Menendez."

"I am Louisa," the woman said.

"I'm backtracking a person you filed complaints about several years ago," he said. "The man's name was Sinclair Forbes."

A short silence. "I remember him," the woman said. "He moved not long after the police came to his apartment the second time."

"The reports here indicate that he had an automobile engine in his apartment, and that solvents and the noise of him running the engine were what you were hearing."

"Yes," she said. "That's what they told me. I told them it wasn't like that at all—that I heard explosions, and they were not anything like the sounds from a car engine. And that the smell I caught was from whatever had exploded. It wasn't no cleaning stuff. But they said it was, and that was that, and then he moved away."

"Do you remember what he looked like?"

"Sure," she said. "He was fish-belly white, and fat, and he had brown eyes and long, greasy brown hair. He looked like a bum, he dressed like a bum, but I heard his parents were rich and important. I'm glad he's gone. Sometimes he looked at me, and, sweet Jesus protect me, it made my blood turn to ice. He had evil eyes."

They talked a bit longer; she didn't know what had

happened to him after he moved, and she had never heard of him or from him again.

When he looked over the reports in more detail, things bothered him. Menendez had been quite certain that Forbes had been doing something bad in his house, but the reports indicated that both times when the police arrived Forbes had been happy to escort them through the place, and to show them his motor, and his cleaning solvents, and to discuss his attempts to soup up the engine. None of the cops responding had been motorheads, so they hadn't been sure how possible what he described doing actually was, but one of them had written that Forbes was a real fanatic about his car, that the apartment was full of *Car and Driver* magazines, and that Forbes was a mind-numbing talker who seemed desperate for someone to describe his latest project to— they had been relieved to escape.

Something about that just didn't feel right.

Car and Driver. The apartment was full of *Car and Driver.*

He left his own cubicle and headed down the rows to see if Aaron Lakemer was in. Luck was with him.

"You still rebuilding engines?" he asked.

"Got a Chrysler Hemi in the workshop right now; aiming to bring it up to nine hundred horsepower in time for the Jeg's Engine Masters Challenge."

"You ever read *Car and Driver?* I mean, as part of rebuilding your engines?"

Lakemer snorted. "That's a generalist magazine. Nice articles, but completely useless for what I do. I get a couple of specialist magazines, but mostly I work from manuals and my own experience."

Brig nodded. "Read this for me, tell me what you think."

Lakemer read the two reports, the expression on his

face getting grimmer and grimmer. "He was bullshitting them. The few things they wrote down as quotes are total crap—and they couldn't even have misunderstood the guy bad enough to have gotten them *this* wrong. He was blue-skying the whole thing, and hoping that they'd do exactly what they did—flee as soon as their eyes glazed over." He handed the reports back to Brig. "Nice catch. I didn't think you knew much about cars."

"I don't. I've read *Car and Driver,* though, and I couldn't see it being the magazine a genuine car geek would line his apartment with."

"So you want to go out and talk to this guy again? I'd drop what I'm doing and come out, just to see what he has on blocks in there."

"This happened almost five years ago. The guy vanished four years ago after what is starting to look like a successfully disguised murder. He's linked into my automotive explosions cases, and to an attempted murder, stalking, and death threats. We think we've tracked him to a monastery in Colorado, but obviously if he's there and his alibi of being there for the past four years holds, my case goes all to hell."

Lakemer whistled. "You do get some strange ones, don't you?"

"A few," Brig said.

He headed back to his own cubicle. He was considering calling Dia, but the news he had complicated things a lot, and didn't offer any upside. He decided to hold off until he managed either to find something good, or until he just needed to check on her to make sure she was all right.

Weezer called.

"Yeah," Brig said. "Give me some good news."

"I can tell you that your package deliverer is Forbes. Biometric measurements on the placement of the nose and mouth, lips and cheekbones, and the distance between the bottom of the nose and the top of the upper lip make me almost one hundred percent certain. I wish we had eyes or ears. That would close this for us. As it is . . . well . . . you have enough for a warrant. I'd take the stand and swear they were the same guy."

Brig grinned. "I'll be interested in who we find in that Colorado monastery, then."

"Let me know how it works out," Weezer said. "Hey, by the way. See if you can find the surgeon who did this guy's nose. He might have info for you."

"Surgeon?"

"Oh, yeah. For some reason he had it thinned. Not shortened, not straightened—just thinned. Looks like hell; it's completely out of proportion. I don't know why this guy wanted a skinny bitch nose but didn't go for the whole stomach-staple and fat-sucking routine, but the doctor who gave it to him is sure to remember him."

"Thanks," Brig said. "That could give us an in."

"Dinner in a nice restaurant," Weezer said mournfully. "And a movie. Nobody ever takes me anywhere."

"I'll see what I can do," Brig said.

The bell rang, and there they were: Kelly and Ryan and Tyler and Sherm and Howie, and a very small U-Haul.

"Guys," she said, feeling happy, "I'm so glad you're here."

"You look better," Kelly said.

"I feel better. You're moving in, and the police identified Forbes as the man at the front door."

"So you're getting close to this being over," Kelly said.

Ryan grinned at her. "That's fantastic. We should have a party."

"More pizza," Sherm agreed. "She gets the best delivery over here."

"I'm two blocks from Vito's," Dia said. "We could walk, and you could taste the stuff fresh."

She felt like she could walk on air. She wasn't free yet, but she was almost free. They'd catch the guy. And then all the weirdness in her life would simply go away. No more writing on mirrors, no more creepy computer behavior, no more letters or boxes or things going wrong with her tanks. She'd be safe. And then maybe she could step back a little and get her head wrapped around Brig and all the implications of a full-scale relationship. She would be able to see if it was him she was in love with, and not just the fact that he was keeping her safe from a nut who was trying to kill her.

The guys hauled in Kelly's bed, and her dresser, and her small, wall-mounted home gym, and her clothes. Kelly was a clotheshorse, and the clothes took time.

"Everything else is in storage," Kelly said. "The rest of my furniture is crappy compared to yours, and there wasn't any sense cluttering up the place. If we like this arrangement, I can see if I can sell my old stuff on eBay."

Dia grinned and did a little dance step. "Excellent idea," she said.

"You seem really, really happy," Kelly said, looking at Dia with a wary expression. "You haven't been, like, into anyone's medical supplies or . . . anything. Have you?"

"Not even aspirin," Dia said. "You have no idea what a relief it's going to be to have you here."

Kelly exhaled. "Okay, then. It's good to be wanted."

The whole crew walked to Vito's for pizza, and then across University Avenue and down the road to the Borders bookstore. They kicked around, looking at books and magazines, in the end none of them buying much. Kelly surprised everyone by picking up a blank book and admitting that she kept a diary and had since she was in grade school. And that she was about ready for a new book.

"I would never have guessed you as a diarist," Howie said. "You're so . . . so surprisingly deep."

"I'm not," she said. "I'm just obsessive-compulsive. I put down a few scrawls about each day, just because I was there. I started, and then I found out I couldn't stop."

"I get that," Ryan said. "I'm not actually obsessive about it, but I keep a journal, too. Not an everyday thing, but big days, you know. Stuff you want to be able to remember the details of later. And goals. New Year's resolutions. Things like that."

They all gave him a huge hard time about New Year's resolutions, which the rest of them, except for Kelly, had quit doing years earlier.

It was a wonderful afternoon, and a wonderful evening. Kelly was amenable to sitting and watching DVDs on television, the two of them discovered that they both loved *Alias,* and when Dia made popcorn, it felt an like overnight party in high school. It felt fun. Happy. Promising.

And Brig called. Twice. Both times just to make sure she was all right.

He seemed amused by her happiness, and though he couldn't talk long either time, he did say they were making progress on locating Forbes.

It was funny, Dia thought as she hung up the phone for the second time. This mess had managed to break her out of her shell of complacency. She had been only half living her life, going though the motions without ever really facing the fact that for four years she hadn't dared to move forward. To take chances. To do things that might make her happy.

All it had taken was one series of events to make her appreciate waking up every morning, to let her explore the possibilities of romance with a man she found attractive, and to get herself a roommate who was funny and fun and who was actually going to lower her expenses, making saving up for a better place a real possibility.

She hated to admit it, but in a way she owed Sinclair Forbes a thank-you.

Sort of.

But she didn't plan to get carried overboard by that.

Chapter 17

Stan called late the next day. "I'm at the airport, on my way back. This has been the most amazing mess I've ever seen," he said.

"I can't say I'm surprised. What's going on there?"

"The monks had to drag out Forbes, who vigorously resisted coming to meet with me. There's a good reason why he did."

"Alibi has holes in it?"

"*His* alibi is perfect. He hasn't been out of the town for four years. And he has, as indicated by Representative Forbes, been withdrawing his trust-fund money from the bank every month. Like clockwork. Care to guess how much?"

"Nope. Just tell me."

"Over eighteen thousand per month. That's just interest off of the apparently quite extensive principle."

"Damn. What is a Taoist monk doing with eighteen thousand dollars a month?"

"Mailing most of it back to South Florida. To a drop box. This guy is a skinny little ex-con who liked the idea of a perpetual paid vacation someplace where criminals who had reason to want him dead would never look for him. Forbes has been letting him keep two thousand a month just for doing what he probably would have done for free. Meanwhile, the real Forbes, who this guy refers to as the Fat Man, could be anywhere, but almost certainly is in the Coral Springs area. Since that's where the money goes."

Brig said, "We're golden on the real Forbes, then. Weezer gave us the green light on Dia's tape. Facial biometrics match. All we need to do now is find out where the bastard is hiding and how he's been keeping such close tabs on Dia."

Stan was quiet for a while. Then he said, "You think maybe the mother knows where he really is? Or was she genuinely surprised to see him outside of a Taoist monastery? And how about the father, who has been mysteriously elusive?"

"I don't know," Brig said. He propped his elbows on his desk and rested his head on the phone. "I just don't know. When you get back, we can call in Mama and Daddy Forbes, and see how they respond to discovering that the man in the monastery isn't, and never has been, their son. Maybe we can shake something loose with them." He looked up at the map with the little pushpins marking the sites of Forbes's accidents and frowned. "I almost have to give this one to Forbes, though: If that woman were my mother, I'd disappear off the face of the earth, too."

"Too true." In the background, Brig could hear a boarding call go over the loudspeaker. Stan said, "That's me. I'll be back in about three hours. We'll see what we can find with this drop box address I got. Bring the parents in again, see if we can round up witnesses. We have the guy. Now we just have to find him."

"Tell me why I think that isn't going to be the easy part."

Forbes walked into the pawnshop, knowing that he would be on camera. He didn't care. He shifted his bulk through the narrow aisles, jammed with everything from guitars to good jewelry to guns to lawn mowers, and sidled up to a counter beneath the glass of which lay an astonishing variety of fancy knives.

"May I help you, sir?" a man at the back asked after Forbes had lingered there for a while.

"I'd like to look at some of these hunting knives."

The man walked behind the counter and unlocked it. "Which one would you like to see?"

Forbes brushed stringy, greasy hair out of his eyes and pointed to an exquisite ten-inch knife with a beautiful hand-carved ebony grip and blood runnels in the blade. The man handed it to him and he hefted it, appreciating the way it fit in the hand, the elegant balance, the wonderful weight of it.

"It's a good knife."

"I can tell," Forbes said. "I'm a collector." He smiled a little. The man was staring at him. That was fine with him, too. He'd remember seeing Sinclair Forbes, but he would remember it only when it was too late to do anyone any good.

Balance would have been righted, and such cold justice as the universe required would have been served.

He paid for the knife with a traveler's check—same as cash—to which he signed his name with a flourish.

And then he walked out, knowing that the man would watch him until he was gone, and got into the very fine '58 Chevy Bel Air coupe that he'd "inherited" from the old man in whose name his house was still listed. He'd inherited the old man's name, too, and the old man's bank account.

The old man had suffered a heart attack, and had suffered the misfortune of telling Forbes that he didn't have anyone left in the world who would miss him when he died.

He didn't die, though. He got better, and he went home, and then one day Forbes dropped in to visit him. And never left. The old man had disappeared into the coral-crusted dirt of his overgrown, walled-in backyard, and Forbes had assumed his life.

It wouldn't be for much longer. He was going to have to shed old Mr. Steenman, just as he was going to have to shed Sinclair Forbes.

He picked up cat food from the grocery store, and then drove home. For a moment he considered not going in; he feared the return of the cold, of the watchful sensations of the room around him, of the words written in steam.

But he overcame his dread at last, and went in.

Returning the world to balance required sacrifice. And sometimes courage.

Chapter 18

Dia sat with Brig on her couch. Kelly kept hovering, clearly worried.

"So," Dia said, "Forbes had everyone who knew him thinking he was a Taoist monk in Colorado?"

"That's what they say they think. We have evidence to the contrary, but none of it leads us to where he is now. Not yet, anyway."

"He had the key to my place. That has to suggest something," Dia said.

"I know. I'm inclined to think someone is working with him. This is why it's so important that you think of anyone else who has been odd around you. Threatening patients or those who tried to get too friendly, people who have made the attempt to get close to you. Utilities people or repair people who had reason to be in your garage, or that you've seen when you didn't see a repair truck nearby." He took her hand and gave it a squeeze. "This is still a dangerous situation, but it won't stay that way. We're closing in on him. There is some clue, some key, that you probably already have in your possession, that will make this whole thing unravel into a perfect straight line."

"What if it doesn't?" Kelly asked.

"That's not an option," Brig said, looking into Dia's

eyes. "That's never going to be an option. We'll solve this."

He pulled Dia into his arms, and in the background heard Kelly moving away, down the hall, closing a door. And the shower running.

"I'm not going to let him hurt you," Brig told Dia. "We'll find him. In the meantime, stay safe, be careful who you trust, don't take any stupid chances. All right? If you think you see something suspicious, or someone suspicious, don't try to handle the situation yourself."

"I won't," she said. "I'll be careful. I promise."

He held her tight, wishing that he could take her to bed and make love to her right then. The roommate who was currently occupying the bathroom was a fine security measure, but a lousy privacy measure. Even if she was polite enough to go someplace else and do something else for a little bit so that he could be with—

He realized the water had cut off at the same instant that he heard screaming.

Dia broke away from him; he pushed past her and raced to the bathroom and kicked in the door, to find Kelly, with a towel mostly wrapped around her, with the room both steamy hot and icy cold, with a message scrawled in the steam that said:

I'LL KILL YOU, BITCH

And with an invisible finger writing

N . . . O . . . T . . .

M . . . E

beneath it.

The handwriting was different. Similar, but different.

NOT ME

He saw it.

Kelly saw it.

Dia saw it, but Dia wasn't screaming, or fainting, or fleeing, or any of the things that he personally felt like doing.

She was going, "No, no, no, it's just a trick, no, no, no, no . . ."

He got them both away from the bathroom, and closed the door, and said, "You both saw the writing underneath the threat appear by itself. Right?"

Kelly, dripping in the hallway, shivering, nodded.

Dia said, "It's just a trick. Forbes has figured out some way to do that. Magnets, or some sort of chemical . . . or . . . something. Right? It's just a trick, right?"

Brig was watching her, not sure where she was coming from, or why she was reacting the way she was, but wanting to understand.

"I don't see any way it could be a trick." He peeked back into the bathroom. "I don't think there's any way to do that. Not the way we saw it. There are no special effects that could make that happen in real time."

"It didn't happen. We didn't see it," Dia said. She had her arms wrapped around herself, and her eyes tightly closed. Kelly was calming down; Brig was shaking on the inside but he was forcing himself to accept what he'd seen; but Dia was crumbling right in front of him.

"Dia? What's going on?" he asked.

"It can't be real, because if it's real, it means Mac is here. Mac isn't here. He's dead. This is all Forbes, and it's all explainable. We get Forbes and everything is going to stop being wrong, and it's going to . . . to . . . to go away."

From her bedroom, music started. Not "Bad Moon

Rising." Instead, Peter Gabriel singing, "In Your Eyes." Loudly.

Dia, her back against the wall, her hands over her face, slid to the floor in a sobbing puddle.

Kelly clutched her towel, her face pale. She looked to Brig, who said, "Get dressed. I'm not sure what we're going to do tonight, but it isn't going to be this."

He crouched beside Dia. "Hey," he said. "You need to talk to me. This happened before, didn't it?"

She was rocking back and forth, sobbing. He wrapped her in his arms and said, "It's a weird world. But, Dia, you have someone looking out for you."

"*Nobody* knew that was our song," she said. "*Nobody*, ever. Just Mac and me."

"It's okay. This is scary, darlin'. Hard to understand. And I'm going to get someone over here and have him check the mirror again. We'll get fingerprints if they're there. We're going to get everyone out while I have a specialist check to see how Forbes got back in here again. Okay—I'm not going to tell you this isn't bad. It looks like Forbes has found his way in here again. Somehow."

"Forbes isn't the problem."

Brig laughed. He couldn't help it. She was less afraid of the man who was trying to kill her than she was of the possibility that some remnant of her dead husband was still with her.

"I don't know what to say. I know that Mac isn't trying to hurt you, sweetheart. And that's my concern; that there's someone who is. But we may not be able to make sense of this situation. Not everything in the world fits into nice, neat categories. Dead seems to be one of the things that sometimes doesn't."

She looked up at him, eyes swollen, nose red, face blotchy. It was an endearing face, he thought.

"If he's still here, is he still my husband?"

Brig said, "No. The vow is 'till death do us part,' and no matter how you look at it, he's still dead. You're still a widow, but he cares enough about you to warn you."

"I can't face this," she said. "It's too much."

He pulled her to her feet and held her tight. Over her shoulder, toward the bedroom where the music was still blaring, he said, "Mac, if you're here, I've got this. I'm on Forbes; I'm going to find the bastard; we're investigating him in relationship to your death as well as the threats against Dia and a whole lot of recent crimes. He's not getting away with what he's done. And I'm not going to let anyone hurt her."

The music stopped in midsong. Nothing else followed it.

Dia looked up at him. She glanced back at the bedroom, and then up to Brig again. She didn't say anything. She shook her head, then pressed her face against his neck.

"Kitchen," he said, and banged on the door to Kelly's room. "We're going to be in the kitchen making something to drink for everyone. Come out when you're done, okay?"

"I'll be out in a minute," she said. "I'm changing."

In the kitchen he started water for tea, which he figured both Dia and Kelly could use.

And then he called Stan. He said, "Yeah, I know you don't want to hear from me at this hour. Sympathy on the jet lag, sorry, sorry. Listen. We're experiencing some serious shit over here. . . . A break-in, another death threat, plus a ghost . . . Do you *hear* me laughing? . . . Three of us were here; all three of us saw it. It wasn't a hallucination; it wasn't something you can just blow off. We're going to have to go over this place with a microscope to see how Forbes managed to get in again in spite of the new locks and the alarm system." He sighed. "No, everyone is fine. We've had a scare but the place is secured."

And then he thought about that. He couldn't actually say that the place was secured. He'd been so shocked by seeing writing appear of its own accord on the bathroom mirror, and by seeing Dia's reaction to the music that began playing from the bedroom, that he'd jumped to a possibly unjustified conclusion. He said, "I'll call you back, Stan."

And he pulled Dia to her feet. "C'mon," he told her. "I'm not going to leave you sitting here by yourself. I have to check out your bedroom. We didn't make sure Forbes wasn't in there."

"Nobody knew about that song," Dia said. "I don't want to say it was Mac. But it was Mac."

"C'mon. We're going to go look anyway. Because I am not going to be able to rest or eat or do anything but worry until I make sure that Forbes isn't in the house right now."

Brig had his service weapon in hand as he led her down the narrow hall, all the way to the back bedroom. He flipped on the lights, checked anyplace where someone could have been hiding, made sure the windows were locked, and told Dia, "Okay. We'll run through the rest of the place, too, just because I'm paranoid."

She nodded and followed along. The bathroom was fine, the high, small window also locked.

He banged on Kelly's door again and said, "I'm clearing the rooms, Kelly. Come on out and let me take a look."

Kelly didn't say anything.

His gut tightened. "Kelly? Open the door."

Nothing.

"Oh, no," Dia whispered behind him.

He tried the handle. It was locked. He gave it a quick,

hard kick, right at the level of the lock, and it blew open,
bits of wood flying from the frame.

Kelly lay sprawled, facedown and naked, on her bed.
The light in the room was on, so he could see the situation clearly, right from the first. He put a hand out to
keep Dia back, but she followed him anyway.

Kelly was dead, her throat cut so deeply her head
looked barely attached to her body. The knife that had
cut her lay on her back, between her shoulder blades,
her blood still on the blade. It was an enormous hunting
knife, one of those handmade art knives that were un-
godly expensive and generally never used for anything
but looking scary on some poser's wall. Kelly's diary
lay in front of her, away from the pool of blood that
soaked the bedspread, her clothes, and the carpet below
the bed.

He could see the page it was open to. In Forbes's
handwriting, it said, *Anyplace I want, anytime I want.*

The door of the wardrobe she'd had brought in that
day stood open. Brig could see where Forbes had
cleared a space for himself—where he'd been hiding.
Though Brig could not begin to imagine how the man
had squashed his enormous body into that limited space.
Brig looked at the window. Closed, not locked.

He looked back at Dia, who was gray, and who suddenly bolted for the bathroom. He could hear her throwing up.

He followed her, just to make sure that the bathroom
was still empty of anyone but her. It was.

Brig hit redial on his cell phone. "Stan," he said when
his partner picked up. "I'm reporting the murder of
Kelly Beam, Dia's colleague and new roommate. Suspect is Sinclair Forbes. He left us a note. I need a full
team over here."

On the other end of the phone, Stan went a little crazy.

"Just get here," Brig said. "Scene is as found, I still have to secure the rest of the house, and I'm not in a position right now to do more than basics. Dia is . . . Well, as soon as everyone arrives, I need to get her out of here."

Chapter 19

Dia couldn't think. She couldn't accept any of this. It was too much, too impossible. Forbes and Mac, writing on the mirror. Kelly dead.

She hung over the toilet, afraid to move even though she knew there was nothing left in her stomach. She couldn't walk past the other bedroom, because if she did Kelly would still be lying in there, and all of a sudden Kelly and Mac looked the same to her, their heads half on their bodies, nothing she could do to save them, both of them dead because of Forbes. Kelly couldn't be dead.

Dia's hands were shaking. And then Brig was with her, pulling her to her feet.

"We're getting out of here and going to my place," he said. "You're staying there until this is over."

She nodded.

"I'm going with you to your bedroom, and I'm going to help you get your things together."

That made sense, she thought as he led her into her room. It wasn't going to be her room anymore. She was never coming back to this place. Never, for any reason. She'd talk the guys into packing her up, and she'd pay them for their help. She'd find a little place somewhere.

She didn't want to think about that, about new places. She didn't want to think about anything. She was suddenly tired. It hit her like a roof collapsing on her head. She looked at her bed, though, and she couldn't sleep there. Forbes had been in the house. He could have touched the bed; he might have been in it. She could tell the guys they didn't need to bring the bed.

Right on the heels of that, she realized that he could have touched everything. Might have tampered with anything. She wanted nothing from this place.

She stood, turning in circles, staring at the room, thinking of Kelly and wondering whom to call to notify about her death. Kelly had been quiet about her personal life. She didn't mention family. She only talked about Sam as always being on call. He was a doctor, but there had to be ten thousand doctors in Broward County. Dia didn't even remember Kelly mentioning his full name. Sometimes she'd call him Sam, and get a dreamy look on her face. But lately she hadn't talked about him much, and Dia wondered if the two of them were still dating.

She wanted to go back in time. She wanted to go to Kelly standing in the hall in her towel, and stop her from walking into that bedroom. She wanted to go back even farther, and tell Kelly she couldn't move in.

"Dia?"

She realized Brig was talking to her. She stopped turning, and looked at him.

"I just went ahead and got some things. We're going to get you home now."

"I want to drive," she said. "I'm going to need my car."

It sounded so sensible coming out of her mouth. So very controlled, so rational. She didn't sound like someone who wanted to scream until she exploded.

"I'd rather you didn't," he said. "You look pretty unsteady."

"I don't want to leave the car here. I'm not taking

anything else from this place, but I'll need the car. Not
tomorrow, maybe. But soon." She was amazed at how
calm she sounded. She didn't sound crazy at all—lucky
for her Brig couldn't see inside, where she was still
turning in circles, screaming.

"All right. Traffic isn't bad right now. You'll follow
me; we'll take our time. If you can't do it, just flash
your headlights and we'll pull over and you can ride
with me the rest of the way."

She nodded. "I can do that."

"Good."

He walked her out of the bedroom and into a throng
of people. "We're getting out of here," he said, and she
recognized Stan, his partner.

"I'm sorry about all of this," Stan said.

She just stared at him.

"I know. We'll get the guy who did it."

She nodded.

Brig backed her car out of her garage and worked it
past all the police cars. "I can have one of the unis bring
this over to my place," he said.

She shook her head. "I need to do this. I need to know
that I'm still capable—that I can still function."

"You don't have to be strong all the time," he told her.

She looked at him, sick with fear, but certain about
what she had to do. "I know that. I won't even try to be.
But . . . I need to be strong right now."

"Fair enough."

He left her car in the street, got his car worked free,
and pulled it in front of hers. And then he walked her to
her door, put her in the car, and waited while she fastened her seat belt.

"Any problems, you flash the lights. You feel too
sleepy to move, you feel sick, you get scared . . .
anything."

She nodded.

He said, "Give me your keys for a minute."

She pulled them out of the ignition and handed them over. He walked to her trunk and opened it, then shut it again. "Nothing in there that shouldn't be."

He handed her the keys, pulled the little flashlight out of his pocket, and crouched down and looked under her car. "I don't see anything down there that shouldn't be there, either."

"Okay," she said.

She shut her door, locked the car, turned the ignition, and waited while Brig got into his own car and started it.

They drove off slowly, away from the lines of yellow crime scene tape, away from the flashing red and blue lights of cop cars and the ambulance that would take Kelly's body away when the investigators were done with it, away from the people gathered in clusters as close to the tape as they could get. But staring at her.

Staring.

She could feel their eyes drilling holes in the back of her neck long after she was out of the neighborhood.

She followed Brig onto University Drive, where the traffic was still heavy. She managed to stay close behind him; she was irrationally terrified of a car cutting between them, and her losing him at a light, and him not being able to get back to her before Forbes got her.

It was crazy. She knew it was crazy. But she was in control. Driving. Still on her feet.

They were heading south, and had hit a point where traffic had cleared just a little, so they were making better time—right at forty-five miles per hour.

Ten P.M., and the road was well lit, fast-food restaurants and real restaurants and an unholy lot of businesses were still open, and the world outside her car seemed normal. Impossibly normal.

The front end of Brig's car exploded in a flash of blue fire, and Dia didn't even think to hit the brakes. She plowed right into the back of it as it spun into the concrete median.

The Crown Vic went up into the grass, and she fought her door open, and, shaken, wobbly, got out of her car and ran to his.

He was fighting with his seat belt. The front of his car was on fire, and she could see flames starting to lick at the fuel dripping from the back.

He got his belt off as she dragged his door open. She grabbed him and hauled him out, and saw that he had a lot of blood on his face. Blood trickling from both ears. He looked stunned. The shock of the blast had probably blown at least one of his eardrums.

She didn't waste time yelling to him. She just grabbed his hand and pulled, and he staggered after her, down the raised median, dodging crape myrtles and palms and palmettos designed to make the median pretty, that instead just made it impossible to run along. Cars were swerving around the accident on one side; they were slowing and rubbernecking on the other. A cop car had spotted the accident, and was coming at them with sirens screaming.

Behind them, the world shook and shrapnel exploded in all directions and the sky, for just a moment, went as bright as the surface of the sun.

On the other side of the road, cars collided.

Dia took Brig's cell phone from his belt. She got him to look at her, and slowly mouthed the words, *I'm going to call Stan.*

He put his fingers to his ears, held the sides of his head, and looked at his hands as they came away covered with blood. He nodded slowly.

She worked her way down his autodial list and found

Stan's name. She pressed the autodial, and when Stan answered with, "Jeezus, what now," she said, "Brig's car just exploded with him in it. He got out. He's hurt, though he looks mostly okay. He can't hear anything, he's bleeding, he's staggering. I rear-ended him. We're both shook up."

The silence at the other end echoed her own feelings of disbelief. After a seemingly endless moment, Stan asked for directions. Dia said, "University, heading south. Just past the bowling alley."

"I know where you are. If you end up in an ambulance before I get there, call me and tell me what hospital you go to."

She clipped Brig's cell phone to the waistband of her jeans, and wrapped her arms around him. She had turned him away from the crashed cars. She saw her own car go up in flames, and heard the fire engines getting closer.

The explosive device had been attached to Brig's car, not hers. Why? To get Brig out of the way in order to clear Forbes's path to Dia? Because Forbes assumed that Dia would leave with Brig instead of driving her own car—had it been an attempt to kill them both?

She held Brig close as a uniformed police officer ran from the remains of their cars to shout, "Did you see what happened?"

News crews were already convening on the site, setting up reporters along the strewn remains of the two cars, pulling witnesses from the sidewalks. Fingers were pointing toward her and Brig.

When the cop led the two of them to the first ambulance to arrive and put them on it, Dia was grateful. She'd had enough of the news.

Chapter 20

Brig had one badly ruptured eardrum, and couldn't hear out of that ear at all. The ER doc put a patch over it, and told him so long as he took his antibiotics, kept foreign objects out of it, and left it the hell alone, it would be better in about two months. Dia had been convinced he'd ruptured both eardrums, but a bit of glass that had lodged itself above the left ear during the collision had proven to be the cause of the bleeding on the other side of his head.

He was getting his hearing back in the other ear. That was good. And according to the doc, he'd only be dizzy and queasy for another twenty-four hours or so. Just a day—if the dizziness went on past that point, he was supposed to report promptly to his own doctor for follow-up.

Brig had been lucky, and he knew it. He could have been dead, and he had to assume that had been Forbes's intent. He could have been maimed, blinded, crippled for life.

Instead, he was going to be deaf in one ear for two months, and hurt like hell for about a week from the multitude of bruises, twists, and hits that he'd endured during the explosion, the collision, and then the shrapnel strikes from the second explosion.

He was so grateful that Dia hadn't been in the car

with him. It hadn't taken her doctor long to pull the bits of glass and metal out of her skin, or to sew up the couple of small lacerations she'd acquired. It was funny, but she hadn't even realized she was hurt. She'd only been afraid for him.

Stan came in while the doc was off reading his X-rays. "Hell of a way to get yourself a week of paid vacation," he said.

To Brig, he sounded like he was whispering. "Going to have to talk louder, pal," he said. "Pretend I'm your great-grandfather."

Stan said, "The guys on-site found bits of an explosive device like the ones we've been finding at our wrecks. So now we have a beautiful link from Forbes through the death threats to Dia, and from the murder at Dia's home to the explosive device on your car. We have all our pieces. All we need is the shitweasel who's been handing them to us."

"Yeah. We broadcast the picture of the guy who delivered Dia's package. Put out an APB with his picture, list everything and the kitchen sink."

Stan nodded. "We do a press conference first thing. Ask people who have seen him to come forward."

Brig was having a hard time focusing on Forbes and the case. Postexplosion, his thinking was fuzzy. He was shaken enough that his concentration was shot for anything but his own pain and his worry that Dia wasn't in his direct line of sight.

The laid-back life in Montana was looking pretty good all of a sudden. Nobody had been trying to kill him or someone he loved back there, and back then.

"You going to be all right with everything until I'm cleared to work again?" he asked Stan.

"I'll be fine. I mean, if you want to cover paperwork for me, I'll be more than happy to bring it over for you to do. But . . . what with your needing to heal up, and your new roommate situation and all . . ." He managed a sly smile that Brig made a point of ignoring. "Yeah, well . . . anyway, I thought you might actually want a couple of real days off. You have them coming, and I can cover the bases until you get back. We're going to have extra help now in tracking down Forbes, which will lighten the caseload a little."

"All right," Brig said. "I'll commit to taking tomorrow off. And just decide day by day after that."

Dia was finished long before Brig. She came in several times to check on him, but her colleagues from Rescue kept showing up. The news about Kelly's death had spread fast, and Dia was in constant demand to explain what had happened to Kelly, and what had happened to her and to Brig.

He watched her, watched the people with her, watched staff and strangers who walked by. He was on edge, wary. Forbes wasn't done with her, and Forbes might be working through other people, which meant every person who walked by Dia constituted a threat.

Dia wanted to be with Brig, but her friends kept dragging her away; they couldn't crowd into the bay he'd been put in, and they wouldn't wait to hear what had happened.

She couldn't blame them . . . not really. Kelly was dead, and no one could quite hold on to that. It had been too sudden—it had happened not because of something Kelly had done wrong, but because of something she had done right: She'd helped her friend. Her colleague.

Any of them would have done the same thing. But Kelly had been the one who paid for it.

"And what about you and Brig?" Ryan asked. "You look a little banged up, but he looks pretty rough."

Dia said, "Most of his damage is superficial. He's going to have a lot of pain the next few days. But nothing did irreparable damage. The biggest problem he'll have is being deaf in one ear for the next couple of months. He's lucky it was just the one ear—when I first saw him, I was sure it was two."

"Where are you going to be staying?" Tyler asked her. "Because, you know, any one of us would be happy to put you up."

Everyone crowded around her agreed, except for Howie. "I'm figuring you'd turn me down. And I can't blame you. So I won't offer. But . . ." He shrugged. "Well, you know."

She knew.

"You guys are great," she said. "I'm not putting anyone else at risk, though. I can't do that. The FLPD has promised me protection." At Brig's insistence, she was not telling anyone where she was staying. He said that she could never be sure who was listening to her, and she needed to do everything she could to prevent anyone from inadvertently saying the wrong thing in front of Forbes.

She was so glad to see Brig walk out from behind the curtain around his bay, accompanied by his doctor. He still looked shaky, and he was definitely pale, but he didn't have that dazed, lost look he'd had when she dragged him out of his car.

She broke away from her friends and joined him.

"News?"

"Twenty-nine stitches in seven different lacerations," he said. "Headache that is going to take the top off of my head any minute now. Ear that has an agony line straight to my brain, and bruises that are going to turn me into Purple Man for a week. . . . Breathing? Priceless."

She laughed. "Yeah. Me, too."

She watched him watching the off-duty guys from the station. "They don't know where you're going to be?"

"Nobody does."

"Good. Stan's driving us, and we'll have a couple of unmarked cars following along making sure that we don't have someone unwelcome following us home. We aren't going to have a repeat of today, I promise. You're going to survive this."

"I will," she said. "And you, too."

He looked like he was going to say more. But then he turned as Stan joined them, and the moment passed.

"Ready?" Stan asked.

"Much as we'll ever be."

Dia had a prescription for pain pills. Brig had a stack of little white sheets. He passed them over to her, and she recognized an antibiotic, a muscle relaxant, a pain reliever, something to help with nausea and dizziness, and a sleeping pill.

If he took everything he'd been prescribed, he'd float through the next week in a happy, dopey daze. She couldn't see him agreeing to that.

She passed his scrips back to him, and as the three of them walked out the door together—a bit of professional courtesy she'd finagled from the staff, who generally insisted that even people who were doing fine on their feet be wheeled to their rides—he told her, "Pick out the ones that won't mess up my reflexes. I'll take them. Everything else can go in the trash."

She nodded. That had been nothing less than what she expected.

The ride to Brig's place was uneventful. It was the only thing that had been for far too long. She let her head rest on his shoulder, he put an arm around her, and both of them closed their eyes.

She didn't want to think. But with her eyes closed, all

the rest of her senses got in on the act, tossing her impressions and pain, noises and scents. The memory of Kelly on the bed, the diary open in front of her. The smell of blood. The roar of the second explosion, the one that had engulfed Brig's car and hers in flames and sent glass and metal flying.

Wrecks. Blood. Twisted metal. Camera crews hovering, trying to get access to victims and responders and bystanders.

The foiled security system in her home. The window shouldn't have opened without setting off the alarm. But it had.

Hadn't it? Or had Forbes found a way to remain inside the house even after Kelly was killed, only to slip out some other way? And the writing on the mirror—the threat, and the other thing. Mac's ghost, undeniable at last.

The car came to a stop, but instead of sitting for a moment, then rolling forward again, Stan turned the engine off.

"Home," Brig told her. "For a while, anyway."

She said good night to Stan, and felt him watching them until Brig used his key code to open the door to the apartment building. He waved, Stan got back into his car, and Brig closed the door and waited for the click that assured them it had locked.

"I'm on the second floor," he said. "I'd say that if I knew I was going to have company, I would have cleaned, but I know that isn't true. I would have started to clean, then gotten sidetracked on work. And it would still look just exactly the way it looks now, only I'd feel guilty about it."

It wasn't bad. He'd made no effort to pretty the place up, but he looked like a habitually neat person. Belongings had places. The place for papers, reports, graphs, charts, and photographs was clearly on the enormous maple kitchen table, but aside from that one lapse, books were in bookshelves and the floor was neatly swept.

She saw no sign of hobbies.

Well, reading. He had an odd library, comprised mostly of nonfiction about detection, crime, techniques, personalities, histories, serial killers. A whole stack of Ann Rule true crime. Robert Parker detective fiction, westerns by a couple of well-known authors, and a smattering of novels in odd genres like fantasy and science fiction written by people she'd never heard of.

He didn't have video games. He didn't have a cat, a dog, or a fish tank. No sports memorabilia. No pictures of people or of places. No art on the walls.

He did have a computer. A standard PC that sat on a prefab desk that had nothing in common with the good furniture in the rest of the place, except for an equal number of horizontal surfaces. An uncomfortable-looking office chair in vivid red and black sat in the corner and made itself the focus of attention.

Because everything—*everything*—else was the creamy beige that spoke of a designer with the soul of a flounder. The furniture fit the place so well, she suspected Brig lived in a furnished rental unit.

He was watching her look around.

"It isn't much," he said. "It's just a place where they can deliver pizza and I can sleep at night between work."

She understood that. "Most of my life has been work, too." She looked and him and said, "I don't even have a toothbrush with me, Brig. I don't have a driver's license anymore. Or my bank card, or my checks, or my clothes. My birth certificate and Social Security card are in my safe-deposit box, but my key to it is with what's left of my car."

Somehow she had managed to forget about that.

About her purse sitting on the floorboard of her car, with all her essential ID in it. About her bill box in her trunk, now certainly reduced to cinders along with the few other essentials she'd thought to take with her.

They had been essentials, the things she'd grabbed. And now she was without them until she could find a way to replace them.

She closed her eyes.

"I can help you get all your paperwork back, Dia. Driver's license, bank card, everything else. It'll be a nuisance, but it isn't the end of the world."

"I know," she said. "I just keep wondering, as the shock wears off, what other surprises I'm going to have waiting for me. Other things I'll have to deal with that I'm not thinking about now."

"You know what?" He smiled down at her. "Don't worry about them. When your brain is ready to deal with them, it will remind you. And even then, there's no sense worrying when you can't do anything about it." He glanced at the clock in the microwave and said, "It's past three in the morning, and the only good thing we can say about this situation right now is, we don't have to get up at any particular time tomorrow."

"I'm tired," she said. That was something else she hadn't noticed. But as soon as she realized what time it was, her body agreed that she needed to be in bed. "God, I can't believe how tired I am."

"My doctor told me not to use the shower for twenty-four hours," Brig said. "How about yours?"

"I'm supposed to keep my stitches dry."

"Straight to bed, then. I have some clothes you can wear. And tomorrow, since we don't have anything else to do, we can get you a few things to tide you over."

His bedroom was as beige as the rest of the condo. He wasn't a bed maker. The comforter and sheets were tangled. But the bedroom, like the rest of the place, was otherwise neat.

He gave her one of his T-shirts and a pair of cotton running shorts, and she slipped into them.

They curled up together in the bed, carefully spooning, both so sore already that they were afraid to move once they got settled.

"Sleep well," he told her. "I've got you, and I won't let anyone hurt you."

She drifted off wishing that she could promise him the same thing.

And there was Mac. She knew she was dreaming, but she couldn't wake up.

He was standing in front of her, but they didn't seem to be anywhere in particular. She couldn't see ground; she couldn't see trees—all she could see, in fact, was Mac, and a sort of gray nothing that was, when she looked around, the sum total of up and down, forward and back. Mac looked faded. Not dead anymore, not all ripped up. But thin and washed out, like he was losing his grip on existence.

"Not safe," he told her. "Not safe."

"I'm not safe. I know," she said.

He shook his head. "Not safe."

"Brig's not safe?" she asked.

She could see frustration on his face.

"Sinclair Forbes killed you, right?"

He nodded. The frustration stayed on his face. He knotted his hands into fists, and she could see him trying to form other words with his mouth. She could see him trying to shape them. But when he spoke, the only words that came out were, "Not safe."

And when they did, she saw what looked like a tear roll down his cheek.

It was, she thought, like speaking with someone who'd had a stroke, and who was just getting back the ability to talk. With them, too, she had always been able to see them trying to say so much more than they could find the words for.

She wondered if it was the same for him.

"I'm sorry," she told him. "I'm so sorry. About everything. About what happened to you. You deserved so much better than that. And about me not wanting to admit you were there. It's hard. I'm trying to move on, and I . . . I just don't know where you fit."

She could see him trembling with effort, his mouth tightening, his body rigid. "Don't . . ." he said. And then, struggling, fighting: "Trust . . ."

He seemed to be fading. His mouth was shaping the third word. The one she needed. And the gray of the place where she was simultaneously filled in around him, through him.

She saw the look of triumph on his face, and he said . . . it. The name.

She could hear him whispering it. It was the answer. The solution. She knew who had been haunting her; she knew where he was. She knew everything.

She woke, excited, and rolled over to wake Brig, to tell him that Mac had told her the killer's name—who he was now, not who he had been then.

And discovered that the final word, the one she needed, the one that was the answer, was gone.

She fought for it, tried to see Mac's lips form the name, tried to hear again what he'd whispered before the gray swallowed him.

It might as well never have been. She couldn't find it, she couldn't bring it back, and she lay there, frustrated and in tears, certain that she had known the truth, but forced to acknowledge at last that nothing she did was going to let her remember it.

At one point in her life, not long before she met Mac, she kept dreaming that she'd found the solution to world peace. She had the dream several times, and she awoke from it each time knowing that the answer would work, that if only she could take it from her sleeping mind into the everyday world, she would make life better for everyone. Everywhere in the world. For all time. It was that big, that comprehensive.

So one night she put a notepad and pen beside her bed, then promised herself every night before she fell asleep that if she had the dream again, she would force herself to wake up afterward.

Eventually she did. She had the dream, it was as perfect as it had been each time before, and when she reached the conclusion, she woke herself up, turned on her night-light, carefully wrote the solution down on the notepad, and, elated that at last she had succeeded, flopped onto her pillow again and went back to sleep.

The next morning, remembering that she had finally won through the solution from her dream, she grabbed the notebook.

And found the word "cigarettes" neatly block-printed across one whole page. And nothing else.

Was Mac in her dreams like her world-peace solution? Was his presence as she slept simply some phantasm that she was conjuring up? But if he was her own creation, how had her dreams managed to lead her to Sinclair Forbes?

If Mac's spirit spoke to Dia in her sleep as it did when she was awake, then why hadn't he been more useful in helping her solve his own murder, or in preventing the man who had killed him from killing Kelly and coming after Dia?

Why didn't he just come out and say, "The person trying to kill you is . . ."

And there it had been again. The certainty that what he had told her was the truth, the answer. But that something—in her, or between the two of them—was blocking her from getting it.

Brig's arm was around her. At least she wasn't in this on her own.

She lay there, not able to go back to sleep, and considered what Mac had given her in her dreams.

The scene of his death—rolled ambulance, wrecked car, the three dead EMTs, Sinclair Forbes still alive as Dia rescued him. Why hadn't Mac ever talked about Forbes? Mac and Forbes had been friends for years, until the day one boy had turned the other boy in to the police for criminal behavior. That had to have been a huge influence on Mac's life; Mac had to have thought about it all those years later.

Did he feel guilty for what he'd done? Did he hate the boy who had once been his friend? Had there been other issues involved that made him keep that part of his past a secret from her? She'd mused on those questions ever since she discovered that Mac had known the man who had been the cause of his death . . . but she hadn't come to any more satisfying answer than that she was unlikely ever to know.

But if Mac haunted her dreams as well as their little duplex, then he'd handed her the connection between himself and Forbes, simply by forcing her to keep looking at it. But . . . the whole scene had been in there.

Ambulance. Car. Wall. Dead men. The music—"Bad Moon Rising"—over and over and over.

Could there have been a message in the song? She knew it word for word—but hurricanes, lightning, floods, and earthquakes had nothing to do with her situation or Mac's death.

The line about the eye taken for an eye seemed promising. But the more she thought about it, the more it didn't take her anyplace she hadn't already been. Forbes was getting his revenge on Mac. Maybe Mac was waiting to take his revenge on Forbes. Either way, it didn't tell her anything she didn't already know.

She couldn't let the dreams go, though. If she'd found the only secret in them when she realized that investigating Sinclair Forbes might be worthwhile, why did she keep dreaming the same scene? Variants of it, certainly, but—ambulance, car, dead men, live man, music—he kept dragging her, or she kept dragging herself, over the same terrain.

"Why are you awake?" Brig asked in a sleepy voice.

She jumped a little. "Nightmare," she said. "How did you know I was awake?"

He chuckled a little, and she could feel the vibration of his laughter against her back. "Your body was giving off enough tension, you probably could have woken me up from across the room."

"Sorry about that."

"You've earned the tension. And the nightmares, though I wish you weren't having them," he said. "Snuggle closer, and I'll think drowsy, fuzzy thoughts at you. You need the sleep."

She liked that. He pulled her closer and the warmth of his breath on the back of her neck, and the weight of his arm on her, and the way their bodies fit together, chased away her worries. She knew she'd be better able to deal with everything in daylight, after she'd slept. The world was going to be a hard place to live in for a while. But it didn't have to be, right at that moment. She had an oasis. A sanctuary. Even if it was just temporary, that safe space and that feeling of being protected and wanted and cared for was something she needed.

It might be that she and Brig had discovered in each other the piece that had been missing from each of their lives.

She wasn't going to hope too much. Not yet. Not while everything was horrible and crazy and deadly.

But she thought she could afford to hope a little.

And if her safety was only illusory, well, she and Brig and the Fort Lauderdale Police Department were working to fix that.

She closed her eyes again, and the next time she managed to drift off to sleep, she didn't dream of anything at all.

Chapter 21

"I hurt too much to cook," he told her when he came into the bedroom. He was carrying bags of food. She smelled breakfastish smells, even though it was well past noon.

"So you went out?" She'd been blissfully asleep, but the idea of having been alone in his apartment, even for a little while, locked her gut into a tight, hard knot. Dia found herself abruptly and completely awake.

"Are you nuts?" He was looking at her with a curious half smile on his face. "I can barely walk, I'm so sore. I ordered delivery from a place I like, and specified a delivery guy I know. No surprises that way, and we get great food fast. And you get to wipe that panicked expression off your face. I'm not going to leave you here asleep and alone."

She stared at him. "My mind is transparent, or my face is. Or you're an amazing mind reader."

"I'm a cop. I think in terms of security." He put the food down in front of them on a towel he spread on the bed. "Sorry I don't have those nifty little bed trays," he told her. "Men don't buy those things, and then we have a day when we need them, and we wonder why we don't."

Dia watched as omelets and link sausages and corned-beef hash—perfectly browned—and pan-fried potatoes seasoned with a wonderful mix of spices appeared from beneath the lid of one Styrofoam tray. Then orange juice in a big cup with a lid and a straw. And some evil combination of cheesecake, pastry crust, and strawberry jam that she'd never seen before.

It all looked too good.

"It's fattening," he told her. "It's the heart attack special, with sides. But it's also only one day. I know neither of us is going to be working out for a couple of days. However . . . there are times when food fills places that nothing else can."

She glanced sidelong at him and said, "Some other day I might be inclined to argue. At the moment, though, comfort food looks like a perfect, if temporary, solution."

She dug in as he settled beside her and opened his own identical tray.

The food was good. Neither of them talked—everything they had to talk about would ruin the wonderful breakfast. He didn't turn on the television at the end of the bed, either. So they sat shoulder-to-shoulder, silent except for the squeak of plastic forks on Styrofoam, and let the food and the companionship of the moment be enough.

She ate everything. It was more food than she would have eaten in any other circumstance. She didn't think about it. Every time she thought, horrible pictures started scrolling across that screen inside her head.

Nothing she could do would make those pictures go away for good. But for the moment, tasting and chewing and swallowing silenced her private horror show.

When they were done, they ignored medical advice and took showers. Neither of them even broached the idea of showering together. Movement hurt, bumping into each other hurt, and in Brig's small closet-type shower, the whole process would have been guaranteed pain.

And then they sprawled on his couch, her at one end, him on the other, their legs tangled together in the middle.

"I don't want to talk about yesterday," she said.

"Neither do I," he agreed. "We'll have to dance around it a little bit, though, but right now, reliving the . . . well . . . supernatural elements of the day is not going to move us forward. Our goal has to be to catch Forbes and make this stop. We need to focus on him and what he did, and mostly on how he did it."

Dia laid her head against the couch arm and stared at his ceiling. "How did he get into the house?" she asked.

"The obvious answer is that he came in through the window in Kelly's room, then hid in the armoire. The first question that brings up is, how did he circumvent the alarm system?"

"The question before that, actually, is why was her window unlocked?"

"People were carrying furniture into her room. Did they open the window for any reason?"

"Kelly opened it, and set off the alarm briefly," Dia said. "I had her shut it, and I reset the alarm."

"Did you make sure she locked the window?"

Dia said, "You mean, did I check behind her? No. Of course not. She knew the situation; she certainly would have had the sense to lock the window."

"It wasn't locked." Brig started to tuck his hands behind his head, winced at the movement, and put his arms carefully across his stomach instead. "But the window is not the only possibility. It's the obvious possibility, because we found it unlocked. But if he'd come in through it or gone out of it, he would have set off the alarm. Right?"

She bit her lip. She hadn't considered that. "Yes, he would have."

"Unless he has alarm system skills—but considering what we know about him, that isn't the most logical assumption. First, he would have had to fit through the window, and I don't think he could have. It's big, but not that big. Second, we know he had a key to your front door before you changed the locks and put in the security system. It isn't impossible to imagine that he might have obtained a new key in the same manner that he obtained the first. The alarm should have been a problem, but clearly it wasn't. If he came in through an alternative route—whether through the front door or through the garage—he might have unlocked the window, either before or after he killed Kelly, to give everyone a plausible method for explaining what he did."

"Why?"

"Because he might have had a much better way into your home that he didn't want to compromise. By giving everyone who was looking for it an obvious entry, he decreased the chance that his less obvious, but better method of getting to you still existed."

Dia considered that. "But no one has found that alternate entry."

"No. They haven't."

"And every possible entry into the house itself is hooked into the alarm system."

"Yes."

"And I had the alarm system on."

Brig sat up and leaned toward her. "A determined enemy can find or create alternate routes to anything, if given enough time and the right resources."

Dia considered that. "He has the resources, doesn't he?"

"He had an enormous amount of money going to him every month. Money-wise, he could have paid for any number of pricey solutions. And time-wise . . . well, we know you were married to Mac when Forbes found him. We know he knows that you exist, and has for at least four years. And we know that he has made at least one aboveboard attempt to contact you."

"Right."

"In four years, a determined man can do a lot of damage. Or make a lot of plans."

She tried to imagine what Forbes had been doing those four years before he started coming after her. Her imagination didn't offer her anything useful, but it didn't take her anywhere good, either.

"I don't know why he's doing what he's doing," she said at last. "I think that is why I don't get this. I can understand how he would go after Mac. There's a direct line between them, and in Forbes's eyes, Mac hurt him. But what do I have to do with this?"

"We don't know that. Motive doesn't always tell you much, anyway. His motives seem very confused. He stalks you, he presents himself as someone who wants to thank you, he gives you gifts, he tries to kill you, he tries to kill me, he does kill Kelly. If we could figure out how each of those events relates to all the others, we might understand why he's doing this—but that would probably not put us closer to catching him."

They leaned back again. Sat looking at each other in silence.

"I'm not good at lying around the house," Dia said after a while. "I don't relax well when I'm still. I relax when I'm running, or swimming, or diving, or rock climbing."

"I prefer horseback riding," he said. "Though at the moment, all I can really think about is how much that would hurt."

And they fell silent again.

Eventually Dia said, "There has to be something we could do."

"Television?" he asked.

"During the daytime? Shoot me now."

He grinned. "No television."

"I meant, something we could do to find Forbes."

"I know what you mean. My personal car is tucked away here. If Forbes has managed to track us down to this apartment complex, we don't want him to know which car that is. So . . . you can borrow another of my T-shirts and a different pair of my shorts. I have no doubt you'll make them look as charming and adorable as the ones you slept in. And when you're dressed, we'll put dark glasses on you, tuck your hair up, and stick a hat on your head. And then we'll drive to the station and go over the casebook. And everything else I can think of. Being there will be better than being here."

"I'm sorry I'm not good at lying around," she said.

"Don't be. I was already going stir-crazy myself."

She looked good in his clothes. He liked the way she'd knotted his FLPD T-shirt on one side, and the way she'd cinched the shorts tight around her waist. Wearing those, her running shoes, one of his baseball caps, and a pair of Ray•Bans, she looked curvy, sleek, and delicious.

Most of her bruises were covered. That was a plus.

His mostly were as well. He also wore a pair of shorts and a T-shirt and running shoes. He also had on a base-ball cap and sunglasses. They looked generic; they could be South Florida residents, tourists, whatever.

His personal car was an Impala, late model, dark green, dark-tinted windows, fully appointed. It bore no bumper stickers or other marks that would identify it as a car belonging to a cop. That was on purpose—but also because he couldn't stand the idea of crudding up a nice car with a lot of crap that wouldn't come off.

They made it from the apartment to the parking lot without incident. He didn't see anyone watching them. He knew that he wouldn't, but he managed to avoid limping and so did she, and he was confident that the two of them would pass even close scrutiny without revealing their identities.

They drove around the streets for a while. He asked her if she wanted to stop off and get some clothes before they headed into the station; she declined the offer.

His station was busy, but then it always was. He led her up the back way, to his cubicle. Stan popped in almost immediately.

"There were bets," he said.

"Bets?" Brig asked.

"Bets. On exactly how long it would take you to wear her down and get her to come in here so that you could work on your day off."

"Who won?"

"Well, since the earliest bet was sometime tomorrow, some of the bettors are arguing that the whole thing should be called off. Clearly you're an evil, evil man, and have no consideration for the needs of your companion."

"Coming in was my idea," Dia said.

Stan shook his head sadly and said to Brig, "*Clearly* we all underestimated you. Not only did you browbeat the poor woman, but you brainwashed her into believing this was all her idea."

"Any news?" Brig asked, changing the subject.

"Not even a little bit."

"Dia and I are going to sit down with photographs and the casebook, then, and see if she can spot anything familiar in the whole mess. She hasn't been looking at this day in and day out. Maybe when she does, something will jump out at her."

Dia was looking at the map Brig had put on his cubicle wall, that had the locations and dates of each of the traffic killer's hits. She was frowning.

"You see a pattern?" he asked her after a while.

"No. I just didn't realize that I'd been to so many of them."

Brig said, "With a likely new wreck that Stan picked up, we've found seven now—including mine. These are the ones where we located explosives matériel at an accident site. There were no doubt others before this."

She nodded, stood and walked over to the map, and started going over dates and times and locations.

"Six," she said.

"What?"

She stood there, a finger resting on one of the pins, reading the details out loud.

"Yes. Six," she said. "You've found seven, and of those seven, I've responded to six. And was involved in the seventh."

He rose and joined her. "Show me."

"These are the cutoff points for anything our station takes that isn't disaster-related. Pickups, I mean—not deliveries. Look at this." She picked up a red pen from his desk and drew a tiny *X* on the map where the station was located. "Here's us, right in the center of our district, more or less. That little jog up there is where we ended up picking up the slack for a station that the city shut down for tax purposes, but other than that, we're right in the middle of your cluster of crimes."

"So your ambulances have been responding to Forbes's crimes."

"Not just our ambulances. *Me.* Personally. Some of these have been major disasters, and even though they weren't in our area, we went in on a county-wide all-available-units disaster call. The one where you and I first ran into each other—we were out of area on that one."

"Right." What she was telling him suggested to him that she was the deciding factor in where Forbes committed his crimes. And when.

She frowned. "I'm trying not to take this personally," she said, "but it looks like these things are somehow connected to me."

"Somehow besides through the killer?"

"Yeah. Besides him."

Brig studied the map and rested a hand on her shoulder. "You probably know him. You might not like him, but you probably see him around the station, or even *in* the station."

"I swear, Brig—I don't know him. I don't know anyone who even looks remotely like him. I'd remember. He doesn't even look like any of the patients we've carried recently—I can't imagine how he's managing to get close to me without my seeing him."

"He is close to you, Dia. Somehow."

She turned pale and stared at him. "That's what Mac told me. That he was close to me."

"For me . . . for my peace of mind . . . go through the photos again. I don't know how a man that big could disguise himself, but I don't know how he hid in Kelly's wardrobe while he was waiting for her, either. All I know is that he did. So humor me, okay?"

"Yeah."

He sat her down and handed her the casebook—a fat ring binder jammed with notes, investigation reports, and other essentials for tracking the crimes and the criminal. In the front he had a plastic holder in which he'd inserted copies of the pictures of Sinclair Forbes when he was younger.

Dia studied Forbes's high school photographs, and later pictures that Brig and Stan had managed to round up, including the one that had been taken shortly before the accident that had killed Mac.

She frowned, pulled out pictures, held them close to her face, held them far from her face, held them up to the side of her so that she caught glimpses of them from the corner of an eye.

He wasn't entirely certain what she was doing, but she was fun to watch.

Finally she put the last of the pictures back in its holder, closed the folder, and handed it back to him.

"And? I'm guessing from your expression that you haven't had a eureka moment."

"There's something familiar about him. I can't place him, exactly. But I may have seen him around. Only . . . why don't I remember where? He isn't exactly nondescript."

"Maybe he's a janitor. A medical supplies representative. That would explain his access to medical-grade nitrous oxide. Maybe he's a friend of some night-shift EMT who only works part-time . . . maybe someone who moonlights when you're shorthanded."

Her frown deepened. "I keep reminding myself that Sinclair Forbes had blood all over his face when I pulled him from the car. To me, that would suggest the possibility of scarring. But he has a lot of money, so maybe he's had a little plastic surgery done to reduce the scars. Or even to change some of his features a bit."

"Weezer told me he had his nose reduced. That it wasn't proportional to the rest of his face. We haven't had any luck finding the surgeon who did the work. The man who sold him the knife came forward. So did the man who works on his car, which is apparently a classic—a 'fifty-eight Chevy Bel Air coupe with original two-tone paint. He might actually be the car nut he was passing himself off as six years ago. But doctors . . . no. They'll claim privilege and hide their connections with the lowest scum on the planet." Then he sighed. "Not all of them. One of my best friends is a doctor. But . . . overall . . ."

Dia looked exasperated. "This is going to bug me. It isn't . . . it isn't that I think I know him. Or that I think I don't. It's that the things about this guy that are familiar aren't. . . . Feh. I don't even know what I'm trying to say. My brain is saying, 'Yes, you've seen him,' but damn, Brig. I sure can't think of anywhere that I have. He's a guy with brown eyes and dark brown hair. In the video he looked like he weighed between four and five hundred pounds. He seems like he ought to be easy as hell to spot. But I'm dead certain that I haven't. Yet he still seems familiar."

"Think peripherally," Brig told her. "Someone who is where EMTs go. You folks have a favorite restaurant or bar? A shop where you pick up supplies for your after-hours activities?" He watched her face, waiting for something to click. He was sure it would; that she would sift through the places she went and the people she saw every day, and suddenly someone would step out of the shadows and reveal himself as Forbes.

But that click never happened. Instead he saw increasing frustration on her face. "He looks a little bit like someone else," she said. "But not much. Not even enough for me to figure out who he reminds me of."

"Nothing, then?" He put the crime book back on his desk and leaned back, looking at Dia and thinking that she was pretty. And that he wanted to sneak her into a back room and have his way with her, even though he was too sore to move. She had that effect on him.

It wasn't what he ought to be thinking about. But

right at the moment, getting her naked was the clearest image in his mind.

"No, nothing," she said. "I'm sorry."

For an instant his mind collided with the picture of her he had there, and he thought that he wasn't sorry a bit.

But of course, that wasn't what she was talking about.

"Right," he agreed. "So maybe Forbes is a sort of EMT fanboy—a groupie who likes to watch all the machines and sirens and people running around in a state of organized chaos. Maybe he likes to see all the blood and hear the screaming. Maybe most of the time he isn't looking for the kill as much as he's looking for the response it brings. Like stirring an anthill with a stick."

"Maybe," she agreed. "Maybe he wants to see himself on television. A lot of his accidents have brought out reporters and camera crews."

Brig nodded. "Or maybe it's just the thrill of playing God. Saving life. Taking it away."

Dia thought about that. There was an element of Godness in what she did. When she had a good win in a bad case, Tyler had on occasion referred to her as Para-God, which invariably pissed Ryan off—so Tyler didn't do it too often. It bugged her a little, but there was a kernel of truth in the nickname. She stepped into situations where people were in the process of dying, and she fought to bring them back to life. Sometimes she succeeded.

She thought of Forbes. Sometimes she succeeded when everyone would have been a whole lot better off if she had failed.

Of course, most of the time it wasn't anywhere near as dramatic as that. Most of the time she ran nuisance calls, pointless calls, situations where people had no idea what an emergency response system was for. . . .

"Maybe," she said softly, "he gets bored, and he just likes to see the big ones." She looked into Brig's eyes, and he realized that something about that had hit her strangely. "Let me look at the photos again. All of them. The pictures you had of our guys, too."

He passed the crime book across to her. And she pulled them out, and sat there placing pieces of paper across various features in each photograph.

"The guys call Tyler the Big One," she said after a minute. "It isn't obscene, though your first guess would probably be that it was."

"Why the Big One?"

"Because he has this uncanny knack for predicting when we're going to have something awful happen. He isn't always right—"

"He'd be an idiot if he was," Brig muttered.

"—but he's right often enough that people have noticed."

"And you didn't think to tell me this?"

"Didn't cross my mind. I mean, half of us have prediction systems going. My favorite is Three-F Night."

"Which is?"

"Friday night, first of the month, full moon."

Brig nodded. "Start of the weekend, government money has gone out, and people have enough light to see while they're in places where they shouldn't be, doing things they shouldn't be doing. Right. I use that one, too. It's a pretty reliable indicator of when more bad things are going to land on my desk. Rapes, stabbings, shootings." He studied her. "But you don't think Tyler's system is like that?"

"I don't even think it was a system to begin with. One day he said, 'It's too quiet. Something bad is going to happen. We're going to get a call on the Big One.' And fifteen, maybe twenty minutes later, we did. And it was huge—a multicar pileup in the intersection in front of the Winn-Dixie. . . ."

"Car wreck."

"Yeah. Not one of the ones on your chart. Before the first one of those—but it could have been one, I guess." She looked pale. "But he was with us the whole time."

"You're sure he predicted it?"

"Not completely sure. Fairly certain. I mean, nobody really thought anything about it at the time. I've said things like that, too, and sometimes something would happen. Most times it wouldn't."

"What was different about Tyler, then?"

"Well, he did it again maybe a week later. Said he felt the Big One coming, and we all got called out within half an hour. Sooner, even, I think."

"And then?"

She leaned forward and clasped her hands on top of the book in her lap. Half closed her eyes. "The same people were around, and a few of us noticed. There were the usual woo-woo noises idiots make, you know. But we all remembered it, because it had been twice in a row, and . . . and both times the accidents were really big."

"Another car accident."

She nodded slowly. Her eyes had gotten rounder, and her skin had gone waxy and pale. "He started making a little bit of a production out of it, then. Silliness, you know. That sort of black humor that fills in when you can't react the way normal people react. You can't scream, or fall apart weeping, or run away, so you laugh."

He was almost holding his breath, but he managed to say, "Yeah, we get a lot of that in Homicide, too."

"Right. Well, he did this sort of magician routine one day. Some of the guys who were going on duty were playing cards in the break room, waiting for a couple of our late trucks to come in. And he grabbed a card, closed his eyes, held it to his head, and said, "I feel the Big One coming.""

"Another accident."

She gave him a funny little smile. "His mouth had no more than shut than we got a call. Slip-and-fall at a twenty-four-hour department store. Everyone is giving him shit as we run out the door, because a slip-and-fall has never been, and will never be, the Big One, right?"

"Right."

"We take the call and are no more than two blocks out when a county-wide all-available-units call goes out. That terrible wreck over by the high school. Bunch of students involved—it was a nightmare."

"I didn't have that one on my map," he said.

"You might want to put it there," she said after a moment. And then her face twisted with pain. "Tyler? Tyler is the sweetest guy I know. I mean, it isn't him doing this, obviously. But they could be . . . brothers, maybe? Brown hair, brown eyes, something sort of similar about the mouths. Cousins? He could know in advance—only I just can't believe it."

She shook her head, and he watched her clench her hands into white-knuckled fists.

"He's always there for our patients. He's careful and conscientious, and after that day and the business with the cards, he never got silly about it again. It was like he'd scared himself. Now one or the other of us will ask him. Like, 'Feel anything out there, Tyler?' But we don't joke about it. Because, well . . ." She shrugged and turned her face to the wall beside her. He could see her taking deep breaths, fighting off tears, doing everything she could just to hang on and get through the moment.

"He ever been right since?"

"Yes," she said.

And then she turned to him. "He didn't kill Kelly. He didn't have anything to do with that at all. He and Kelly were great friends. He couldn't have done that to her. It isn't possible."

"He could have fit into the wardrobe a lot easier than Forbes, and if they're working together, it would explain how Forbes knows your schedule and has such clear access to you."

"No."

"Yes. It might be possible that he's involved. I'm not saying that he is, but it's something we can look into." He put his hand over hers and said, "I've been over his record, and there is *nothing* in it that would support this. We have him making statements, and bad things happening, but at the moment that's purely circumstantial evidence."

He didn't think it was a fluke, though. He didn't want to upset her, but if Tyler was accurately predicting only vehicular wrecks involving explosives, odds were hugely in favor of his having been involved in them.

Dia looked miserable. "He's been accurately predicting big accidents that involve motor vehicles." She looked at his wall chart. "And explosives. He hasn't said something before every one of them. But . . . most, I think." She hung her head. "I feel sick."

Brig looked at her and wanted to give her some hope. He could understand her anguish. He and Stan depended on each other for their very lives—it would be like finding out that in his spare time, Stan was blowing people up. Working both sides of the street. What the hell was up with that?

He tried to give her a little comfort. "He might be a genuine psychic."

She stared at him, disbelief on her face. "You're joking, right? Please tell me you're joking."

"I'm not. I've dealt with people who had genuine psychic ability—well, *one*. I don't think that happens often, but I'm convinced it happens sometimes." He shrugged. "And for the moment, what you've presented isn't hard evidence against Tyler. It's circumstantial until and unless there is some sort of physical evidence or eyewitness account linking him to a crime." He thought for a moment. "We'll have him come back in to go over his statements again. If we ask the right questions, he might be inclined to tell us something he doesn't mean to."

Dia was still for a moment. Then she said, "Kelly would have opened her window for Tyler. If he'd tapped on it, I mean."

"While she was naked?"

"Well . . . no. Probably not."

"And even if she would have, that still doesn't explain how she got it open without setting off the alarm."

"Maybe she let him in the front door. I'd shown her how to use the alarm."

"Maybe," Brig agreed.

Stan stopped in. "Any luck?"

"Maybe," Brig said.

Brig fished out the picture of Tyler he'd had enlarged preparatory to taking it and the other EMTs' photos in to Weezer. He studied it, and studied the much smaller pictures of Forbes.

Dia was right: They didn't look much alike. He started mentally rearranging features to see if he could imagine turning one face into the other. Nose would have to have been narrowed. Eyebrows lifted and reshaped. Chin and jaw reworked. He didn't think they were brothers. He might buy half brothers. Or cousins.

A blood relationship between the two didn't matter, he decided. The connection between them could be anything if it would give a judge justification to issue a warrant for a search of Frakes's home.

"We need more background on Tyler Frakes," he told Stan. "We need to see how he connects to Forbes."

Stan looked startled. "Really?"

"Apparently Mr. Frakes had recently demonstrated an uncanny knack for predicting large, messy traffic accidents within half an hour of their occurrence."

A happy smile spread across Stan's face. "*Really* . . . ? If we could bring him in and get him to give up Forbes, that would be . . . sweet."

"We need more than what we have," Brig said.

"Not enough for a warrant?"

"Nah. So far we just have circumstantial evidence. It's pretty compelling . . . but not good enough."

"Okay," Stan said. "We'll get him down here and see what we can find."

"Let's do it," Brig said.

Stan raised his eyebrows. "When I said, 'We'll,' I wasn't referring to you and me. You're not here today," Stan said. "Shorts and a T-shirt? My man, it will not pass. And you have Forbes's would-be next target with you, when the official story is that she's tucked away in a safe place."

Brig sighed and said, "We'll get out of here. Just do right by us, okay?"

"It will be done."

They went shopping—nothing fancy, just things like toiletries, underwear, and a few changes of clothes, plus a couple of critical purchases that Dia explained she couldn't live without: a replacement bag, a good pair of trauma scissors, and a stethoscope to replace those she'd lost when her car burned. Dia enjoyed the mundane simplicity of walking down the aisles with Brig, looking at things, talking about nothing in particular, pretending for a little while that her life was no more complicated than making decisions about new shampoo and the right toothpaste.

Brig insisted on paying for things—he said he had lots of paid sick days and vacation and hadn't been spending money on much of anything lately. Dia didn't. She wouldn't be paid for the days she missed. She had combined vacation/sick days, and she used them as she got them, taking vacations faithfully each year.

She found herself wishing she hadn't, even though she'd enjoyed the mountain climbing out west and her trip to Alaska to go kayaking with some of the other EMTs. All that fun wasn't doing much for her right then.

She was going to have to buy a new car. Well, not new. But she was going to have to scrape together the money for another used car, and there would be no insurance to cover the demise of the old one. All she had on it was the state's required liability and PIP, and even that had cost her over three hundred dollars a month.

South Florida was the worst place in the world to drive, people told her. She'd heard there were actually places in California that were more expensive. But she was outside her budget where she was—she didn't need to know about worse. Trying to figure out where the money for another car would come from, she found herself getting more and more depressed.

"Hey," Brig said, putting an arm around her shoulders. "Had enough shopping?"

"Definitely," she told him. "We need to do something that has nothing to do with spending money. It's depressing me."

"Why?" He laughed, and kissed her forehead in a gesture that melted her inside.

"Because I don't have any. And I keep thinking about my car. I'm going to have to get a new one—and I had that car for eight years. It was completely paid for; it was in good shape; I made sure to keep up with all its needs. And now I'm going to have to have payments again. Or one big lump that I can use to buy some ancient, ratty beater that was somebody else's problem." She sighed. "If I get new, there's the insurance leap. If I get old, it'll be a bunch of money up front. Either way . . ."

He stopped walking and turned her around to face him. He took her chin in his hand and said, "Is there anything you can do about this problem right now?"

"No. But—"

"Are you making the situation better by worrying about it?"

"No. But—"

"No buts. Let it go. You don't know what the future may bring. My buddy Bob Scotty is reliable. He could fix you up with something older but decent. A brand-new, wonderful car may rain out of the heavens and fall in your parking space. You might not need a car. Some friend could give you a car he had sitting in his garage." He grinned at her. "I see all sorts of good possibilities."

"Why?"

"Because I'm with you," he said, and turned them both around and aimed her toward the checkout. "Remarkable the effect you have on me. But you need food," he said. "We'll eat. We'll go home. We'll tell each other stories about our childhoods and all the trouble we each got into. It will make for an entertaining evening, and maybe after our pain meds kick in, we can do things that hurt in good ways before we go to sleep."

She smiled at him. She was, she thought, falling far too much in love with him. It seemed like a good idea to be in love with him—and she didn't trust that impulse. But it also seemed like a terrible risk for him, and the idea that she was risking his life as well as her own terrified her.

Forbes had already killed one man she loved, as well as the woman she considered her best female friend. She couldn't stand the idea of anything more happening to Brig because of his association with her.

She simply didn't know what to do about keeping him safe.

Larry lay in his bed staring up at the ceiling. He had his hands tucked behind his head, and he was grinning.

It had gone just perfectly. He'd bypassed Dia's security system and gone in through the unlocked window in Kelly's room. He'd written a note on the bathroom mirror in big block letters, then waited patiently in Kelly's wardrobe.

He'd had a bad moment in that wardrobe, though. It was claustrophobically tight, and it got worse when Mac showed up.

Larry could see Mac's ghost, standing *through* Larry's own body, staring down into Larry's eyes. In that pitch blackness, he glowed like . . . like . . . like a poisonous mushroom in a cave. He was saying something, but no sound reached Larry's ears. He looked . . . dead, his throat slashed clear to his spine, his arm off. But he was smiling.

Larry knew Mac couldn't do anything to him, but Larry also couldn't stop his heart from racing or his skin from prickling and sweating. He couldn't make himself not want to run away.

When Mac's ghost finally faded, Larry had never been more grateful for anything in his life.

There was, eventually, a fuss. And then the fuss died down, and Kelly came into her room, and he let her tell them she'd be out soon. Then he'd killed her, and left his note, locked the door, and slipped back out the window, making sure that the alarm system was back on before he fled.

He'd considered raping Kelly, but he wasn't about rape. Rape was low—a form of cowardice, really, that had nothing to do with balance.

Larry kept giving Dia chances to choose to live a balanced life. To come to him, to lean on him . . . to *see* him.

She kept turning away.

The time was coming when he would have to choose for her. Either she would come to him, or she would die.

He preferred to live his life in balance—for every step he took in the light, he took a step in the darkness. He was both hero and villain. He carried his own weight in the world. But he was struggling to offset her behavior; she kept pushing the light to the detriment of darkness, and he had to walk more in darkness to compensate. He wasn't willing to continue to make that sacrifice.

It was only when he had discovered the Tao that he understood, at last, how he could be both a hero and a villain inside—and how it was right that he should be. He came to understand that what he wanted to do, what he *needed* to do, he needed because it was right, not because there was something wrong with him.

The universe needed his balance. It needed him, and the critical services he supplied. And Dia needed him, too.

One way or the other.

He knew her, and because of that, he knew where she would be. When she would be there. Whom she would be with. He'd just gotten word from the captain, and everything else fell into place for him.

She got one last chance to make the right choice.

He had the bomb that would help her make her decision.

Chapter 22

Brig and Dia were halfway through a movie and dinner eaten on the couch, but the movie wasn't worth watching, and when she turned to him in one particularly slow part of it and asked him, "So how *did* you end up leaving Montana?" he was happy enough to turn the damned thing off.

"You really want to know?"

"I do," she said. "I was born here. Lived my whole life here. I want to know what sort of insanity would drive someone to move here voluntarily."

He raised an eyebrow. "Love," he said. "Or what I thought love was. We had cattle, my family did, and a nice spread of land. And a handful of boys who could help my father branding cattle and stretching barbed wire and digging postholes and doing all the feeding and veterinarying and everything else that comes with the territory. But it's not work that pays a living wage some years, running cattle. So most of us had other jobs, too. Mine was policing. I liked it well enough. Being a beat cop, you're outdoors as much as you want to be, and I knew the people where I lived and they knew me. It worked."

She gave him a dreamy smile. "I can see you on horseback on a ranch. You seem to fit there so much better than you do in a police car."

"Well, your job is your job, but it isn't who you are. Inside, I am and always will be a cowboy. I'm a good detective; I work hard at it; I know it matters. But it isn't who I am."

"And yet you're still doing it."

It was a point, and one he'd been giving a lot of thought to lately. "Anyway," he said, "I met a girl. Pretty, sharp, sort of a traditional girl, I thought. I could see us settling down and raising a family together. But she had other dreams. She hated the ranch, but she thought police work was interesting, and she loved Sonny Crockett—you ever see *Miami Vice?*"

Dia made a face. "A couple of times, I suppose. On reruns, maybe. It wasn't something that stuck in my mind."

"It stuck in hers. She thought Miami would be the most glamorous place in the world to live, and I'd made detective by then. And Miami didn't interest me, but I thought to give her a taste of the sun and the beaches and the palm trees, we could try Fort Lauderdale, which I thought might be less of a crime haven."

"We all make mistakes," Dia said.

"Oh, indeed we do," he answered. He hoped the fervency in his voice didn't sound as crazed to her as it did to him.

"So you came here, and . . . didn't have your family."

"Being pregnant and being a mom were not glamorous. Plastic surgery was glamorous. Nightclubs were glamorous. Fancy cars and expensive restaurants, designer clothes. I got a big raise by moving here—at least on paper. Our cost of living skyrocketed, too, though, and she couldn't do all the expensive things she wanted to do, and didn't want to live the life I thought we'd planned." He shrugged. "She was pretty, and she didn't have any trouble attracting men who were happy to spend money on her."

"She ran around on you."

"She ran like Flo-Jo."

"Who?"

He sighed. "Florence Griffith Joyner. Astonishing female runner. Gold medalist, 1988 Summer Olympics—she still holds the world records in the hundred meter and two hundred meters. Or did the last time I checked. She died of cavernous hemangioma ten years after she won her gold."

"You sound like a fan."

"I am . . . *was*. Watching her run was like watching someone defy gravity by sheer force of will. It was beautiful." He glanced over at Dia. "But by not knowing who she was, you totally wrecked my great analogy."

"But now, thanks to your great analogy, I know who she was."

He grinned a little. "There's that."

"So . . . you moved here, and then you stayed here, and now you're still here. And I can see the first, and maybe the second. But why have you stayed?"

"I don't know. Maybe because I'm always in the middle of something I can't put down, because nobody else will go after it the way I will. I keep looking back to the mountains, and to my folks and their ranch, but there's never a good time to just put this down and walk away. I have to know how things end."

Dia said, "I wish I didn't get that. I do, though. I almost never manage to see how things end, and when I do, it's only because they end both badly and fast." She leaned back on his couch and studied him. "Things don't really ever end until you die, you know. You want to make a change, there's never going to be a time when you can make a clean break of it. You'll always be leaving things undone. So really, if there's never a good time, there's never a bad time, either. You do it when you're ready."

He was watching her. "I'm not quite ready. Yet."

She started to say something, but his cell phone rang right then, and she waved it off.

Caller ID said it was Stan. He said, "Tell me something good."

"Sorry, man. Not happening today. Tyler Frakes isn't related to Sinclair Forbes. He doesn't appear to be associated in any way with Forbes. He is, in fact, the busiest little bastard on the planet, and I honest-to-God don't see how he could find the time to do more than he already does. Are they *all* like this?"

"Like what?"

"He's a full-time EMT, which means he takes a lot of continuing education to keep his job. Add to that the fact that he's a part-time dive instructor, and a volunteer Big Brother who makes sure he takes time for his Little Brother. He helps coach the Little League team the kid plays on. He dates regularly, but apparently not any one girl for long—they get a look at his calendar and move on, I'd guess."

"His calendar?"

"Funny story. I dropped by his house. Social call, just wanted to see how he was doing and if he'd remembered anything else about Kelly or anything that might help us. He invited me in, made me coffee, showed me around. I looked at his calendar, and I tell you, this is a man who can account for every minute of his time since the beginning of the year. And before that. He saw me looking through previous months on the calendar, and told me he hung on to the old ones because they were sort of like diaries. He could remember what he did each day, just because of the entries."

"Compulsive."

"Busy," Stan said. "And frighteningly organized. If he hung out with a psychopathic bomb builder, there would be entries that said, 'Visit PSB—nine P.M. to eleven P.M., bring explosives and cookies.' Trust me on this."

"So you're saying he's not even inadvertently linked?"

"I'm saying his mother and little brother stopped by to give him some homemade cookies, and I got to talk to the mother. He gets his energy from her. I'm so tired just from being in the same room with these two people that I need to sleep for a week. And to answer your question, if this guy has anything to do with blowing up cars, my great-grandmother is out robbing banks."

"Nice old lady, your great-grandma?"

"Salt of the earth," Stan said. "Abso-fucking-lutely salt of the earth. Only speaks Chinese, is four and a half feet tall, and weighs about eighty pounds dressed in her winter clothes, makes a great bird's nest soup."

Silence hung between them for a moment. "Well, Dia will be happy," Brig told him, and sighed. "She's been upset about the idea that he might be involved."

"We're still digging," Stan said. "Just because I can't stand to let a lead go at this point, when we have so few. But—gut here—he has nothing at all to do with this."

"And the predictions?"

"No clue. I don't believe in psychics."

"Have a good night, Stan," Brig said, and dropped the cell phone on the table, wondering if he looked as haggard and weary as he felt.

"Tyler seems to be clean," he told Dia. "Because of his seeming foreknowledge of the accidents and his close connection with you, we'll continue looking into him. But Stan's impression is that he has nothing to do with this. From my own experience, Stan's gut checks are usually right."

She leaned back on the couch and he saw her fingers relax. "I didn't believe he would voluntarily be a part of this." She smiled at him wearily. "Brig, none of them would. They're the brothers I never had. They're my family."

"I know." In spite of how much he hurt, and how much he suspected she hurt, he wrapped his arms around her and held her. "The problem from my perspective," he said, "is that sometimes families do some horrifying things to each other. I've seen it too many times to be willing to trust. We have to keep digging, even in the places where you don't want to dig. It might be that one of your other colleagues doesn't realize that he knows Forbes."

She seemed lost and fragile. She didn't say anything. She just looked at him with those wide, sad, scared eyes.

I'll save you, he thought. *No matter what, I'll save you from the bastard who's after you.*

By the third day of mostly hiding out in Brig's apartment, Dia was about to go crazy. The two of them were feeling better, and while he still couldn't hear out of one ear, everything else was getting back to normal for him. He had the most amazing collection of bruises she'd ever seen, but the department had cleared him to come back in to work at the desk.

Dia felt good enough to work, too. And she needed the money; her meager savings wouldn't get her through a whole month.

She wanted to get back to work. Brig didn't like the idea, but Brig didn't have her bills to pay, either.

And she needed to be with the guys. She needed to reconnect with them, and mourn Kelly with people who knew and loved her. She understood that there could be some danger in doing that—but she had never been threatened at the station, or while out on calls. She'd never had anything at all threaten her while she was doing her job. The danger had always been at home, where she expected to feel safe.

She called the station, telling herself it was just to talk. Just to hear friends.

The captain answered.

"This is Dia," she said. "Ryan or Sherm or Howie or anyone around?"

"All on calls," he said. "At the moment you have me and Clearwater." Clearwater was the day-shift lieutenant.

"Figures." She heard what she'd said to him, and cringed. "I didn't mean it that way, Perry. I was just hoping to talk to the guys, and hear what will be happening with Kelly."

"Nobody told you about Kelly?"

"I haven't heard from anybody."

"I told them not to bother you." He laughed a little. "I just didn't expect them to listen to me. Kelly's parents are holding the funeral for her on Saturday. They'll have the wake tonight. I thought you knew. I know we'd all love to see you; everyone from the station will be there."

She said, "I will be, too." She hesitated for a moment, then said, "I have my cell phone with me. Tell the guys I asked them to call me, would you? I feel so alone."

"Where are you?" he asked her.

Her pulse started to race; her heart started to hammer. It was probably an innocent question, but she couldn't allow herself to think of any questions as innocent. She had to assume that everyone was her enemy until she could find the person who truly was.

And then she got hold of herself. Sinclair Forbes was only a couple years older than she was. Captain Hall, who had been her partner after Mac died and before she moved up, was in his early fifties, and talking about retirement. He had a wife and two kids in college, and a Basset hound, a bad sportfishing habit that he supported with difficulty, and hopes of grandchildren before he got too old to enjoy them. She could trust him. She knew she could trust him.

She paced back and forth. "I'm not telling anyone where I am," she said. "I don't want to put the person I'm staying with in any danger." And then, although she knew she shouldn't, she said, "I need to get back to work, Perry. I have to be able to buy myself a car, and pay rent and utilities, and find someplace else to live. I can't sponge off someone else."

"If you need a place to stay for a while," the captain said, "both of our kids have rooms that aren't being used. The wife calls them guest rooms, but we don't have guests. You can stay in one while you get your money together." He said, "I've always been proud of you, Dia. You've been with us a long time; I've watched you grow up and go through hard times, and I couldn't be any more proud of you if you were one of my own kids. If you need help, you tell someone. I'll see that you have help. We all will."

Her eyes filled and she couldn't get any sounds to come out of her mouth. That was the way she felt about them. All of them. She finally managed to squeak out a strangled, "Thank you."

"You're family."

I love you, she thought. "You, too," she said, wishing she could say what she felt; wishing that workplace regulations and personal boundaries didn't stand in the way of her telling him.

When she hung up the phone, she had a tentative schedule. She'd told Perry she wanted to run it by the police before she committed to it, considering the possible risk her presence might cause to all involved.

She didn't think Brig would be happy. But she would take every precaution. She was willing to turn her life upside down to stay safe. She did, however, have to work. Unemployed destitution was not an option.

"You told your captain to put you back on the schedule?" Brig couldn't believe what he was hearing. "When someone you work with might be trying to kill you?"

She said, "I'll give you the possibility that someone I work with has accidentally given information about me to Forbes. But everything you've pursued on Tyler has been a bust, right?"

"Yes. We cannot find anything connecting him to any of the crimes, except for the fact that in a joking fashion he may or may not have predicted several of them, with no specific descriptions and with imperfect reliability."

"Right. And no one else is a genuine suspect, either." He nodded.

"You've gone over my colleagues from top to bottom."

"I can't definitely rule them out. We've been limited to meeting with your fellow EMTs individually or in pairs at odd times because of their erratic schedules; no one has given us any cause to be suspicious. All of them seem to have completely open lives."

"So where else are you looking?" She was so defiant. Almost as if she blamed him for not trusting the men she worked with.

"We're looking," he said, maintaining calm he didn't feel, "into every possible lead. We have several. We'll find him."

She shook off the defiance, smiled at him, and sat at his kitchen table. "I know you will. I have faith. But in the meantime I have rent to pay, Brig. Bills, a car to buy, about two hundred dollars in savings, a checking account that's down to the last twenty or thirty bucks."

"I could give you money."

"No. You can't. And I have to maintain my good credit, what little of it there is, or I won't be able to get another place to rent, or buy another car. And I'm out of time. I have no sick days or vacation days left to use. I'm not one of those people who can afford to take off until everything is better."

"You could always marry me," Brig said, and the moment the words were out of his mouth, he wished to hell he could stuff them back in and swallow them.

Because her eyes went wide and her jaw dropped, and her head started shaking side to side. For a stretch of time that seemed like forever but that probably wasn't, she sputtered and gasped. Then she said, "We're in the middle of major trauma." She stood up and started to pace. "Bad idea. Bad. You and I have had so much happen to us lately—and me especially. Everyone says that you should never make a life-altering decision in the middle of a disaster, because the odds are good that you'll make a mistake."

She stopped pacing and stared at him. "Forbes killed the last husband I had."

She started pacing again. "No. No, no—he's killed Mac, and he's killed Kelly, and he's tried to kill you."

"Whoa," he said. "Dia. Hold on. I know who he is. I know what he's doing. I'm a big boy. I can take care of myself."

She turned to face him again, biting her lip. Pale. "Look, cowboy. Mac was an Air Force PJ. Nobody makes men any tougher than that. He knew Forbes, too. He knew what Forbes was doing back when the bastard first started doing it. And Forbes succeeded in killing him, and in doing it so slickly that nobody even realized it was murder for four years. How, exactly, are you going to protect yourself from that?" She took a step closer to him, so that their faces were inches away. "How?"

"My first concern is protecting you."

"It isn't my first concern," she said. "My first concern is knowing that you're not going to get killed. And that doesn't answer my question, either." She took another step closer, so that their bodies touched. So that her face pressed against the side of his neck. He could feel her body, muscles coiled, trembling; he could feel the heat of her. She kept her arms tight against her sides. "Because I love you," she whispered. "Maybe I shouldn't. Maybe you aren't who I need. But you're who I want."

He swallowed hard and pulled her tight against him. "I love you, too. And you wouldn't have to marry me. Not right away. You could live with me, and I'd take care of you."

"Not while he's out there," she said. "Not while he could take you away from me. I need to get back on my feet and put some distance between you and me, Brig, at least until you find him, so that you won't be his target anymore." She didn't pull away from him. Instead she relaxed into him. But her words were carving distance between the two of them just as plainly as if she were running away. "He finds out where people are weak," she said. "And the funny thing about our weaknesses is that they're almost always the parts of ourselves that we don't recognize. He'll find a way to you that you haven't prepared against. Just like he wrecked your car instead of mine. You were watching me, so you forgot to watch you." Finally her arms wrapped around him. "That would make me your weakness."

He hadn't meant to ask her to marry him, but once he'd said it, he knew he meant it. He loved her. He wanted to be with her. He wanted the two of them to have a future, and as he saw it, the best way to make sure that they did was to keep her close. To keep all his eggs in one basket, and watch that basket.

And she was rejecting that.

"You aren't my weakness." She was, really, because he would do anything to protect her, including take a bullet for her. But he couldn't see her that way. "You're . . . Dia, you're *joy*. You're my *passion*. You're my *hunger*. We belong together—always."

At last she pulled out of his embrace. "I won't let you be the next one who dies."

"It's my job to protect you," he said. "Not your job to protect me."

"I love you," she said. "This isn't about jobs, but if it were, that would fit, too, because my job is to save lives. I'm going to save yours by not marrying you and by not living with you. Not now. Not while he's out there."

She turned away from him. "I'm tired. I'm worried. And I'm going to go ahead in to work tomorrow. I'm calling the station to have whoever's on put me back on the schedule." She was staring down at her feet, her thumbs jammed into her pockets. "The captain offered to let me stay in one of his kids' rooms for a while, rent-free. I can't take him up on his offer, either. I'm going to have to come up with something on my own that won't risk anyone."

"The mystical free place where you can live while not putting anyone else at risk isn't going to happen. You're going to have to stay somewhere; you can't stay at your place, and you're better off here than with some unarmed, unprepared old guy and his wife who will provide no barrier between Forbes and you."

"I'm going to call the station. Tell them I need a ride in tomorrow, see if they can have one of the guys pick me up."

"One of the *guys?* Are you trying to get yourself killed?"

She walked over to the phone. "Yeah, that's what I'm trying to do. You and your partner have been investigating my friends—my second family—and you've come up with nothing. We know we're after Forbes—none of my guys is Forbes; they sure as hell aren't going to *give* me to Forbes. So relax. You're getting call-ins from people all over offering tips, and one of those tips will pan out. Somebody has seen the bastard; somebody knows where he is and what he's up to. Somebody will sell him out when the price is right."

"You can't know that."

"I can't know *anything*. Except that I have to get back to work."

"Fine," he said. "Get back to work. I'll drop you off and pick you up."

Dia's cell phone rang. She glared at Brig as she answered it. An angry smile spread across her face, and she said, "It's the guys."

And went into the bedroom and closed the door to take the call.

Chapter 23

Brig had asked Dia to marry him, and all she wanted to do was say yes. It was all she could think about as she stormed into his bedroom and closed the door behind herself.

Howie was on the phone, and with him in the background, what sounded like the rest of Alpha shift. She didn't really want to talk to him, or to any of them, right then. She wanted to tell Brig, *If you could promise me you wouldn't die, I'd marry you tonight.*

But Brig couldn't promise that. And she needed to draw a line between him and her, so that he stopped being in the target zone. If Forbes was listening to someone at the station, she wanted to make sure he heard the right thing.

She told Howie, "Hey, I can talk now."

Howie said, "Captain told us you were ready to get back to work."

"I'm going stir-crazy. Bossy cop thinks the best thing to do with me is to keep me in a cage."

"I thought . . . um, we all thought . . . you and bossy cop were a . . . a *thing.*"

"No. We were a stressed-out accident, and my urgent, urgent need is to get into my own place. Fast as possible. Also, to get a replacement car."

"Can't help you with the place," Howie said. "I'm sharing mine with Stolhnik from Beta shift, and it's a studio. It's way cozier than I like. But hang on." And then, though he was muffled a bit by his hand partially covering the mouthpiece of the phone, she heard him say, "Dia needs a place to stay. The cop is apparently not a keeper."

Low voices.

Ryan came on the phone. "You're not coming back to work yet."

"Yeah, I am," she said. "Life isn't free, you know?"

"It's a bad idea. You need to be more concerned about your own survival, Dia. We miss you—don't get me wrong. The guy who's subbing for you is . . . Well, he's not you; let me put it that way. But if the cop thinks you should stay with him, you should. And if he thinks you shouldn't come back to work yet, you shouldn't."

"Nice to talk to you, too, Ryan," she growled.

He laughed. "You know I'm on your side. But . . . I happen to think that your side would include your living to keep defending it. If the guy could get to Kelly, and if he could get to Detective Hafferty, he can get to you. If you come back to work or find a place to live where you don't have someone watching your back, you're just going to make it easy on him."

She flopped back on Brig's bed and sighed. She could hear him stomping around out in the kitchen, clattering things. He sounded pissed. He had a right to be.

"So I take it you're not going to offer me a room?"

Ryan didn't answer her for a moment. "Don't get me wrong," he said. "You'd be a great roommate; I have no doubt. But . . . ah . . . your last roommate ended up dead, and I heard that your current one nearly did. And I have an irrational attachment to my own skin. Besides, the old guy I lease my room from won't even let me have visitors. He wrote that into the lease. He doesn't like noise."

"I know, I know. I wasn't really asking. You said what I told Brig. That I shouldn't be living with *any-body.* I'm a death magnet."

"You have some crazed, obsessive recluse after you. Stay with the guy with a gun, and let your credit go downhill for a little while if it has to. Good credit is going to be worthless if you're dead."

He was making sense, and she didn't want him to make sense. She wanted to know that she could keep Brig out of the line of fire.

"Stop nagging her," Tyler said in the background. "You sound like her maiden aunt. Gimme that."

And Dia found herself talking to Tyler.

"Your temp replacement sucks," he said. "He has hands of stone. He can't start an IV in a moving truck; he can't hear a blood pressure or get a pulse in a moving truck. He came in here from Pompano, and we're going to be *so* damned happy to send him back."

She smiled a little. "You need me, then?"

"The patients do. This guy's only one third of an EMT. He's the *E.*"

"I'll be in tomorrow," she said. "Tell the captain to confirm me on the schedule." She looked at her watch. "I have to go. All my clothes are gone and I need a dress. I've got to get ready for the wake."

"You're going? We'll all see you there, then."

"Tell Howie thanks for calling."

Tyler said, "I will. And all the rest of the guys say hi, but we'll see you later. They can tell you themselves."

Larry put the cats out and shut the door behind them. They didn't know it, but they wouldn't be coming back in again. Sinclair Lawrence Forbes was going away.

Shadow and sunlight were mixing again; he was bringing himself back into balance. He was going to end the double life he'd led, and shed both of his alter egos. He had a new life already waiting for him. A new name, new papers, a new past—and as Jon Howards, in Taos, New Mexico, he would live in perfect balance.

Tonight he started resetting the scales.

He stood naked in the center of the room. Slowly, carefully, with great ceremony, he pulled off the prosthetics that made his cheeks and face broader and created the massive double chin. He'd had eye, nose, and forehead prosthetics made when he had the film team make the suit for him, but they had proven too difficult to wear publicly for any length of time. He'd compensated for skipping some of the facial prosthetics by wearing a long, shaggy brown wig that he'd worked hard to make look real.

When the few prosthetics he did wear were gone, he stripped out of the fat suit. It was difficult—donning the skin of his shadow self, the man he would have been had not Dia intervened, required a great deal of physical strength, determination, and dedication. So did shedding that skin. He'd had the creators of the suit make it in pieces so that he could handle it alone, instead of with a team of dressers, but even so, dressing in it, moving in it, and working with it required a tremendous amount of effort.

He would miss the sense of presence for a while. But Jon Howards would be a heavy man—naturally heavy. Not as heavy as Larry's Forbes alter ego. Heavier than his other self, though.

He left the fat suit where it lay. It would be a fine way of giving the finger to the police after he was gone. They'd find the old man, they'd find the suit, they'd find the bomb room. And a few other surprises, too.

But not until he was ready for them to. He'd drop them a letter in the mail on the way out the door in the morning.

For the moment, however, he had places to be and things to do.

He wasn't happy about it, but Brig took Dia to the wake with him. The ride over was grim. They were barely speaking to each other. He didn't understand how the two of them had gone so wrong so quickly. He hated it. And he didn't know how to fix it.

She was angry with him because he wanted to protect her. He was angry with her because she didn't think he could, and his anger was, he had to admit, a testosterone-driven response. She was challenging his manhood. He hadn't been neutered; she loved him, and he loved her, and the need to protect was still built into him, and he could not understand why she couldn't see that, or why she wouldn't accommodate herself to the idea of letting someone else watch out for her. He wasn't telling her she shouldn't take responsibility for her own safety. Far from it. But he wanted to have her let him be the second layer of protection.

The wake was being held in a private residence—the home of the doctor who had been Kelly's on-again, off-again lover. Apparently her parents had known of the relationship and been comfortable enough with it to permit that final intimacy.

Brig parked out in the street. Uniformed cops were visible, plainclothes detectives only slightly less so. This would be the first time Dia had been in an open, public space where Forbes would expect to find her since Kelly's death. As such, the department had hopes that he would be present in person, and that they could identify him and arrest him.

Brig watched Dia slowly working her way through the crowd. He kept close as she met Kelly's parents, as she met the girlfriend and gracefully negotiated her surprise that "Sam" was Samantha and not Samuel, as she talked to women whose interest in how she had known Kelly was obviously more personal than informational. She was good at comforting people, he realized. Good at knowing what to say—in dealing with death. That was something he had never managed with any skill.

She met up with her own friends, the people she called her second family. He saw a lot of hugging, then, and more than a few tears.

Kelly looked small in the coffin. Young. Pretty, in that strange, horribly still, alien way that could be managed only by a relatively neat death and a skilled mortician. The slash across her throat was completely invisible.

Dia wept on her friends' shoulders, not on his. They all ended up in a corner together, talking, telling stories, trying to make sense of it. Meanwhile, he kept close, but scanned the crowd, hoping to see the small, wide-set brown eyes and thick lips of Forbes on one of those many faces.

He saw a couple of big men who looked possible, and he noticed colleagues taking note of the same men he'd seen, surreptitiously picking dropped cups and paper plates out of trash cans and hurrying them away.

Something. They'd get something. Forbes was there; his gut told him the bastard was close.

She'd wept with Kelly's friends. Comforted Kelly's girlfriend. It made Dia sad that Kelly hadn't felt safe enough with any of her friends to tell the truth about Sam, who seemed like a remarkably nice woman, and one who was devastated by Kelly's death.

When it became too much, Dia retreated to the corner where the guys were. When she joined them, they were telling stories about Kelly's great saves, about her moments of craziness, about the time she'd run through gunfire to get to a kid who was bleeding out, and taken a bullet herself. In the butt. They managed to laugh though tears at that.

And to find time to be angry that, somehow, the only part of that story that had hit the press was how the kid was in critical condition and not expected to live, and how the gangs were fighting because they were the American dispossessed. There had been no mention of Kelly's heroism.

"The press isn't looking for heroes anymore," Ryan said. "It has no use for them."

And Dia disagreed. "There are always stories about a kid who saved his parents or a dog who saved a drowning kid, or . . . things like that."

Sherm said, "Those aren't hero stories. They're freak stories. They're *Ripley's Believe It or Not!* played out in real life, and the people who read those stories want to be surprised by how weird the situation is, not by how moving or uplifting it is. Not by how heroes are just the everyday Joe standing next to you at the checkout line, who stepped up one day because nobody else could. Or would."

Ryan said, "The press wants victims, and it wants villains. It wants the victims so it can tell stories that sell pity and weakness, and it wants villains so it can sell fear and making excuses. Heroes sell hope. And the fact that ordinary people can be heroes sells idealism. And hope and idealism aren't on the current agenda."

Perry Hall had been listening. He nodded and added, "And white men are at the top of the list of heroes the current agenda doesn't want."

Dia was leaning against a wall. "I'll buy that white men have been made the idiots in every commercial and every sitcom," she said. "But that's Hollywood. Everyone knows Hollywood is the next bastion of evil." She laughed. "But even Hollywood loves heroes. *Everyone* loves heroes."

"Everyone used to," Perry said. "But when is the last time you read a story about a white male who risked his life to save someone else? Aside from nine-eleven?"

Dia thought about it. She hadn't read anything of the sort in ages, actually. Come to think of it, she hadn't read or seen any news in ages that emphasized any acts of heroism. She didn't trust the news anymore, admittedly. Reporter biases had become far too pervasive for her to believe anything anyone on *either* side of any issue said. Bias was bias, and right and left both stewed in it, and as far as she could tell, there was no such thing as a middle.

But she still sometimes watched one news program or another, trying to glean simple details from the ever-present slant.

Some stories that should have been in the news simply weren't there. And most of those stories were about human beings risking themselves to help others. Military troops in far-flung places rebuilding schools, restoring power and water, protecting the freedom not just of Americans but of foreigners who were trying to find their own way to freedom. People at home stepping between the helpless and the dangerous at their own risk. People who, with their own lives and courage, affirmed that the lives of others mattered. That had been news when she was a child. It briefly became news again in the wake of September 11, 2001.

And then . . . nothing.

"All I ever wanted to be when I was a kid was a

hero," Ryan said. "Superhero was my first job pick, you know."

The other men around her were nodding. "I figured I would be a cop like my dad," Sherm said. "That was as close to a superhero as I needed to get."

Howie said, "I wanted to be a ninja. I would have been really happy to be a mutated turtle ninja, but any ninja would do."

"I thought I could grow up to be Spider-Man," Tyler said. "He had the best superpowers. I spent a lot of time trying to figure out how to mutate a spider so it could bite me."

Ryan nodded. "Mutation was very important. It was all about the superpowers."

Dia had never dreamed of being a superhero. She'd wanted to be a princess, and was deeply disappointed to discover that there were no job openings in her preferred career field. Following that, she wanted to ride horses, but was too tall to be a jockey, and then to be a ballerina, but she was too tall and big-boned for that, too. Mostly, though, she hadn't wanted anything in particular. She'd simply fallen into work she liked while waiting for her life to resolve itself into something that offered a clear sign saying, "This is your purpose."

It never had. For these men, life had been a steady line from superhero to real, if invisible, hero.

"Was it the tights?" she asked.

A couple of them laughed, but it was Sherm who said, "The uniform was a part of it. But part of it was knowing that if you did those big, brave, dangerous things, people would love you."

"*Women*," Howie said. "Let's be real. The hope was that *women* would love us. We could take or leave love from the men. Mostly leave it."

Ryan agreed. "Some of that is there. But when Superman saves the day, everyone cheers. When we save the day? Well, we go home, we come back the next day, we save the day again. Sometimes we get shot at. Sometimes we get punched. We get bled on, and stuck by dirty needles, and sworn at. Sometimes we get sued. We get puked on, pissed on, shit on; we get hurt; we get killed. Hasn't been a ticker-tape parade for us yet, you know?"

"I never really thought about it," Dia said.

"You wouldn't. You're a woman. There's a whole different chemistry going on in there. Being a man," Sherm said, "well . . . you'll crawl on your lips across broken glass to do the right thing . . . if someone appreciates it afterward."

She looked at them. "Really?"

"That's it," Ryan said. "We're still little boys inside, and we'll do anything to be appreciated." At that moment, with his tousled blond hair and his sad blue eyes, he looked very sweet, and sort of needy. The rest of them, she realized, wore minor variations of that same expression. It was like being surrounded by a litter of large, wistful puppies. She almost laughed—but men appreciated being laughed at only when they were trying to be funny, something she'd learned the hard way, after too many hurt feelings. Her guys weren't being funny right then. They were dead serious.

So instead she hugged each of them in turn. "You know *I* appreciate you."

And then the floor of the house shook beneath her feet. The lights went out, fire illuminated the darkness outside, and everyone began screaming.

Brig had taken up an observation post near the front door when everything changed. He heard a crack, a roar; he caught a flash of searing blue-white light out the window. The lights in the house went out; thunder shook the ground; glass shattered. People surged around him, some charging forward to see what had happened, some falling back to hide. All of them buffeted against him.

His first thought was that a freak lightning strike had hit the house. His second, however, was the realization that there had been another explosion. Outside. With the cars.

He could hear Dia and the other EMTs; they were shouting for calm; they were determining if anyone had been hurt. They were doing what they did, and for a moment he was going to have to let them so that he could do what he did.

He ran outside, looking for anyone fleeing, or for anyone watching too intently or with too much pleasure.

Car alarms up and down the street shrieked and wailed; people hurried out of their homes to see what had happened, because people didn't have a lot of sense when shit went down. They were okay about staying inside if they heard gunshots, but blow something up or set it on fire, and they were all over one another fighting for the best view.

Forbes could be one of them. Hell, looking at them standing in little clusters, he could see several possibilities. Overweight men in America were hardly a rarity.

His personal car burned before his eyes, its doors all blown open, its glass exploded outward in glittering fragments that shimmered across the pavement like blood-reddened stars. The cars in front of and behind his car had caught fire, and the force of the explosion had blown out the picture window at the front of the doctor's house. But the warning had been for him, and he suspected that it was *about* Dia.

That he couldn't keep her safe.

He was fighting his way through a spider's web,

through obstacles he couldn't see and against an enemy he couldn't find, yet who had no problem finding him.

She was vulnerable. And he felt increasingly helpless to intervene against whatever Forbes was bringing to bear against her.

He turned his attention to the rest of the crime scene. He started clearing people back. The EMTs, he noted, had made their way outside and were triaging the wounded—there were a few, though as far as he could tell, no one had been badly hurt.

He began working his way through the bystanders, asking them if they had seen anyone. Anything. It was a bitter, fruitless, futile procedure; they had seen nothing, they had been nowhere around, they were all neighbors who minded their own business, didn't know the woman in front of whose house they gawped and stared, had no idea how the car had come to explode in their quiet, polite, sequestered neighborhood. They were useless, all of them, and as he moved from blank face to blank face, he found himself wanting to shake them, to scream at them, *Pay attention, would you? A woman's life is in danger, a killer is wandering right past you, and your ignorance will not save you!*

The problem was, against the invisible enemy he found himself fighting, he did not know what would.

Chapter 24

"Would it be better if we ran away?" Dia asked him.

"It would be better if we caught that motherf—" Brig glanced at her, and cut off in midsyllable the word he'd intended to say. He refused to swear in front of her, and she found that charming. Almost Old World courtly. "It would be better if we caught Forbes," he said. "Promptly."

She smiled at him. "How about if I promise you that I will not take any chances, and I will not do anything stupid, and most of all, that I will not in any way, shape, or form get myself killed today?"

"If you could promise that and mean it, I'd be fine."

"Then be fine. *I* will be. The guys and I worked it out last night after the explosion—Sherm is picking me up this morning, and Ryan will drop me off tonight."

"I'm walking out with you. I'm going to check Sherm's car to make sure it hasn't been booby-trapped. I want to know you're going to get there safe."

"Your ride's going to be here first."

"Stan can wait. And we can be late for once."

She nodded. Now that she'd reached the time when she actually had to head out the door, she wasn't sure it was the right thing to do. Ryan had been right when he told her that perfect credit would be worthless if she were dead. Brig was right in telling her that a couple more days could give the police critical information toward finding Forbes.

But neither of them was in her position, with her bills, with the uncertainty that Forbes would ever be caught. Neither of them could tell her that this would all go away if she hid for another week, or another month. Or another year.

She was taking every precaution. She was being as smart as she could.

She was in uniform, fed, as ready as she was going to get.

Brig looked out the window. "Tell me Sherm doesn't have the new Mustang GT."

"Well, he didn't." She looked out the window with him. "That's not Sherm. That's Ryan. And that's a new car for him." She stared at it. "God . . . *nice* car."

Her cell phone rang. It was Sherm. "Got a flat partway to your house," he said. He sounded furious. Dia couldn't remember ever hearing him sound angry before. "I called Ryan. He'll pick you up this morning. I'll take you home tonight."

"Ryan's already here," Dia told him. "So no problem. I'm sorry about your tire, though."

"Me, too," he said.

"Gotta run."

She and Brig went down to meet Ryan.

"Sherm had a flat," Ryan said as they stepped out of the building. "He was *pissed.*"

Dia said, "He already called. He said he'd drive me home tonight."

"Works for me." He turned to Brig. "Hey, man, what's the news on your car?"

"Insurance is going to total it. I'll get enough back to put a down payment on a replacement."

"That's good. I guess." He shook his head.

"Dia said yours is new," Brig said, eyeing the Mustang.

Ryan nodded. "I got it a few days ago—went up to my eyeballs in debt with a ruinous lease to get it, too, but I had to get a decent car. My other one was so bad the dealer wouldn't even take it. I know I didn't need a car this cool . . . but I wanted it, you know? Six years of driving a Fiat made it too tempting to resist when I found out that the dealership would let me have the Mustang."

Dia laughed. "I have to admit, I was looking forward to riding with Sherm a lot more than you. He has a *nice* car. But now so do you."

"Let's make sure it stays nice," Brig said. "I want to check it. Make sure it doesn't have any explosives attached. If Forbes thought Sherm was picking her up, you're probably okay. For now. But let me look anyway."

"I should be okay," Ryan said. "But I don't want to be surprised, either."

Brig got down on hands and knees, and with great care checked the undercarriage from front to back. "It looks clean," he said. "Don't go by any usual route today, okay? If he has something planned on her normal route, you could end up in the middle."

"You sure you want to go to work today?" Ryan asked her. "Staying home another couple of days, just to be safe, sounds like sort of a good idea."

Dia bit her lip. "I want to go to work. But I don't want to put you in any danger." She looked at the Mustang. "Or your new car."

"Screw the car. It's insured," Ryan said. "I'm concerned about you."

Brig hugged her and said, "Go. You'll go nuts in the house by yourself, and we've taken every possible precaution. I'll make it a point to be here tonight when Sherm drops you off."

Dia hugged him tight, and then stepped back and looked at them—her lover and one of her brothers. She was putting both of them in danger just by being near them.

The best thing she could do for everyone involved in this mess would be to change her name and move across country somewhere. She was selfish—that was her problem. She had a solution that wouldn't risk anyone's life but her own, but she was so greedy that she wouldn't give up the people she loved to keep them safe.

She thought about everyone talking about heroes the night before. And she thought, *If I were a real hero, I'd walk away. I'd give them up. They'd live, and whatever happened to me would happen, but there would be no more Kellys dying because I didn't have the guts to do what needed to be done.*

She had enough money for a bus ticket. Enough to maybe get herself a cheap room someplace for a few nights.

If she was a paramedic again, the license would have to be transferred, she'd have to give references, her new address would be in the system and linked to her old address. And thus she'd become visible to Forbes. At least, as long as Forbes was able to keep his connection to the system hidden. She could get a job doing something else, though—something menial, where the employers didn't ask too many questions, and she could gradually build herself a new life.

After work, she decided, she was going to do what she had to do. She'd beg off the ride with Sherm, tell him Brig was going to pick her up. As soon as everyone was out of sight, she'd take a taxi to the bus station and just disappear. No superhero tights for her, no news story, nothing like that. She'd send Brig a postcard to let him know she was all right. And he, and all her guys, would live.

Brig came over to her and gave her a hug and a quick kiss. "I'm going. See you after work tonight."

"Be safe," she told him.

"I will," he said. "You, too."

And she nodded, and gave him another hard hug and a deep kiss. A good-bye kiss. She looked at him too long, knowing it would be the last time for a while. Maybe, if Forbes found her anyway, the last time ever. "That's the plan," she said.

Brig got into Stan's unmarked, and Dia started toward the passenger side of the Mustang.

"You want to drive it?" Ryan asked.

Dia stared at him. "It's brand new."

He grinned. "Okay. Whose driving do you trust most in the ambulance?"

"When we're in a hurry, or driving like sane people?"

"Either."

"Mine, frankly."

"Right. Me, too. So, if I trust you with my life when you're driving that big damned box on wheels, why wouldn't I trust you with my car? Besides—you know you want to."

She nodded. "So very much." It would help her take her mind off that evening. Off of what was coming. And it was *such* a hot car. Ryan had chosen the hardtop version in gorgeous rich red. The interior was black, the seats leather. She settled into the driver's seat, snapped on her seat belt, then studied the instrument cluster. She didn't have to do much to adjust the seat or the mirrors—being tall had its advantages.

"Wow," she told him.

"Awesome, isn't it?"

"How much did you have to pay?"

"I leased. I know that's a terrible idea financially, but it was the only way I could get into it. I figure if I eat less, and only use electricity twice a month, I won't have to get a second job to support it."

She started it up, and the eight-cylinder engine under the hood rumbled to life. "Ohhhh. Oh, *wow.*"

"Something, isn't it?"

"I want one."

"You should have one. You look good in it."

She quickly familiarized herself with the placement of the controls. Shifted, and felt the smooth engagement of the stick into reverse. "Like butter," she said.

"You have no idea. You open it up, it digs in and grabs the road, and you can just feel its muscles bunching."

"Unfortunately," she said, giving him a sidelong look and a wry grin, "I'm not going to get to open it up. Because we're headed for work."

He laughed. "Spoilsport."

She backed down the drive, and he said, "Head west first."

"West?"

"I promised Brig we wouldn't go the usual way."

"Well, away from work is definitely not the usual way."

"He's worried. He's right to be."

"All right," she said, and sighed, and started westward. "Sherm sounded really bent out of shape about his tire," she told him.

He settled into his own seat and said, "He sounded weird when I talked to him on the phone. Pissed about the tire, but about his plans, too. Very un-Sherm-like. He made it sound like picking you up this morning was a big deal. I told him if it mattered that much, I'd give up my regular turn tonight. He didn't sound like he thought that was much of an alternative."

"Well, things have been stressful lately. But it does seem odd. Sherm is always so quiet. I wouldn't have thought he cared one way or the other."

"You never know about people," Ryan said.

They drove in silence for a few minutes, and then Ryan said, "Since last night, I've been thinking about that hero talk we had."

"Really?"

"Yeah. Trying to remember when heroes went out of fashion. The last person I knew who was treated as a hero was this teenage kid. He was at a park one day with a bunch of his friends, and one of the friends did something stupid. That kid was running along with a metal rod in his hands, and it hit a power line. He went down like a dropped brick, and lay there twitching.

"No one knew what to do except for this one kid. He was my age, but he was different, you know? He got out, he did things. Everyone admired him. His parents trusted him. He was just a kid, but he already knew what he was going to be—he was a junior EMT. He'd learned CPR and basic rescue techniques. The hurt kid lay there, twitching, frying, dying. And his friend found something nonconductive, and got the stick off the line and out of the way of the kid. Grounded the kid. And then, after he sent the friends to go for help, he started CPR.

"He saved the kid's life, and everyone made a huge deal about it. His picture was in the paper, it got picked up by national news for a day, he got some sort of Boy Scout award for it. He was as big and bright and shiny as Superman after he saved all of Metropolis, and that shine never went away."

Dia said, "That's funny. Mac did something like that once. He never made a big deal about it, but we were talking about things we did when we were kids. His story was a lot like that."

She heard a metallic click to her right. She looked over, and found herself on the wrong end of a handgun. "It *is* funny," Ryan said. "Because Mac came out of that day shining like the neighborhood god. Meanwhile, the kid Mac saved was labeled the stupid moron who didn't have the sense to keep a swimming pool strainer away from power lines, and had even more restrictions put on his life after he recovered. Mac never told you that kid's name, did he? Never really talked about him. Never mentioned that they'd been best friends, that the kid he saved had worshiped the ground he walked on. Nothing like that, right?"

Dia was having a hard time breathing. "You're . . . Sinclair Forbes?"

"Hell, no," Ryan said. "Sinclair Forbes suffered from an overprotective, overbearing, distant mother and a spineless absentee father. Sinclair Forbes tried to be a hero, and discovered that he didn't have what it took— and then his friend turned him in to the police for even trying. Larry Forbes, on the other hand, embraced the Tao and learned about balance."

"What?"

"Balance," Ryan said, "Mac saved my life, and everybody loved him. Nobody loved me, so I thought, Hey, I could save somebody's life, and then I'd be like that, too. Only it's not so easy to be in the right place at the right time to save somebody. I eventually shoved a little kid into a swimming pool so I could get him back out again and save him. Only I wasn't such a good swimmer. The kid drowned, and I almost did." He shrugged. "I tried a couple other things, but they didn't work out. So I climbed into a tree that hung over the street in front of our house. This was before the city started clearing out all the overhanging limbs, you know? I was up on the limb, and right in the intersection, and I dropped a cat onto a car windshield, and the driver swerved head-on into another car." He said, "Just keep going straight here. We'll be driving to the Everglades today."

"What?"

"I've been giving this a lot of thought. I don't want Brig to have anything left of you to bury. I don't even want him to know that you're dead. We're going to disappear. They'll figure out that I'm Forbes, of course. And sooner, rather than later. But they'll waste at least a little time looking for this car, which is, in fact, stolen. This car is going to disappear with you. I'm glad you like it, because at least you'll have the comfort of knowing that you get a pretty coffin."

He laughed. "You won't want to get out. You know how the alligators are in the Everglades."

Dia disguised the motion of hitting the autodial on her cell phone as trying to unbuckle her seat belt. She had Brig set as *1. She hoped she'd hit the right buttons.

"I'm going to give you a choice," he said, grabbing her wrist, "and the choice does not include taking off your seat belt and jumping out of the car. Alive, you'll be able to hope for rescue. Dead, you won't. You're going to drive the car into the Everglades, Dia. Or else I'm going to shoot you and shove the car into the water. I have my spot picked out, the place on the fence is already cut away, my getaway car and my new identity are already waiting for me. If you drive in, you can call Brig on your cell phone and hope he and a rescue team that doesn't mind alligators get to you before you run out of air. If I shoot you, well, that's the end of hope, isn't it?"

She heard the soft clicking of the cell phone connecting, and knew Brig's voice would follow. So she screamed at Ryan, "Why are you doing this, Forbes? Ryan? I'm not going to drive into the Everglades! I'm not going to just let you kill me!"

"Don't get hysterical. I never, ever took you as the hysterical type, and I really don't feel like having my illusions shattered at this late date."

Dia put her foot on the gas and started accelerating. "No," she shouted. "I'm not. I'm not hysterical, you creep. You murderous, psychopathic freak! Don't wave your gun in my face and tell me not to be hysterical. I'm *not* hysterical. I'm just *pissed.*"

On the other end of that cell phone call, Brig felt the air getting thin around him. He was walking into his cubicle when the call came through, and, answering it, he'd expected that Dia would be calling him to tell him she and Ryan were safely at the station. Instead, as he picked up, he heard her screaming, and made out that she was being instructed to drive to the Everglades.

It took a second for his heart to start beating again. Another couple of seconds for his brain to start working. And then he went into Stan's cubicle next door, and said, "Forbes has Dia. He's planning to have her drive into thc Everglades."

Stan looked at him blankly. "How the hell did Forbes get to Dia?"

Brig still had the cell phone pressed to his ear, listening to Dia shouting, to the sounds of motor noise, and squealing tires, and Ryan shouting, "Not so fast; are you *crazy?*"

"Ryan Williams *is* Forbes," he said.

"Five hundred pounds, two hundred pounds," Stan said. "I don't think so. Besides, we checked the hell out of him. We checked all of them."

"Not well enough, apparently. We can recriminate ourselves for being sloppy afterward. Right now, she's still alive, and she's heading west in a late-model red Mustang, and apparently driving recklessly."

"I'll shoot you, you stupid bitch!" Ryan shouted in his ear.

"At this speed, if you do, we'll both die. So long as I can kill you while you kill me, I'm okay with that."

"You whore. You filthy *whore!*" Ryan screamed.

There were no gunshots.

"We can triangulate her position from her cell phone," Stan said.

"We need to get choppers in the air over her. We need to have diving rescue on standby, or following along." He kept his ear pressed to the phone.

Stan put the wheels in motion, and the helicopters into the air. A uniformed patrol quickly spotted the car in traffic, and officers suggested roadblocks.

Brig stood still, forcing himself to think. The problem was that as soon as Forbes knew they were being tracked, he would have less reason to keep Dia alive. As it was, he was trying to get her to the Everglades. He had his little scenario in mind, and he planned to leave her alive so that he could watch it play out.

Brig didn't think that he would be the type to go quietly if he realized that he was going to end up in jail. No one ever knew, of course—but to Brig, Forbes's actions to that point suggested a certain recklessness. He was a good planner—no doubt about that. But he also liked to get in close, to thumb his nose. He'd been in the house with the detective who'd been trying to find him when he'd killed Kelly Beam. He'd installed Dia's security system, and Brig would bet everything he owned that the bastard had given himself a set of keys and maybe a way to turn the system on and off from outside. He'd had fun leaving his packages at her front door. He'd played with everyone, somehow making them think he was fat, brown-haired, brown-eyed, when in fact he had transformed himself into a lean blue-eyed blond. Hair dye, contact lenses, and big weight loss did a lot to change anyone's appearance. He'd given himself every possible access to her, and then he'd used it just to show them how helpless they were against him.

If it came down to last minutes and last chances, Brig figured Ryan—Forbes—was the sort of man who'd choose to go out in a blaze of glory. If he could not be the superhero, then he'd be the supervillain.

"Everything is up and running," Stan said. "The helicopter is hanging back, but it has them. Patrol cars are catching up—having to run without lights or sirens is hampering them a bit. A dive rescue has been dispatched toward Alligator Alley."

"We need to get out there."

"Yeah. Everything else will wait. Let's go."

They didn't walk. They ran. The news had started spreading already. Nobody asked where the fire was, nobody got in their way. Stan drove, which was just as well, because Brig didn't think that he would have been safe on the roads in his current frame of mind.

He kept running everything over in his mind, and no matter how many times he went back over it, he couldn't see where Ryan Williams had slipped. There wasn't a single time that he'd looked like anything other than another of Dia's work-obsessed, gung-ho EMT brothers. Not one.

He'd saved her life with the scuba tank. Of course, he'd also been the one to put nitrous in her tank. Brig couldn't figure out what that had been about—the incident, then, hadn't been about killing her, but about . . . what? Winning her complete trust? He'd already had that.

Winning Brig's trust?

Maybe.

Playing with his prey, the way a cat played with a captured mouse before eating it?

Probably.

Chances were, they would never know.

Chapter 25

If she'd managed to dial the right number, help would be on the way. If she hadn't, she was on her own. The problem was that she had no idea if she'd pushed the right buttons or not. She couldn't see what she was doing, she was driving, she was scared, she was shaky—the odds of things going wrong were high.

Her cell phone was dead quiet. She hoped Brig was listening. That he was there. She had so many things she wanted to tell him, but she'd already told him that she loved him. He knew that, and if she never got to say anything else to him in person, at least she'd said that.

She didn't think Ryan—*Forbes;* why couldn't she think of him as Forbes?—was going to let her live. She knew damned well that if she could, she was going to take him down with her.

"They're going to catch on to us," he said suddenly.

"Shut up. I don't want to hear your voice," she shouted.

"I'm the one with the gun!" he yelled. "If you keep driving like this, some cop will try to pull us over. Is that your plan?"

"You're not as stupid as you look," she said.

She had a plan, actually. It was a lot like suicide, or like the old nuclear mutual assured destruction plan of the unmourned Cold War.

But it was a plan.

She knew a place where she could hurt him, kill him, make sure he never got to do to anyone else what he'd done to Mac, and Kelly, and all those people in the wrecks he caused.

"If you think I'll let you stop for lights and sirens, you're stupider than *you* look," he said. "You kept choosing wrong, choosing imbalance over balance. I'm correcting that. You're not getting out of this alive."

She'd already figured that.

They were getting close to the spot. He was going to shoot her; she knew it. He was going to kill her while she was driving, and take his chance. She was afraid to look at him, because his eyes were so crazy. So wild.

"Contact lenses," she said.

"What?"

"Your eyes. Blue. Because of contact lenses."

"And my weight, down because of intensive body-building and getting out from under my mother's thumb. Yeah. I made a few changes. And had enough money that I could have a fat suit made, too."

She swerved, jammed on the brakes as an old man gave her the finger and tried to pull out in front of her just because he could. She got around him by running up onto the median, then swerving back onto the pavement as quickly as she could. Horns all around her blared, and the old passive-aggressive behind her bleated his horn and cussed her out in the rearview mirror. His car sat sideways in traffic, with another car locked onto the bumper.

She was being a lot of people's bad day right then.

"Why, Ryan?" she asked. "Why did you kill Mac? Why did you kill Kelly? And all those people in the accidents? Everyone loved you. You had friends, you had work you were good at, you were making progress toward your EMT-paramedic. Why? And why did you come after me?"

"You emasculated me. You took away my dignity. And then you did nothing to help me get it back—either of you."

"Mac *saved your life!*" she shouted.

"And put me in his debt. And became everyone's golden boy because of it. Meanwhile, in everyone's eyes I became forever after the overweight, inept lump who needed to be rescued."

"You're *alive* because he saved your life."

"He did not take responsibility for his actions. For my future. He should have. I restored balance—I killed him. And *you* saved my life, then turned your back on me just as he had. Funny how that works, isn't it? There's a Chinese proverb about saving people's lives. How, if you do that, you're responsible for them forever." He stared over at her as if he were willing her to understand him.

"You're saying that Mac owed you something for saving your life? That I owed you something? That just saving your life wasn't enough?"

"Yes. He should have understood when I told him about the cat and the tree. He should have seen that I wasn't doing anything he hadn't done. I wanted to save people; I was doing what I had to do to do that."

He moved the gun, and she felt the presence of that cold metal in the car like a physical blow. "You should have come to see me in the hospital. You should have cared what happened to me. You should have spent time with me, gotten to know me, and fallen in love with me. You had every chance. That would have restored balance. It would have made things right. Instead you did nothing. And that's what you do with all your patients. Nothing. They could be anyone, doing anything, but you pay no attention to who they are. To what kind of people they are. You care nothing for balance."

She accelerated, cut in front of someone because she had to be in the right lane to do what she had to do. She had to. She'd already passed a couple of possible targets, but she wanted the best one—a spot with specific characteristics, specific challenges. She knew the place; she was almost to it, and she couldn't let her nerve fail her. Traffic was picking up. She knew she needed to hit her spot hard. She'd get only one shot at this.

Ryan-Forbes wasn't walking away from what he'd done. She probably wasn't, either, but she was going to make sure that he didn't get the chance to fade into the background again, that he never got to pick up where he'd left off.

She'd never yearned for tights or a cape. She had no illusions about any glory conferred by heroism. For her, heroism was doing what had to be done when no one else could, and as often as not, it didn't end well for the hero.

Ahead, to her right, the ground beside the road curved gently downward, that golf-course-perfect curve created by people who had carved Fort Lauderdale and the surrounding towns into the canal-riddled Venice of the West. The slope ended in a concrete-sided canal. It was the deepest, widest one she could get to quickly.

She knew she was going to flinch, and she was afraid her face was going to give her away. He couldn't realize what she was doing, or he'd try to stop her. He might succeed.

"You know," she said, "I think the Chinese might have been on to something. We are, perhaps, responsible for the people whose lives we save."

"Bit late to come around to my way of thinking," he said, and she smoothly eased the steering wheel to the right and floored the gas pedal. The Mustang had a lot of kick. She'd give it that. They shot off the road and off that gentle curve of land into the air like they'd been launched by a catapult.

Ryan screamed—a flat-out girl-in-a-horror-movie scream that Dia would have felt a hell of a lot better about if there had been dirt under the tires and the the nose of the car hadn't been arcing down into the canal. Down.

Down.

The world rolled into slow time, with Ryan's scream stretched out long and high-pitched and crazy, almost, she thought, like a siren.

The car hit the water like a diver, slicing into the black void in a neat, nose-first arc. The air bags deployed. She slammed into hers, and time sped up. The engine died. The sounds around her were of water, bubbling, gurgling, coming into the car through all its many seams. She could already feel it around her feet. Cold, surprisingly cold.

Her handbag was on the seat behind her—or at least it had been when the car hit. No telling where it had landed. It didn't matter—she hadn't yet replaced the handgun she'd lost in Brig's wreck.

Even if she had replaced the gun, though, it wouldn't have done her any good. Not lying in a bag she couldn't find or reach.

Her trauma scissors, though, might. They were in her jacket pocket. She pulled them out, keeping an eye on Ryan as she did. He wasn't moving. If she was lucky, he was dead already.

She jammed one half of the trauma scissors into the air bag, cut viciously, and deflated it. She cut through her seat belt.

The water was up to her knees, and she knew even before she unlocked the door and tried to open it that the pressure outside the car would be higher than the pressure inside. The doors wouldn't open until pressure equalized—until, in other words, the car filled up with water. She had to get into the backseat, quickly.

Ryan turned his head to look at her. His nose was bloody. He was grinning. The gun was in his right hand, pointed at her again. "This will do," he said. "Doesn't matter to me where you die. Canal is just fine."

She stabbed at his right wrist with the scissors, holding the blade without the safety edge on it like a knife. He pulled the trigger, the gun shot, but the scissors hit his wrist as he did and the shot went up and to the left of Dia. The gun blew a hole in the windshield, and the water blasted in like it was coming through a fire hose. Dia's scissors dug deeper into Ryan's wrist. She'd been working for an artery, and she hit one. His blood pulsed out, the pressure squirting it like the water through the windshield. He shouted; she screamed; she grabbed for the gun as it dangled in his fingers; he clutched for her.

The water was up to her waist. She didn't have a lot of time. And he was strong. To her advantage, his movements were severely hampered by his air bag. And she'd hurt him with the scissors. He was going to have to stanch the bleeding.

But he was fighting her instead. Fighting to get control of the gun, to get his fingers wrapped tight around it again, so he could kill her. He wanted her dead; he wanted to be the one who swam away, and then walked away.

And the water was rising. Their arms dipped below the water, but the gun stayed above it.

She kept fighting, and felt him regain control of the gun—felt the cold metal steady in his hand as he started to swing it around toward her.

With everything she had in her, she shoved. Hard,

upward, away from her, toward him. The gun went off as the barrel snapped toward him, and she had a retina-burning flash-image of an explosion, of blood and bone, of a face twisting, rippling, and contorting. Ryan's face was a ruin, and he wasn't moving.

She exhaled in relief.

Something heavy dragged along the windshield, a sort of claws-on-blackboard sound, and she didn't look because she couldn't. She got the gun, untangled it from Ryan's limp hand, and carefully jammed it into her pocket.

The water was up to her neck. She tried the door again, but the pressure still hadn't equalized. The car sat nose-down at the bottom of the canal, resting at about a thirty-degree angle. She stood up, letting the water take as much of her weight as she could, and scrambled over the front seat into the back.

She was shaking, breathing hard, scared to death. But she tried to steady herself. In her situation, a hardtop sedan was the best vehicle to be in. The hardtop would hold a pocket of air even after the rest of the car filled up. All she had to do was keep to the back, to the high point of the roof, and keep her nose above water until the rest of the vehicle filled. Then the pressure would equalize and the doors would open easily, and she could swim out.

She got her head up into the pocket, and breathed.

And felt another heavy thud on the outside of the car. And heard that scraping again. She looked up, out of the rear window, into the water above. She was hoping to see rescuers, people diving in to force the doors open and drag her out.

What she saw instead was the shape of an enormous alligator, swimming overhead.

*　　　*　　　*

"She drove into the canal! She drove into the canal!" the helicopter pilot shouted, for a moment forgetting professionalism out of sheer shock.

Brig, listening in on the radio, felt himself go numb.

It was a mistake. She hadn't done that; she was still safe, on dry land, where he and the men converging on her could get to her.

But they were calling the dive team back to the canal by the road and cross street, calling in two people trapped in a submerged vehicle, and one of those people was Dia. Brig turned to Stan, tasting ashes and blood in his mouth. He was so scared he couldn't place the canal. "Where is she?" he asked.

"We're almost there," Stan told him. "We can get to her. The car will take a little time to fill. It'll be all right. She's smart. She's tough. She'll make it out of this."

"She's in a car with an armed monster, and we can't even see him to kill him."

Stan pointed. "Over there." He skidded across traffic and off the road onto the bank—a patrol car was already on the grass in front of him. The cop was out of the car, on his radio, telling the dive team where to go.

"How long?" Brig shouted to the cop.

"Divers are ten minutes out."

Brig looked at Stan; Stan looked at Brig.

"Too long," Brig said.

He ran to the bank and looked down.

He could make out nothing of the car in the murky water. However, he couldn't miss the alligator that surfaced briefly in front of him, then submerged again. By his best guess, it was easily sixteen feet long. They got bigger, though, and he'd seen only segments of the monster. It might be even larger than sixteen feet. It was enormous. That he knew.

And Dia was down there, underneath the water, still

alive, he hoped, still breathing, but between him and her, there was water, a psychopath, and an alligator.

The water and the alligator he could deal with. "Stan!" Brig shouted, "Rifle! Fast!"

Stan dove for the trunk of his car and came up with a rifle; he raced to the water's edge. "You see Forbes?" he asked. "He getting away?"

Brig pointed to the alligator. "Kill it," he told Stan.

And then he kicked off his shoes and shrugged out of his jacket and his shoulder holster.

And dove in.

Chapter 26

Dia saw the alligator circling. She tried to get an idea of its swimming rhythm—its pattern—because she was going to have to get out there with it above her. The pressure had equalized, the doors would be openable, and the Mustang didn't hold much air up against its roof. She found herself wishing for the days of the steel monster Chevys— those old cars had enormous amounts of headroom, and all that headroom would have held air.

At least she wasn't in an SUV, she thought. All the air would have leaked out the back.

She wouldn't have had an air pocket where she could watch the alligator circle.

She quit staring out the back window. She had to go. She could take her chances with drowning, or with suffocating, or with the gator. She chose the gator. The other two options were death's sure things.

Dia took one last deep breath, praying that she would make it, that she could hang on. She thought, just as she dove, that she saw movement from the passenger side of the car. She didn't have time to question it; she was on her last air, submerged in blood-filled water, and when she opened the door, the tiny trickle that had been swirling into the canal before, enticing the gator, would turn into a flood. She had to move fast; she had to move smoothly and without struggle; she had to hope that the gator would find Ryan before it found her.

All she could do was hope, hold her breath, and keep moving.

She swam over the front seat, hung on to the driver's-side door, and opened it.

And a hand, still strong, clamped around her ankle.

At the same moment, the circling gator bumped against the open car door.

Dia's heart thudded in her chest, her mind went blank for just an instant, and then she twisted, hard, and pulled the gun out of her pocket, and fired in the direction of the hand. Underwater.

The Glock had every reason not to work, but it fired once.

Then again.

The third time it jammed, and she let go of it. The hand around her ankle had gone limp anyway.

But she was out of air. She wouldn't make it to the surface. One last time she shoved her face upward into the air pocket along the roof of the Mustang, knowing as she did that she was giving up. That she was going to die.

She exhaled. Then inhaled, fighting to find oxygen that simply wasn't there. She felt everything going dark.

And very, very cold.

"You're not alone, sweetheart."

Mac stood beside her. They were both in the Mustang; her half leaning on the back of the driver's seat, facing backward, her head tipped up so that her nose and mouth were still in the stale pocket of air; him standing beside her through the seat, holding her head up. Keeping her steady.

"I'm dying. Or dead."

"You're alive, and you're not alone."

In the distance she heard rifle shots—funny the way the water muffled them. One. Two. Three. Four.

"I'm going to give you one last breath," Mac told her. "It's all I've got left in me, love—a little air. I'm done here. Free at last. You stopped the man who killed me, and now I can rest."

"Why can you talk to me now?"

"Because I'm not chained to my death anymore. I'm moving . . . onward. This is my good-bye. And the last help I can offer.

"I'm going," he said.

That part was clear.

"You're . . . going wherever you were supposed to go when this started."

He nodded.

"You know I still love you, right?" she asked. "I always will."

He smiled that crooked smile she had always found so endearing. And he reached out and put his hand on hers, and for just a fraction of an instant when they first touched, he was real and warm and solid. Her Mac again, whom she had missed so much, whom she had mourned so long. Her wild, crazy daredevil, her best friend, her hero, her first love.

And he bent down and kissed her, a bitter-cold kiss that forced air like ice into her lungs.

She started to cry, and her tears blurred him.

No. Not the tears.

He was fading. He was mist, he was a vague shape in the air, and then he was gone. All the way gone.

In her heart, in her gut, she knew he wasn't coming back. That he had held on as long as he could, that he had given her as much as he could, and that at last, having done everything he had hung around to do, he had run out of time.

She was conscious again, her lungs full of air, and a man's hand was grabbing her wrist, pulling her under the water.

She panicked and tried to fight. The gun . . . she'd dropped the gun. Where was it?

But the dark shape in the bloody water tightened on her hand, pulled her out of the car into the canal . . .

—and the alligator, where was the alligator?—

. . . and started dragging her toward the surface, swimming hard, pulling her upward.

Hadn't come to kill her. Came to save her.

Rescue.

Hanging on to that one last breath, her lungs aching, her head throbbing, she managed to start kicking herself toward the surface, helping her rescuer out. She squeezed his hand, and felt him squeeze back.

And then their heads broke the surface, and she exhaled that last breath and treaded water, facing Brig. Brig. Not just some diver who had come in to save her, but Brig.

"Alligators," he said, and dragged her toward the bank. "Have to . . . get out of here. Got one . . . there are more."

She swam hard, and they reached the bank, and cops and EMTs pulled her and Brig out.

She dropped to her knees, shaking hard, and Brig collapsed beside her.

She stared at him—he was shirtless, with his chest gouged and scratched, and blood oozing everywhere. He was pale; he looked like hell.

"What happened to your shirt?" she asked. "And . . ." She touched the bleeding gouges.

He rested his head on her shoulder.

"Big alligator," he said. "Circling the . . . car when I . . . jumped in. Came after me . . . bit the shirt." He closed his eyes and exhaled slowly. "He dragged me under, tried to roll with me—to drown me—and I managed to get out of the shirt and tangle it around his mouth so he couldn't open it again. Got scratched up in the process, swallowed half the canal—but made it back up for air, which is when Stan shot the gator." He gave her a tired smile. "And I came back for you. I didn't think you were going to . . . well . . . you know. But I couldn't leave you down there."

"You were just in time."

"What happened?"

And what did she say to that? She knew a lot of what had happened, but certainly not all of it.

"Ryan's dead. I got the gun away from him and shot him. The rest of it? I'm not even sure I believe it."

He looked at her sidelong, started to ask her something, and then shook his head and changed his mind.

"What?" she said.

"Nothing we can't discuss later. I have only one urgent question right now." He turned to her, and stood up shakily, and helped her to her feet. And then he dropped to one knee and said, "Will you marry me *now,* Dia Courvant?"

She burst out laughing. "Good God, yes, Brig. How could I not?"

The cops, the Rescue guys, the newly arrived dive team, all stood there applauding, and Dia pulled Brig back to his feet so she could hug him. Bloody, dirty, soaking wet, he was the most beautiful sight she had ever seen.

"And I can fight all your alligators for you from now on."

She pulled back so she could stare up into his eyes. "Brig," she said solemnly, "I hate alligators. If I never see another alligator again, it'll be too soon."

A smile slowly spread across his face. "How do you feel about cattle?"